Romantic Reveries

Romance, Volume 6

Jessica Marie Garcia

Published by Wonderland Press, 2024.

This is a work of fiction. Similarities to real people, places, or events are entirely coincidental.

ROMANTIC REVERIES

First edition. July 21, 2024.

ISBN: 979-8227607751

Written by Jessica Marie Garcia.

Table of Contents

For all the dreamers who believe in the magic of love,

and the storytellers who capture its many wonders.

To those who find beauty in fleeting moments and eternal bonds alike,

may these pages inspire you to cherish, embrace, and celebrate love in all its forms.

With heartfelt gratitude to those who journey with us through these romantic rever

ies.

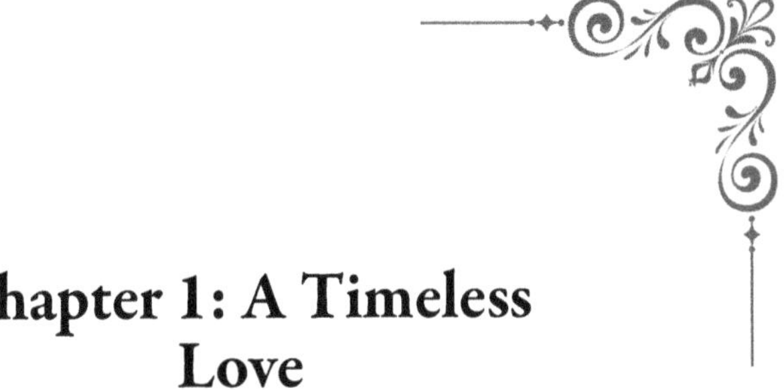

Chapter 1: A Timeless Love

Introduction to the Anthology and Its Theme

Love is a universal language that transcends time, culture, and circumstance. It is the thread that weaves through the fabric of human experience, binding us together in a shared tapestry of emotions, memories, and dreams. "Romantic Reveries" is an anthology that celebrates this enduring power of love, offering readers a collection of stories that span various sub-genres and styles, each capturing the essence of romance in its many forms.

From the innocence of first love to the passion of rekindled flames, from the historical settings of yesteryear to the fantastical realms of magic and myth, this anthology explores the myriad ways in which love manifests itself. As you journey through these pages, you will encounter characters who reflect your own hopes and fears, triumphs and trials, and above all, your longing for connection and belonging.

The Importance of Love Stories Through the Ages

LOVE STORIES HAVE ALWAYS held a special place in the human heart. They are the mirrors in which we see our own desires and the maps that guide us through the complex terrain of relationships. From the ancient epics of Homer to the modern-day romances of Nicholas

Sparks, love stories have captivated audiences for millennia, offering a glimpse into the deepest recesses of the human soul.

In ancient times, love stories were often interwoven with myths and legends, reflecting the cultural values and societal norms of the era. Tales of gods and goddesses, heroes and heroines, conveyed not only the romantic ideals of the time but also the moral lessons and philosophical beliefs of the people. The story of Orpheus and Eurydice, for example, speaks to the power of love to transcend even death, while the tale of Tristan and Isolde explores the themes of forbidden love and sacrifice.

As societies evolved, so too did their love stories. The medieval period saw the rise of courtly love, a literary concept that emphasized chivalry, honor, and the nobility of love. Stories such as "Lancelot and Guinevere" and "Tristan and Isolde" depicted the knight's devotion to his lady, often portraying love as an ennobling and transformative force.

The Renaissance brought a renewed interest in the human experience, and with it, a more nuanced exploration of love. Shakespeare's plays, such as "Romeo and Juliet" and "Much Ado About Nothing," delved into the complexities of romantic relationships, highlighting the interplay of passion, conflict, and reconciliation.

In the 19th century, the Romantic movement emphasized the emotional and individualistic aspects of love. Writers like Jane Austen and the Brontë sisters crafted intricate portraits of love and society, examining the ways in which personal desires intersect with social expectations. "Pride and Prejudice" and "Wuthering Heights" remain enduring classics, celebrated for their deep characterizations and insightful commentary on love and human nature.

The 20th century saw the diversification of romantic narratives, with the advent of new genres and styles. From the sweeping historical romances of Kathleen Woodiwiss to the contemporary love stories of Nora Roberts, romance literature expanded to include a wide array of themes and settings. The rise of genre fiction, such as paranormal romance and romantic suspense, further broadened the scope of romantic storytelling, catering to the varied tastes and preferences of readers.

Brief Overview of the Different Sub-Genres and Styles Included

IN "ROMANTIC REVERIES," we have curated a diverse selection of love stories that reflect the rich tapestry of romance literature. Each sub-genre and style offers a unique perspective on love, capturing its beauty, complexity, and transformative power.

Historical Romance

HISTORICAL ROMANCE transports readers to bygone eras, where love unfolds against the backdrop of historical events and settings. These stories often feature meticulously researched details that bring the past to life, allowing readers to immerse themselves in the romance and drama of different time periods. From the elegance of Regency England to the rugged landscapes of the American West, historical romance explores the timeless nature of love amidst the constraints and challenges of history.

Contemporary Romance

CONTEMPORARY ROMANCE focuses on modern-day relationships, exploring the dynamics of love in the context of today's world. These stories often delve into themes such as career, family, and social issues, offering a realistic portrayal of the joys and struggles of contemporary romance. With relatable characters and contemporary settings, these tales resonate with readers who see their own lives reflected in the pages.

Paranormal Romance

PARANORMAL ROMANCE blends elements of romance with the supernatural, creating a unique and captivating genre. These stories feature characters with extraordinary abilities, such as vampires, werewolves, and witches, navigating love in a world where the boundaries between reality and fantasy blur. The heightened stakes and fantastical elements add an extra layer of excitement and intrigue to the romance.

Fantasy Romance

FANTASY ROMANCE TRANSPORTS readers to magical realms and enchanted worlds, where love is intertwined with adventure and myth. These stories often feature epic quests, mythical creatures, and fantastical landscapes, offering a sense of wonder and escapism. The blending of romance and fantasy creates a rich and imaginative tapestry that captivates the imagination.

Romantic Suspense

ROMANTIC SUSPENSE COMBINES the thrill of mystery and danger with the allure of romance. These stories often feature protagonists who find love while facing perilous situations, such as solving crimes or uncovering secrets. The tension and suspense heighten the emotional stakes, creating a gripping and compelling narrative.

Erotic Romance

EROTIC ROMANCE EXPLORES the sensual and passionate aspects of love, focusing on the physical and emotional intimacy between characters. These stories often feature explicit scenes and explore themes of desire, pleasure, and sexual exploration. The intensity of the romance is heightened by the deep connection between the characters, creating a powerful and evocative experience.

Sweet and Wholesome Romance

SWEET AND WHOLESOME romance emphasizes emotional connection and pure love, often avoiding explicit scenes. These stories focus on the development of relationships and the heartfelt moments that define romance. With their gentle and heartwarming narratives, sweet romances offer a comforting and uplifting reading experience.

LGBTQ+ Romance

LGBTQ+ ROMANCE CELEBRATES love in all its forms, featuring relationships between characters of diverse sexual orientations and gender identities. These stories offer representation and visibility to LGBTQ+ individuals, exploring the unique challenges and joys of their romantic journeys. The inclusive nature of LGBTQ+ romance enriches the genre, reflecting the diversity of love in the real world.

Interracial and Multicultural Romance

INTERRACIAL AND MULTICULTURAL romance explores love across cultural and racial boundaries, highlighting the beauty of diversity and the power of connection. These stories often delve into the complexities of navigating cultural differences and societal expectations, offering a rich and nuanced portrayal of love that transcends borders.

Anthologies and Collections

ANTHOLOGIES AND COLLECTIONS bring together a variety of love stories, offering readers a diverse and engaging selection of narratives. These compilations often feature contributions from multiple authors, each bringing their unique voice and perspective to the anthology. The varied themes and styles create a rich tapestry of romance, allowing readers to experience love in its many forms.

AS YOU EMBARK ON THIS journey through "Romantic Reveries," we invite you to lose yourself in the timeless allure of love. Each story in this anthology is a testament to the enduring power of romance, capturing the essence of what it means to love and be loved. Whether you are a longtime fan of romance fiction or a newcomer to the genre, we hope that these tales will inspire, uplift, and resonate with you, reminding you of the beauty and magic of love.

The Enduring Power of Romance

THE STORIES THAT FOLLOW in this anthology are more than just tales of love; they are reflections of our deepest desires and our most profound connections. Romance fiction has the unique ability to transport us to different worlds, to make us feel the intensity of first love, the heartache of separation, and the joy of reunion. It reminds us that love is a universal experience, one that binds us together despite our differences.

In a world that is constantly changing, where the pace of life seems ever faster and the pressures ever greater, romance fiction offers a sanctuary. It allows us to slow down, to savor the moments of connection, to dream of possibilities, and to believe in the transformative power of love. It is a genre that celebrates the human spirit, our capacity for empathy, and our longing for connection.

As you read through "Romantic Reveries," may you find stories that speak to your heart, that resonate with your own experiences, and that inspire you to believe in the timeless power of love. Whether you find yourself drawn to the passionate embraces of historical lovers, the magical bonds of fantasy realms, or the tender connections of contemporary romance, may each story remind you that love is a journey worth taking, a dream worth dreaming, and a reverie worth cherishing.

Welcome to "Romantic Reveries" – a celebration of love in all its forms, a testament to its enduring power, and a journey through the timeless landscape of romance.

Chapter 2: First Love's Whisper

A Collection of Stories About First Loves

First love is a universal experience, a rite of passage that lingers in our memories long after the initial excitement has faded. It's the moment when our hearts first learn to beat to the rhythm of another's, when our eyes light up at the mere sight of someone special, and when we first begin to understand the complexity and beauty of human connection. This chapter is dedicated to capturing the essence of first love through a collection of heartwarming stories that explore the innocence, joy, and poignancy of young romance.

Story 1: The Playground Crush

Setting the Scene

IT WAS A SUNNY AFTERNOON in May when Emma first noticed Jake on the playground. They were both in the fifth grade, and while Emma had always been more interested in books than boys, something about Jake caught her attention. Maybe it was the way his hair fell over his forehead when he ran, or the way his laughter seemed to fill the entire playground. Whatever it was, it made Emma's heart race in a way she had never experienced before.

The First Interaction

DURING RECESS, EMMA found herself gravitating towards the basketball court where Jake was playing. She watched from a distance, her heart pounding in her chest. When Jake finally noticed her, he smiled and waved, causing Emma to blush furiously. Mustering all her courage, she walked over to him.

"Hi, Jake," she said, trying to keep her voice steady.

"Hey, Emma," Jake replied, his eyes twinkling. "Wanna shoot some hoops?"

Emma nodded, and as they played, she found herself laughing and feeling more at ease. By the end of recess, they had made plans to meet up again the next day. That afternoon marked the beginning of a beautiful friendship that would eventually blossom into something more.

The First Kiss

AS THE SCHOOL YEAR progressed, Emma and Jake became inseparable. They spent their days exploring the playground, sharing secrets, and dreaming about the future. One day, as they sat under the big oak tree behind the school, Jake leaned in and kissed Emma on the cheek. It was a simple, innocent gesture, but it made Emma's heart soar. She knew in that moment that Jake was her first love.

Story 2: The Summer Fling

A Chance Meeting

SAMANTHA HAD ALWAYS looked forward to summer vacation. It was a time to escape the pressures of school and enjoy the freedom of long, lazy days. That summer, she was staying with her grandparents in a small beach town. She had never expected to find love there, but fate had other plans.

One evening, while walking along the shoreline, Samantha met Alex. He was a local boy, a year older than her, with a charming smile and a mischievous glint in his eyes. They struck up a conversation, and before long, they were inseparable.

The Joy of First Love

SAMANTHA AND ALEX SPENT the summer exploring the town, swimming in the ocean, and sharing their dreams for the future. They laughed, held hands, and watched sunsets together. Each moment felt magical, like they were the only two people in the world.

One night, as they sat on the beach, Alex turned to Samantha and said, "I don't want this summer to end."

"Neither do I," Samantha replied, her heart full of love and longing.

The Bittersweet Goodbye

AS THE END OF SUMMER approached, Samantha and Alex knew they would have to say goodbye. On their last evening together, they walked along the beach, their hands intertwined. When they reached the spot where they had first met, Alex kissed Samantha gently on the lips. It was a sweet, tender kiss that left them both breathless.

"I'll never forget you," Alex whispered.

"Me neither," Samantha replied, tears streaming down her cheeks.

Though their time together was short, the memories of that summer would stay with them forever, a reminder of the innocence and beauty of first love.

Story 3: The High School Sweethearts

Meeting in the Hallway

SARAH AND DANIEL FIRST met in the crowded hallway of their high school. It was the first day of freshman year, and both were feeling overwhelmed by the chaos of the new environment. Sarah, with her nose buried in her schedule, accidentally bumped into Daniel, causing his books to scatter across the floor.

"I'm so sorry!" Sarah exclaimed, kneeling to help pick up the books.

"It's okay," Daniel said with a smile. "I'm Daniel, by the way."

"Sarah," she replied, blushing slightly.

The Blossoming Friendship

OVER THE NEXT FEW WEEKS, Sarah and Daniel found themselves in several classes together. They quickly became friends, bonding over their shared love of literature and music. They spent hours talking about their favorite books and bands, and soon, their friendship deepened into something more.

The First Date

ONE FRIDAY EVENING, Daniel mustered the courage to ask Sarah out on a date. They went to a local diner and then to a movie. It was a simple, sweet evening, filled with nervous laughter and shy glances. After the movie, Daniel walked Sarah home, and as they stood on her doorstep, he leaned in and kissed her. It was a gentle, tentative kiss that left them both smiling.

The Challenges of Young Love

AS THEIR RELATIONSHIP grew, Sarah and Daniel faced the typical challenges of young love. They navigated the ups and downs of high school, from exams and extracurricular activities to misunderstandings and insecurities. But through it all, they supported each other, their love growing stronger with each passing day.

The Prom Night Promise

BY THE TIME SENIOR prom rolled around, Sarah and Daniel were inseparable. That night, under the twinkling lights of the dance floor, Daniel took Sarah's hand and led her outside to the school garden.

"Sarah," he said, looking into her eyes, "I know we're young, but I love you more than anything. I promise that no matter what happens, I'll always be here for you."

Tears welled up in Sarah's eyes as she replied, "I love you too, Daniel. Forever and always."

Their first love was a beautiful, innocent journey that would shape their futures and leave an indelible mark on their hearts.

Story 4: The College Romance

A NEW BEGINNING

When Emma arrived at college, she was both excited and nervous about the new chapter in her life. She was eager to meet new people and experience new things, but she never expected to find love so quickly.

During her first week on campus, Emma attended a welcome party hosted by her dorm. It was there that she met Ethan, a charming sophomore with a passion for art and a knack for making her laugh. They spent the entire evening talking, and by the end of the night, Emma felt a connection she had never experienced before.

The Spark of Attraction

EMMA AND ETHAN QUICKLY became close friends, bonding over their shared interests and late-night conversations. They studied together, attended events, and explored the campus. The more time they spent together, the more Emma realized that her feelings for Ethan were growing into something deeper.

One evening, as they were sitting on a bench overlooking the campus, Ethan turned to Emma and said, "I think I'm falling for you."

Emma's heart skipped a beat as she replied, "I think I'm falling for you too."

The First Kiss

WITH THOSE WORDS, THEIR relationship blossomed into a full-fledged romance. Their first kiss was under the stars, a moment of pure magic that left them both breathless. From that night on, they were inseparable, their love growing stronger with each passing day.

Navigating College Life

EMMA AND ETHAN FACED the typical challenges of college life, from balancing coursework and extracurricular activities to dealing with homesickness and stress. But through it all, they supported each other, their love providing a source of strength and comfort.

A Love That Endures

AS GRADUATION APPROACHED, Emma and Ethan knew that their time in college was coming to an end, but their love was just beginning. They made plans for the future, excited to see where life would take them.

Their college romance was a journey of discovery, growth, and deep connection, a testament to the beauty and innocence of first love.

Story 5: The Unexpected Connection

A Chance Encounter

LILY HAD ALWAYS BEEN a romantic at heart, but she never expected to find love in the most unexpected place. It was a rainy afternoon when she took shelter in a small café near her apartment.

As she sipped her coffee and watched the raindrops fall, she noticed a young man sitting alone at a nearby table, sketching in a notebook.

Curiosity got the better of her, and she approached him. "Hi, I'm Lily. What are you drawing?"

The young man looked up and smiled. "I'm Max. Just sketching the view outside."

A Shared Passion

LILY AND MAX STRUCK up a conversation, discovering that they shared a love for art and creativity. They spent hours talking, completely losing track of time. By the end of the afternoon, they had exchanged phone numbers and made plans to meet again.

The Blossoming Romance

OVER THE NEXT FEW WEEKS, Lily and Max's connection deepened. They visited art galleries, attended painting classes, and spent countless hours creating together. Their shared passion for art brought them closer, and soon, their friendship blossomed into a beautiful romance.

The First Kiss

ONE EVENING, AS THEY were walking through the city, Max took Lily's hand and led her to a quiet park. Under the soft glow of the streetlights, he leaned in and kissed her. It was a tender, sweet kiss that made Lily's heart soar.

"I've never felt this way before," Max whispered.

"Me neither," Lily replied, smiling.

A Love That Inspires

LILY AND MAX'S LOVE story was one of unexpected connection and shared passion. Their first love was a source of inspiration and joy, a beautiful reminder that love can be found in the most surprising places.

Story 6: The Childhood Friends

Growing Up Together

EMILY AND JACK HAD known each other since they were toddlers. Their families lived next door to each other, and they had grown up playing in each other's backyards, sharing secrets, and dreaming about the future. They were best friends, and their bond was unbreakable.

The Realization

As they entered their teenage years, Emily began to notice a change in her feelings towards Jack. She found herself thinking about him more often, her heart fluttering whenever he was near. She wasn't sure when it happened, but she realized that she was in love with her best friend.

The Confession

One summer evening, as they sat on the swings in the park, Emily gathered her courage and turned to Jack. "Jack, I need to tell you something."

Jack looked at her, his expression curious. "What is it, Em?"

Taking a deep breath, Emily said, "I think I'm in love with you."

For a moment, there was silence. Then Jack smiled and replied, "I've been waiting for the right moment to tell you that I feel the same way."

The First Kiss

WITH THEIR FEELINGS out in the open, Emily and Jack's friendship blossomed into a beautiful romance. Their first kiss was under the stars, a moment of pure magic that left them both breathless.

From that night on, they were inseparable, their love growing stronger with each passing day.

A Love That Lasts

EMILY AND JACK'S LOVE story was a testament to the power of friendship and the beauty of first love. They faced the challenges of growing up together, supporting each other through the ups and downs of life. Their love was a source of strength and comfort, a reminder that true love can be found in the heart of a best friend.

Story 7: The Foreign Exchange Student

A NEW BEGINNING

When Isabella arrived in a small town in the United States as a foreign exchange student from Spain, she was both excited and nervous about the new chapter in her life. She was eager to experience a new culture and make new friends, but she never expected to find love so quickly.

During her first week at the local high school, Isabella met David, a charming junior with a passion for photography and a kind heart. They were assigned as partners for a school project, and from that moment on, they became inseparable.

The Spark of Attraction

ISABELLA AND DAVID quickly became close friends, bonding over their shared interests and late-night conversations. They studied together, attended school events, and explored the town. The more time they spent together, the more Isabella realized that her feelings for David were growing into something deeper.

One evening, as they were walking through the town's picturesque streets, David turned to Isabella and said, "I think I'm falling for you."

Isabella's heart skipped a beat as she replied, "I think I'm falling for you too."

The First Kiss

WITH THOSE WORDS, THEIR relationship blossomed into a full-fledged romance. Their first kiss was under the moonlight, a moment of pure magic that left them both breathless. From that night on, they were inseparable, their love growing stronger with each passing day.

Navigating Cultural Differences

ISABELLA AND DAVID faced the typical challenges of young love, from balancing schoolwork and extracurricular activities to dealing with cultural differences and homesickness. But through it all, they supported each other, their love providing a source of strength and comfort.

A Love That Endures

AS THE END OF ISABELLA'S exchange program approached, they knew they would have to say goodbye. On their last evening together, they walked through the town's streets, their hands intertwined. When they reached the spot where they had first met, David kissed Isabella gently on the lips. It was a sweet, tender kiss that left them both breathless.

"I'll never forget you," David whispered.

"Me neither," Isabella replied, tears streaming down her cheeks.

Though their time together was short, the memories of that year would stay with them forever, a reminder of the innocence and beauty of first love.

Story 8: The Love Letter

A Hidden Message

IN A DUSTY ATTIC OF an old family home, young Clara discovered a box filled with letters. These letters, yellowed with age, were tied with a delicate ribbon. As she untied the ribbon and opened the first letter, she realized they were love letters written by her grandmother, Elizabeth, to her first love, James.

The Romance Unfolds

THROUGH THESE LETTERS, Clara pieced together the story of her grandmother's first love. Elizabeth and James had met in the summer of 1952, in a small town where James was visiting his relatives. They had shared a whirlwind romance, full of laughter, stolen glances, and secret meetings.

The First Kiss

ONE EVENING, UNDER the stars, James confessed his love for Elizabeth. With trembling hands, he handed her a small bouquet of wildflowers and said, "I love you, Elizabeth."

Elizabeth's heart soared as she replied, "I love you too, James."

Their first kiss was under the soft glow of the moonlight, a moment of pure magic that left them both breathless.

The Challenges of Distance

As the summer came to an end, James had to return to his hometown. They promised to write to each other every day, and through their letters, they kept their love alive. Each letter was filled with words of longing, hope, and dreams for the future.

A Love That Endures

THOUGH THEY FACED THE challenges of distance and time, their love remained strong. The letters were a testament to their enduring love, a beautiful reminder of the innocence and beauty of first love.

As Clara read the last letter, tears filled her eyes. She felt a deep connection to her grandmother, understanding the power of first love and the beauty of the written word.

Story 9: The High School Crush

A SECRET ADMIRATION

Megan had always admired Jake from afar. He was the star quarterback of the high school football team, with a charming smile and a kind heart. Megan, on the other hand, was a shy bookworm who preferred the company of her favorite novels to the crowded hallways of high school.

The Unexpected Meeting

ONE DAY, FATE INTERVENED. Megan was walking home from school when she noticed Jake struggling with a flat tire on his car. Summoning all her courage, she approached him and offered to help.

"Hi, Jake. Need some help?" Megan asked, trying to keep her voice steady.

"Hey, Megan! That would be great, thanks," Jake replied with a grateful smile.

The Blossoming Friendship

AS THEY WORKED TOGETHER to fix the tire, they struck up a conversation. Megan was surprised to find that Jake was not only friendly but also shared her love for books and literature. They exchanged phone numbers and began texting each other, quickly becoming friends.

The First Date

AFTER WEEKS OF GETTING to know each other, Jake asked Megan out on a date. They went to a local coffee shop and spent hours talking about their favorite books and dreams for the future. It was a simple, sweet evening that left Megan's heart fluttering.

The First Kiss

AFTER THEIR DATE, JAKE walked Megan home. As they stood on her doorstep, he leaned in and kissed her gently on the lips. It was a tender, innocent kiss that left them both smiling.

"I've had a crush on you for a long time," Jake confessed.

"Me too," Megan replied, her cheeks blushing.

A Love That Grows

MEGAN AND JAKE'S LOVE story was a journey of discovery and growth. Their first love was a beautiful, innocent connection that blossomed into something deeper. They supported each other through the ups and downs of high school, their love growing stronger with each passing day.

Story 10: The Dance Partner

A Chance Encounter

WHEN LILY SIGNED UP for the school's dance competition, she never expected to be paired with Mark, the quiet, introverted boy from her math class. They were an unlikely pair, but from the moment they started practicing together, sparks flew.

The Practice Sessions

LILY AND MARK SPENT countless hours practicing their dance routine, learning to trust and rely on each other. They shared laughter, frustrations, and triumphs as they perfected their moves. The more time they spent together, the more they realized their connection was more than just a dance partnership.

The First Kiss

ONE EVENING, AFTER a particularly intense practice session, they found themselves alone in the empty gym. With the music still playing softly in the background, Mark took Lily's hand and pulled her close. Their eyes met, and without a word, he leaned in and kissed her. It was a gentle, tender kiss that left them both breathless.

The Dance Competition

THE NIGHT OF THE DANCE competition was filled with nerves and excitement. As they took to the stage, Lily and Mark felt a sense of unity and trust. Their performance was flawless, and as they finished their routine, the audience erupted in applause.

A Love That Dances

LILY AND MARK'S LOVE story was a beautiful dance of emotions and connection. Their first love was a journey of trust and discovery, a reminder that sometimes the most unexpected connections can lead to the most beautiful love stories.

Story 11: The Library Encounter

A Shared Passion

SOPHIA HAD ALWAYS FOUND solace in the quiet corners of the library. It was her sanctuary, a place where she could lose herself in the world of books. One afternoon, while searching for a novel in the fiction section, she noticed a young man engrossed in a book she had recently read.

"Excuse me," Sophia said softly, "I couldn't help but notice you're reading 'The Great Gatsby.' It's one of my favorites."

The young man looked up and smiled. "It's a great book. I'm Ethan, by the way."

The Blossoming Friendship

SOPHIA AND ETHAN STRUCK up a conversation about their favorite books and authors. They discovered a shared passion for literature and quickly became friends. They spent countless hours in the library, discussing books, life, and everything in between.

The First Date

AFTER WEEKS OF GETTING to know each other, Ethan asked Sophia out on a date. They went to a cozy café and spent the evening talking about their dreams and aspirations. It was a simple, sweet evening that left Sophia's heart fluttering.

The First Kiss

AFTER THEIR DATE, ETHAN walked Sophia home. As they stood on her doorstep, he leaned in and kissed her gently on the lips. It was a tender, innocent kiss that left them both smiling.

"I think I'm falling for you," Ethan confessed.

"Me too," Sophia replied, her cheeks blushing.

A Love That Grows

SOPHIA AND ETHAN'S love story was a beautiful journey of discovery and connection. Their first love was a source of inspiration and joy, a reminder that love can be found in the most unexpected places.

Story 12: The Childhood Sweethearts

Growing Up Together

EMILY AND JACK HAD known each other since they were toddlers. Their families lived next door to each other, and they had grown up playing in each other's backyards, sharing secrets, and dreaming about the future. They were best friends, and their bond was unbreakable.

The Realization

As they entered their teenage years, Emily began to notice a change in her feelings towards Jack. She found herself thinking about him more often, her heart fluttering whenever he was near. She wasn't sure when it happened, but she realized that she was in love with her best friend.

The Confession

One summer evening, as they sat on the swings in the park, Emily gathered her courage and turned to Jack. "Jack, I need to tell you something."

Jack looked at her, his expression curious. "What is it, Em?"

Taking a deep breath, Emily said, "I think I'm in love with you."

For a moment, there was silence. Then Jack smiled and replied, "I've been waiting for the right moment to tell you that I feel the same way."

The First Kiss

WITH THEIR FEELINGS out in the open, Emily and Jack's friendship blossomed into a beautiful romance. Their first kiss was under the stars, a moment of pure magic that left them both breathless. From that night on, they were inseparable, their love growing stronger with each passing day.

A Love That Lasts

EMILY AND JACK'S LOVE story was a testament to the power of friendship and the beauty of first love. They faced the challenges of growing up together, supporting each other through the ups and downs of life. Their love was a source of strength and comfort, a reminder that true love can be found in the heart of a best friend.

Story 13: The Foreign Exchange Student

A New Beginning

WHEN ISABELLA ARRIVED in a small town in the United States as a foreign exchange student from Spain, she was both excited and nervous about the new chapter in her life. She was eager to experience a new culture and make new friends, but she never expected to find love so quickly.

During her first week at the local high school, Isabella met David, a charming junior with a passion for photography and a kind heart. They were assigned as partners for a school project, and from that moment on, they became inseparable.

The Spark of Attraction

ISABELLA AND DAVID quickly became close friends, bonding over their shared interests and late-night conversations. They studied together, attended school events, and explored the town. The more time they spent together, the more Isabella realized that her feelings for David were growing into something deeper.

One evening, as they were walking through the town's picturesque streets, David turned to Isabella and said, "I think I'm falling for you."

Isabella's heart skipped a beat as she replied, "I think I'm falling for you too."

The First Kiss

WITH THOSE WORDS, THEIR relationship blossomed into a full-fledged romance. Their first kiss was under the moonlight, a moment of pure magic that left them both breathless. From that night on, they were inseparable, their love growing stronger with each passing day.

Navigating Cultural Differences

ISABELLA AND DAVID faced the typical challenges of young love, from balancing schoolwork and extracurricular activities to dealing with cultural differences and homesickness. But through it all, they supported each other, their love providing a source of strength and comfort.

A Love That Endures

AS THE END OF ISABELLA'S exchange program approached, they knew they would have to say goodbye. On their last evening together, they walked through the town's streets, their hands intertwined. When they reached the spot where they had first met, David kissed Isabella gently on the lips. It was a sweet, tender kiss that left them both breathless.

"I'll never forget you," David whispered.

"Me neither," Isabella replied, tears streaming down her cheeks.

Though their time together was short, the memories of that year would stay with them forever, a reminder of the innocence and beauty of first love.

Story 14: The Love Letter

A Hidden Message

IN A DUSTY ATTIC OF an old family home, young Clara discovered a box filled with letters. These letters, yellowed with age, were tied with a delicate ribbon. As she untied the ribbon and opened the first letter, she realized they were love letters written by her grandmother, Elizabeth, to her first love, James.

The Romance Unfolds

THROUGH THESE LETTERS, Clara pieced together the story of her grandmother's first love. Elizabeth and James had met in the summer of 1952, in a small town where James was visiting his relatives. They had shared a whirlwind romance, full of laughter, stolen glances, and secret meetings.

The First Kiss

ONE EVENING, UNDER the stars, James confessed his love for Elizabeth. With trembling hands, he handed her a small bouquet of wildflowers and said, "I love you, Elizabeth."

Elizabeth's heart soared as she replied, "I love you too, James."

Their first kiss was under the soft glow of the moonlight, a moment of pure magic that left them both breathless.

The Challenges of Distance

AS THE SUMMER CAME to an end, James had to return to his hometown. They promised to write to each other every day, and through their letters, they kept their love alive. Each letter was filled with words of longing, hope, and dreams for the future.

A Love That Endures

THOUGH THEY FACED THE challenges of distance and time, their love remained strong. The letters were a testament to their enduring love, a beautiful reminder of the innocence and beauty of first love.

As Clara read the last letter, tears filled her eyes. She felt a deep connection to her grandmother, understanding the power of first love and the beauty of the written word.

Story 15: The High School Crush

A Secret Admiration

MEGAN HAD ALWAYS ADMIRED Jake from afar. He was the star quarterback of the high school football team, with a charming smile and a kind heart. Megan, on the other hand, was a shy bookworm who preferred the company of her favorite novels to the crowded hallways of high school.

The Unexpected Meeting

ONE DAY, FATE INTERVENED. Megan was walking home from school when she noticed Jake struggling with a flat tire on his car. Summoning all her courage, she approached him and offered to help.

"Hi, Jake. Need some help?" Megan asked, trying to keep her voice steady.

"Hey, Megan! That would be great, thanks," Jake replied with a grateful smile.

The Blossoming Friendship

AS THEY WORKED TOGETHER to fix the tire, they struck up a conversation. Megan was surprised to find that Jake was not only friendly but also shared her love for books and literature. They exchanged phone numbers and began texting each other, quickly becoming friends.

The First Date

AFTER WEEKS OF GETTING to know each other, Jake asked Megan out on a date. They went to a local coffee shop and spent hours talking about their favorite books and dreams for the future. It was a simple, sweet evening that left Megan's heart fluttering.

The First Kiss

AFTER THEIR DATE, JAKE walked Megan home. As they stood on her doorstep, he leaned in and kissed her gently on the lips. It was a tender, innocent kiss that left them both smiling.

"I've had a crush on you for a long time," Jake confessed.

"Me too," Megan replied, her cheeks blushing.

A Love That Grows

MEGAN AND JAKE'S LOVE story was a journey of discovery and growth. Their first love was a beautiful, innocent connection that blossomed into something deeper. They supported each other through the ups and downs of high school, their love growing stronger with each passing day.

Story 16: The Dance Partner

A CHANCE ENCOUNTER

When Lily signed up for the school's dance competition, she never expected to be paired with Mark, the quiet, introverted boy from her math class. They were an unlikely pair, but from the moment they started practicing together, sparks flew.

The Practice Sessions

LILY AND MARK SPENT countless hours practicing their dance routine, learning to trust and rely on each other. They shared laughter, frustrations, and triumphs as they perfected their moves. The more time they spent together, the more they realized their connection was more than just a dance partnership.

The First Kiss

ONE EVENING, AFTER a particularly intense practice session, they found themselves alone in the empty gym. With the music still playing softly in the background, Mark took Lily's hand and pulled her close. Their eyes met, and without a word, he leaned in and kissed her. It was a gentle, tender kiss that left them both breathless.

The Dance Competition

THE NIGHT OF THE DANCE competition was filled with nerves and excitement. As they took to the stage, Lily and Mark felt a sense of unity and trust. Their performance was flawless, and as they finished their routine, the audience erupted in applause.

A Love That Dances

LILY AND MARK'S LOVE story was a beautiful dance of emotions and connection. Their first love was a journey of trust and discovery, a reminder that sometimes the most unexpected connections can lead to the most beautiful love stories.

Story 17: The Library Encounter

A Shared Passion

SOPHIA HAD ALWAYS FOUND solace in the quiet corners of the library. It was her sanctuary, a place where she could lose herself in the world of books. One afternoon, while searching for a novel in the fiction section, she noticed a young man engrossed in a book she had recently read.

"Excuse me," Sophia said softly, "I couldn't help but notice you're reading 'The Great Gatsby.' It's one of my favorites."

The young man looked up and smiled. "It's a great book. I'm Ethan, by the way."

The Blossoming Friendship

SOPHIA AND ETHAN STRUCK up a conversation about their favorite books and authors. They discovered a shared passion for literature and quickly became friends. They spent countless hours in the library, discussing books, life, and everything in between.

The First Date

AFTER WEEKS OF GETTING to know each other, Ethan asked Sophia out on a date. They went to a cozy café and spent the evening talking about their dreams and aspirations. It was a simple, sweet evening that left Sophia's heart fluttering.

The First Kiss

AFTER THEIR DATE, ETHAN walked Sophia home. As they stood on her doorstep, he leaned in and kissed her gently on the lips. It was a tender, innocent kiss that left them both smiling.

"I think I'm falling for you," Ethan confessed.

"Me too," Sophia replied, her cheeks blushing.

A Love That Grows

SOPHIA AND ETHAN'S love story was a beautiful journey of discovery and connection. Their first love was a source of inspiration and joy, a reminder that love can be found in the most unexpected places.

Story 18: The Childhood Sweethearts

Growing Up Together

EMILY AND JACK HAD known each other since they were toddlers. Their families lived next door to each other, and they had grown up playing in each other's backyards, sharing secrets, and dreaming about the future. They were best friends, and their bond was unbreakable.

The Realization

As they entered their teenage years, Emily began to notice a change in her feelings towards Jack. She found herself thinking about him more often, her heart fluttering whenever he was near. She wasn't sure when it happened, but she realized that she was in love with her best friend.

The Confession

One summer evening, as they sat on the swings in the park, Emily gathered her courage and turned to Jack. "Jack, I need to tell you something."

Jack looked at her, his expression curious. "What is it, Em?"

Taking a deep breath, Emily said, "I think I'm in love with you."

For a moment, there was silence. Then Jack smiled and replied, "I've been waiting for the right moment to tell you that I feel the same way."

The First Kiss

WITH THEIR FEELINGS out in the open, Emily and Jack's friendship blossomed into a beautiful romance. Their first kiss was under the stars, a moment of pure magic that left them both breathless. From that night on, they were inseparable, their love growing stronger with each passing day.

A Love That Lasts

EMILY AND JACK'S LOVE story was a testament to the power of friendship and the beauty of first love. They faced the challenges of growing up together, supporting each other through the ups and downs of life. Their love was a source of strength and comfort, a reminder that true love can be found in the heart of a best friend.

Exploration of Young, Innocent Romance

FIRST LOVE IS OFTEN characterized by its innocence and purity. It's a time when emotions are raw and unfiltered, when every glance, touch, and word is imbued with a sense of wonder and excitement. These stories capture the essence of young romance, exploring the joy, tenderness, and sometimes heartache that comes with falling in love for the first time.

The beauty of first love lies in its simplicity. There are no hidden agendas or ulterior motives, just a genuine connection between two people who are discovering their feelings for each other. It's a time of exploration, where every moment is a new experience, and every emotion is felt deeply and intensely.

In these stories, we see characters navigating the complexities of their feelings, experiencing the highs and lows of first love. From the shy glances and nervous smiles to the sweet, tentative kisses, these tales capture the magic and innocence of young romance.

Heartwarming Tales of First Kisses and Initial

Connections

THE FIRST KISS IS A pivotal moment in any romance. It's a moment of vulnerability and courage, where two people take a leap of faith and open their hearts to each other. In these stories, the first kiss is a symbol of the characters' growing connection and deepening feelings.

These heartwarming tales highlight the beauty and tenderness of first kisses. Whether it's under the stars, in a quiet library, or on a crowded dance floor, each first kiss is a unique and unforgettable experience. It's a moment that leaves the characters breathless, their hearts racing, and their spirits soaring.

The initial connections between the characters are also a central theme in these stories. From chance encounters and shared passions to childhood friendships and unexpected meetings, these tales showcase the myriad ways in which love can blossom. Each connection is a spark that ignites a beautiful romance, leading to moments of joy, laughter, and deep emotional connection.

AS YOU READ THROUGH these stories of first love, may you be reminded of your own experiences and the magic of falling in love for the first time. These tales are a celebration of young, innocent romance, capturing the beauty, wonder, and heartwarming moments that make first love a cherished memory. Whether you're reminiscing about your own first love or dreaming of future connections, may these stories inspire and uplift you, reminding you of the timeless power of love.

Chapter 3: Rekindled Flames

Stories About Love Rekindled After Years Apart

There's a unique magic in stories where lovers find their way back to each other after years apart. Time has a way of maturing hearts, healing old wounds, and sometimes, clarifying what truly matters. This chapter is dedicated to those powerful narratives of lost lovers who rediscover each other, reigniting old flames with a depth and intensity that only time and separation can bring.

Story 1: The High School Sweethearts

The Innocent Beginning

SOPHIA AND MICHAEL were inseparable during high school. They met during their freshman year and quickly became best friends. By their junior year, their friendship had blossomed into a romantic relationship that everyone at school admired. They spent their days dreaming about the future, promising each other that they would always be together.

The Painful Separation

HOWEVER, LIFE HAD OTHER plans. After graduation, Michael received a scholarship to a prestigious university across the country, while Sophia stayed behind to help with her family business. The distance, coupled with the pressures of their new lives, eventually led to their heartbreaking decision to part ways. They promised to stay friends, but as time passed, they lost touch completely.

Years Later

TEN YEARS LATER, SOPHIA was running a successful café in their hometown, while Michael had become a renowned journalist traveling the world. One rainy afternoon, as Sophia was closing up shop, a familiar figure walked through the door. It was Michael, looking just as handsome and charming as she remembered.

"Sophia," he said, his voice filled with a mix of surprise and longing.

"Michael," she replied, her heart racing.

The Reconnection

They sat down and talked for hours, catching up on the years they had missed. Michael revealed that he had recently moved back to town to take care of his ailing mother. As they reminisced about their past, old feelings began to resurface. Michael asked if they could meet again, and Sophia agreed, feeling a spark of hope in her heart.

The Rekindling of Love

OVER THE NEXT FEW MONTHS, Sophia and Michael spent more time together, rekindling their old bond. They went on dates, revisited old haunts, and slowly fell back in love. One evening, under the stars, Michael took Sophia's hand and said, "I've never stopped loving you, Sophia."

Tears filled Sophia's eyes as she replied, "I love you too, Michael. I've always loved you."

Their love, once lost to time and distance, was reignited with a passion and depth that only years apart could bring. They had found their way back to each other, proving that true love can withstand the test of time.

Story 2: The College Sweethearts

The Blossoming Romance

EMILY AND DAVID MET during their sophomore year of college. They were both studying literature and bonded over their shared love of poetry and classic novels. Their relationship blossomed quickly, and they became inseparable. They dreamed of a future together, imagining a life filled with love and literary adventures.

The Unexpected Turn

HOWEVER, LIFE TOOK an unexpected turn when David received a job offer in another state after graduation. Emily had just been accepted into a prestigious graduate program, and they faced the difficult decision of pursuing their careers separately. They promised to stay in touch, but the distance and the demands of their new lives eventually caused them to drift apart.

A Chance Encounter

FIFTEEN YEARS LATER, Emily was a successful author, while David had become a respected professor. They had both moved on with their lives, but neither had forgotten their college romance. One day, while attending a literary conference, Emily spotted a familiar face in the crowd. It was David, and their eyes met across the room.

"Emily?" David called out, his voice filled with surprise and joy.

"David," Emily replied, her heart skipping a beat.

The Reconnection

They spent the evening catching up, reminiscing about their college days and sharing stories of their lives since then. The connection between them was still strong, and as they talked, old feelings began to resurface. David asked if they could meet again, and Emily agreed, feeling a spark of hope in her heart.

The Rekindling of Love

OVER THE NEXT FEW MONTHS, Emily and David rekindled their old bond. They went on dates, attended literary events together, and slowly fell back in love. One evening, as they walked along the beach, David took Emily's hand and said, "I've never stopped loving you, Emily."

Tears filled Emily's eyes as she replied, "I love you too, David. I've always loved you."

Their love, once lost to time and distance, was reignited with a passion and depth that only years apart could bring. They had found their way back to each other, proving that true love can withstand the test of time.

Story 3: The Childhood Friends

The Early Years

LILY AND JACK HAD BEEN best friends since they were children. They grew up in the same neighborhood, went to the same schools, and shared countless adventures together. As they entered their teenage years, their friendship blossomed into a romantic relationship. They were inseparable, and everyone believed they were meant to be together forever.

The Painful Separation

HOWEVER, AFTER HIGH school, Jack's family moved to another state, and they were forced to part ways. They promised to stay in touch, but the distance and the demands of their new lives eventually caused them to drift apart. They both moved on, but neither could forget the bond they once shared.

A Surprise Reunion

TWENTY YEARS LATER, Lily was a successful businesswoman, while Jack had become a firefighter. One day, while attending a charity event, Lily saw a familiar face across the room. It was Jack, and their eyes met, igniting a spark of recognition and longing.

"Lily?" Jack called out, his voice filled with surprise and joy.

"Jack," Lily replied, her heart racing.

The Reconnection

They spent the evening catching up, reminiscing about their childhood and sharing stories of their lives since then. The connection between them was still strong, and as they talked, old feelings began to resurface. Jack asked if they could meet again, and Lily agreed, feeling a spark of hope in her heart.

The Rekindling of Love

OVER THE NEXT FEW MONTHS, Lily and Jack rekindled their old bond. They went on dates, revisited their old neighborhood, and slowly fell back in love. One evening, as they sat on the swings in the park where they had spent so much time as children, Jack took Lily's hand and said, "I've never stopped loving you, Lily."

Tears filled Lily's eyes as she replied, "I love you too, Jack. I've always loved you."

Their love, once lost to time and distance, was reignited with a passion and depth that only years apart could bring. They had found their way back to each other, proving that true love can withstand the test of time.

Story 4: The Lost Letters

The Young Lovers

HANNAH AND ETHAN MET during their senior year of high school. They fell in love quickly and deeply, sharing dreams of a future together. Ethan was drafted into the military shortly after graduation, and they promised to write to each other every day. Their letters were filled with love, hope, and dreams of their future.

The Heartbreaking Silence

HOWEVER, AS TIME PASSED, the letters from Ethan stopped coming. Hannah was heartbroken, believing that Ethan had moved on or, worse, had been lost in the war. She tried to move on with her life, but the pain of losing Ethan never truly went away.

The Rediscovery

Thirty years later, while cleaning out her parents' attic, Hannah discovered a box filled with unopened letters. They were the letters Ethan had written to her, somehow lost and never delivered. With trembling hands, she opened the first letter and began to read. The words of love and longing brought tears to her eyes, and she realized that Ethan had never stopped loving her.

The Search

Determined to find Ethan, Hannah began searching for him, reaching out to old friends and military contacts. After months of searching, she finally found him living in a small town, working as a mechanic. Nervously, she made the journey to see him.

The Reunion

When Ethan opened the door and saw Hannah standing there, his eyes filled with tears. "Hannah," he said, his voice choked with emotion.

"Ethan," she replied, her heart racing.

They spent hours talking, sharing their stories and the pain of the years they had lost. As they reconnected, old feelings began to resurface, and they realized that their love had never truly faded.

The Rekindling of Love

OVER THE NEXT FEW MONTHS, Hannah and Ethan rekindled their old bond. They went on dates, shared their dreams for the future, and slowly fell back in love. One evening, as they sat on the porch of Ethan's home, he took her hand and said, "I've never stopped loving you, Hannah."

Tears filled Hannah's eyes as she replied, "I love you too, Ethan. I've always loved you."

Their love, once lost to time and distance, was reignited with a passion and depth that only years apart could bring. They had found their way back to each other, proving that true love can withstand the test of time.

Story 5: The Second Chance

The Broken Engagement

LAURA AND MARK HAD been engaged to be married, but a misunderstanding and a series of unfortunate events led to their painful breakup. They went their separate ways, both heartbroken and wondering what could have been.

The Unexpected Encounter

FIFTEEN YEARS LATER, Laura was a successful lawyer, while Mark had become a renowned architect. They had both moved on with their lives, but neither had forgotten their love for each other. One day, while attending a mutual friend's wedding, they saw each other for the first time since their breakup.

"Laura?" Mark called out, his voice filled with surprise and longing.

"Mark," Laura replied, her heart skipping a beat.

The Reconnection

They spent the evening catching up, reminiscing about their past and sharing stories of their lives since then. The connection between them was still strong, and as they talked, old feelings began to resurface. Mark asked if they could meet again, and Laura agreed, feeling a spark of hope in her heart.

The Rekindling of Love

OVER THE NEXT FEW MONTHS, Laura and Mark rekindled their old bond. They went on dates, revisited old haunts, and slowly fell back in love. One evening, as they stood on the rooftop of Mark's building, looking out over the city, Mark took Laura's hand and said, "I've never stopped loving you, Laura."

Tears filled Laura's eyes as she replied, "I love you too, Mark. I've always loved you."

Their love, once lost to misunderstandings and time, was reignited with a passion and depth that only years apart could bring. They had found their way back to each other, proving that true love can withstand the test of time.

Story 6: The Childhood Crush

The Innocent Beginning

MEGAN AND RYAN HAD been best friends since they were children. They grew up in the same neighborhood, went to the same schools, and shared countless adventures together. As they entered their teenage years, Megan developed a crush on Ryan, but she never told him, afraid it would ruin their friendship.

The Painful Separation

AFTER HIGH SCHOOL, Ryan moved to another state for college, and they were forced to part ways. They promised to stay in touch, but the distance and the demands of their new lives eventually caused them to drift apart. Megan moved on, but she never forgot her first love.

A Surprise Reunion

TWENTY YEARS LATER, Megan was a successful businesswoman, while Ryan had become a doctor. One day, while attending a high school reunion, Megan saw a familiar face across the room. It was Ryan, and their eyes met, igniting a spark of recognition and longing.

"Megan?" Ryan called out, his voice filled with surprise and joy.

"Ryan," Megan replied, her heart racing.

The Reconnection

They spent the evening catching up, reminiscing about their childhood and sharing stories of their lives since then. The connection between them was still strong, and as they talked, old feelings began to resurface. Ryan asked if they could meet again, and Megan agreed, feeling a spark of hope in her heart.

The Rekindling of Love

OVER THE NEXT FEW MONTHS, Megan and Ryan rekindled their old bond. They went on dates, revisited their old neighborhood, and slowly fell back in love. One evening, as they sat on the swings in the park where they had spent so much time as children, Ryan took Megan's hand and said, "I've never stopped loving you, Megan."

Tears filled Megan's eyes as she replied, "I love you too, Ryan. I've always loved you."

Their love, once lost to time and distance, was reignited with a passion and depth that only years apart could bring. They had found their way back to each other, proving that true love can withstand the test of time.

Story 7: The High School Crush

THE SECRET ADMIRATION

Olivia had always admired Jake from afar. He was the star quarterback of the high school football team, with a charming smile and a kind heart. Olivia, on the other hand, was a shy bookworm who preferred the company of her favorite novels to the crowded hallways of high school.

The Painful Separation

AFTER GRADUATION, JAKE moved to another state for college, and they were forced to part ways. They promised to stay in touch, but the distance and the demands of their new lives eventually caused them to drift apart. Olivia moved on, but she never forgot her first love.

A Surprise Reunion

TWENTY YEARS LATER, Olivia was a successful businesswoman, while Jake had become a lawyer. One day, while attending a high school reunion, Olivia saw a familiar face across the room. It was Jake, and their eyes met, igniting a spark of recognition and longing.

"Olivia?" Jake called out, his voice filled with surprise and joy.

"Jake," Olivia replied, her heart racing.

The Reconnection

They spent the evening catching up, reminiscing about their high school days and sharing stories of their lives since then. The connection between them was still strong, and as they talked, old feelings began to resurface. Jake asked if they could meet again, and Olivia agreed, feeling a spark of hope in her heart.

The Rekindling of Love

OVER THE NEXT FEW MONTHS, Olivia and Jake rekindled their old bond. They went on dates, revisited old haunts, and slowly fell back in love. One evening, as they stood on the rooftop of Jake's building, looking out over the city, Jake took Olivia's hand and said, "I've never stopped loving you, Olivia."

Tears filled Olivia's eyes as she replied, "I love you too, Jake. I've always loved you."

Their love, once lost to time and distance, was reignited with a passion and depth that only years apart could bring. They had found their way back to each other, proving that true love can withstand the test of time.

Story 8: The Lost Love

The Young Lovers

GRACE AND DANIEL MET during their sophomore year of college. They were both studying literature and bonded over their shared love of poetry and classic novels. Their relationship blossomed quickly, and they became inseparable. They dreamed of a future together, imagining a life filled with love and literary adventures.

The Unexpected Turn

HOWEVER, LIFE TOOK an unexpected turn when Daniel received a job offer in another state after graduation. Grace had just been accepted into a prestigious graduate program, and they faced the difficult decision of pursuing their careers separately. They promised to stay in touch, but the distance and the demands of their new lives eventually caused them to drift apart.

A Chance Encounter

FIFTEEN YEARS LATER, Grace was a successful author, while Daniel had become a respected professor. They had both moved on with their lives, but neither had forgotten their college romance. One day, while attending a literary conference, Grace spotted a familiar face in the crowd. It was Daniel, and their eyes met across the room.

"Grace?" Daniel called out, his voice filled with surprise and joy.

"Daniel," Grace replied, her heart skipping a beat.

The Reconnection

They spent the evening catching up, reminiscing about their college days and sharing stories of their lives since then. The connection between them was still strong, and as they talked, old feelings began to resurface. Daniel asked if they could meet again, and Grace agreed, feeling a spark of hope in her heart.

The Rekindling of Love

OVER THE NEXT FEW MONTHS, Grace and Daniel rekindled their old bond. They went on dates, attended literary events together, and slowly fell back in love. One evening, as they walked along the beach, Daniel took Grace's hand and said, "I've never stopped loving you, Grace."

Tears filled Grace's eyes as she replied, "I love you too, Daniel. I've always loved you."

Their love, once lost to time and distance, was reignited with a passion and depth that only years apart could bring. They had found their way back to each other, proving that true love can withstand the test of time.

Story 9: The High School Sweethearts

The Innocent Beginning

SOPHIA AND MICHAEL were inseparable during high school. They met during their freshman year and quickly became best friends. By their junior year, their friendship had blossomed into a romantic relationship that everyone at school admired. They spent their days dreaming about the future, promising each other that they would always be together.

The Painful Separation

HOWEVER, LIFE HAD OTHER plans. After graduation, Michael received a scholarship to a prestigious university across the country, while Sophia stayed behind to help with her family business. The distance, coupled with the pressures of their new lives, eventually led to their heartbreaking decision to part ways. They promised to stay friends, but as time passed, they lost touch completely.

Years Later

TEN YEARS LATER, SOPHIA was running a successful café in their hometown, while Michael had become a renowned journalist traveling the world. One rainy afternoon, as Sophia was closing up shop, a familiar figure walked through the door. It was Michael, looking just as handsome and charming as she remembered.

"Sophia," he said, his voice filled with a mix of surprise and longing.

"Michael," she replied, her heart racing.

The Reconnection

They sat down and talked for hours, catching up on the years they had missed. Michael revealed that he had recently moved back to town to take care of his ailing mother. As they reminisced about their past, old feelings began to resurface. Michael asked if they could meet again, and Sophia agreed, feeling a spark of hope in her heart.

The Rekindling of Love

OVER THE NEXT FEW MONTHS, Sophia and Michael spent more time together, rekindling their old bond. They went on dates, revisited old haunts, and slowly fell back in love. One evening, under the stars, Michael took Sophia's hand and said, "I've never stopped loving you, Sophia."

Tears filled Sophia's eyes as she replied, "I love you too, Michael. I've always loved you."

Their love, once lost to time and distance, was reignited with a passion and depth that only years apart could bring. They had found their way

back to each other, proving that true love can withstand the test of time.

Story 10: The College Sweethearts

The Blossoming Romance

EMILY AND DAVID MET during their sophomore year of college. They were both studying literature and bonded over their shared love of poetry and classic novels. Their relationship blossomed quickly, and they became inseparable. They dreamed of a future together, imagining a life filled with love and literary adventures.

The Unexpected Turn

HOWEVER, LIFE TOOK an unexpected turn when David received a job offer in another state after graduation. Emily had just been accepted into a prestigious graduate program, and they faced the difficult decision of pursuing their careers separately. They promised to stay in touch, but the distance and the demands of their new lives eventually caused them to drift apart.

A Chance Encounter

FIFTEEN YEARS LATER, Emily was a successful author, while David had become a respected professor. They had both moved on with their lives, but neither had forgotten their college romance. One day, while attending a literary conference, Emily spotted a familiar face in the crowd. It was David, and their eyes met across the room.

"Emily?" David called out, his voice filled with surprise and joy.

"David," Emily replied, her heart skipping a beat.

The Reconnection

They spent the evening catching up, reminiscing about their college days and sharing stories of their lives since then. The connection between them was still strong, and as they talked, old feelings began to resurface. David asked if they could meet again, and Emily agreed, feeling a spark of hope in her heart.

The Rekindling of Love

OVER THE NEXT FEW MONTHS, Emily and David rekindled their old bond. They went on dates, attended literary events together, and slowly fell back in love. One evening, as they walked along the beach, David took Emily's hand and said, "I've never stopped loving you, Emily."

Tears filled Emily's eyes as she replied, "I love you too, David. I've always loved you."

Their love, once lost to time and distance, was reignited with a passion and depth that only years apart could bring. They had found their way back to each other, proving that true love can withstand the test of time.

The Power of Forgiveness and Second Chances

REKINDLED LOVE STORIES are powerful narratives that demonstrate the resilience of the human heart and the transformative power of forgiveness. These tales remind us that love, even when lost, can be found again, and that the bonds we form with others can withstand the test of time.

Forgiveness is a central theme in these stories. The characters often have to confront past hurts and misunderstandings, finding the strength to forgive and move forward. This process of forgiveness not only heals old wounds but also paves the way for a deeper and more enduring love.

Second chances are another key element. These stories celebrate the idea that it's never too late to find love again, and that sometimes, the love we thought was lost can be rekindled with a new sense of understanding and appreciation.

As you read through these stories of rekindled flames, may you be inspired by the resilience of the human heart and the enduring power of love. These tales are a testament to the beauty of second chances and the transformative power of forgiveness, reminding us that true love can withstand the test of time.

Chapter 4: Love Across Time

Introduction to Love Across Time

Love is a timeless emotion that has been a central theme in literature throughout history. It transcends the boundaries of time and societal norms, binding people together in an enduring embrace. This chapter is dedicated to exploring historical romances set in various eras, where love defies the constraints of society and time. From the medieval period to the Renaissance and beyond, these stories capture the essence of passionate, timeless love.

Story 1: The Knight and the Lady

The Medieval Period

IN THE HEART OF MEDIEVAL England, amidst the towering castles and verdant landscapes, lived Lady Isabella, the daughter of a nobleman. Isabella was known for her beauty and grace, but she was also fiercely independent and intelligent. She had grown up in a world where marriages were arranged for political alliances rather than love.

The Forbidden Love

SIR ROBERT WAS A KNIGHT of humble origins, known for his bravery and honor. He had risen through the ranks of the king's army due to his valor on the battlefield. When he was appointed to guard the castle where Lady Isabella resided, he never expected to find love.

Isabella and Robert's paths crossed during a summer festival. The moment their eyes met, they felt an inexplicable connection. They began to steal moments together, meeting in secret to talk about their dreams and fears. Their love grew in the shadows, forbidden by the societal boundaries that separated them.

The First Kiss

ONE EVENING, UNDER the cover of darkness, Robert and Isabella met in the castle gardens. The moonlight cast a soft glow on Isabella's face as Robert took her hand. "My lady," he whispered, "I cannot deny my feelings any longer. I love you."

Tears welled up in Isabella's eyes as she replied, "And I love you, Sir Robert." Their first kiss was tender and filled with promise, a moment of pure magic amidst the constraints of their world.

The Battle for Love

THEIR LOVE, HOWEVER, was discovered by Isabella's father, who was furious at the thought of his daughter with a common knight. He ordered Robert to leave the castle and never return. But Isabella and Robert were determined to be together. They planned to escape and start a new life where they could love freely.

On the night of their planned escape, the castle was attacked by a rival lord. Robert fought valiantly to protect Isabella and the people of the castle. In the chaos, Isabella's father saw the true bravery and honor of Robert. After the battle was won, he gave his blessing to their union, realizing that true love was more powerful than societal boundaries.

A Love That Transcends Time

ISABELLA AND ROBERT'S love story became a legend, a testament to the power of love to transcend time and societal norms. They lived a long and happy life together, their love growing stronger with each passing year.

Story 2: The Renaissance Lovers

The Renaissance Period

IN THE VIBRANT CITY of Florence during the Renaissance, art and culture flourished. It was a time of great intellectual and artistic achievement. Among the bustling streets and grand palaces lived Elena, a talented painter who defied the conventions of her time. Women were not often allowed to pursue careers, but Elena's talent could not be ignored.

The Unexpected Meeting

LORENZO WAS A WEALTHY merchant, known for his patronage of the arts. He had commissioned many works from the most renowned artists of the time. One day, while visiting an art studio, he saw Elena's work and was captivated by her talent. He requested a portrait, not realizing that his heart would soon be captivated by more than just her art.

The Blossoming Romance

AS ELENA WORKED ON Lorenzo's portrait, they spent hours together, talking about art, philosophy, and their dreams. Lorenzo was enchanted by Elena's intelligence and passion, while Elena found in Lorenzo a kindred spirit who appreciated her for who she was, not just her beauty or her art.

One evening, as they walked through the streets of Florence, Lorenzo took Elena's hand and said, "Elena, your art has touched my soul, but it is you who has captured my heart. I love you."

Elena's heart raced as she replied, "And I love you, Lorenzo. But how can we be together when society does not approve of our union?"

The First Kiss

UNDER THE MOONLIT SKY, Lorenzo leaned in and kissed Elena. It was a kiss filled with hope and defiance, a promise that their love would overcome any obstacle.

The Struggle Against Society

THEIR LOVE FACED MANY challenges. Elena's family disapproved of her relationship with a wealthy merchant, fearing it would ruin her reputation. Lorenzo's peers looked down upon his association with a female artist. But their love only grew stronger in the face of adversity.

Lorenzo decided to use his influence to support Elena's career, commissioning her to paint for the most prestigious clients in Florence. Her work gained acclaim, and she became one of the most celebrated artists of her time.

A Love That Endures

ELENA AND LORENZO'S love story was one of passion and resilience. They proved that love could transcend societal boundaries and bring about positive change. Their story became an inspiration to many, a reminder that true love knows no limits.

Story 3: The Victorian Romance

The Victorian Era

IN THE ELEGANT YET restrictive society of Victorian England, social class dictated every aspect of life, including love. Lady Catherine was the daughter of a wealthy nobleman, destined to marry someone of equal standing. But her heart had other plans.

The Secret Love

JAMES WAS A HUMBLE but intelligent scholar who worked as a tutor for Lady Catherine's younger brother. From the moment they met, there was an undeniable connection between Catherine and James. They shared a love of literature and spent hours discussing their favorite books and poets.

The Growing Bond

AS THEIR FRIENDSHIP deepened, so did their feelings for each other. Catherine admired James's intellect and kindness, while James was captivated by Catherine's beauty and spirit. They knew their love was forbidden, but they could not help their growing affection.

One rainy afternoon, as they read poetry in the library, Catherine turned to James and said, "James, I know our love is impossible, but I cannot deny my feelings any longer. I love you."

James's heart soared as he replied, "And I love you, Catherine. But how can we be together in a world that will never accept us?"

The First Kiss

IN A MOMENT OF PASSION and defiance, James kissed Catherine. It was a kiss filled with longing and desperation, a moment of pure connection amidst the constraints of their society.

The Struggle for Acceptance

THEIR LOVE FACED NUMEROUS obstacles. Catherine's family forbade her from seeing James, threatening to disown her if she continued the relationship. James faced ridicule and scorn from his peers. But their love only grew stronger in the face of adversity.

Determined to be together, Catherine and James devised a plan to escape to America, where they could build a life together away from the strict societal norms of England. They faced many challenges along the way, but their love and determination kept them going.

A New Beginning

In America, Catherine and James built a life together filled with love and happiness. They proved that love could transcend societal boundaries and bring about a new beginning. Their story became a symbol of hope and defiance, a reminder that true love knows no limits.

Story 4: The World War II Romance

The War-Torn Era

DURING THE CHAOS AND uncertainty of World War II, love was a beacon of hope amidst the darkness. In a small village in France, Claire, a brave and compassionate nurse, worked tirelessly to care for the wounded soldiers. Her life changed forever when she met David, an American pilot whose plane had been shot down.

The Unexpected Meeting

DAVID WAS BROUGHT TO the makeshift hospital where Claire worked, injured but determined to continue the fight. From the moment their eyes met, Claire felt an inexplicable connection. She nursed him back to health, and in the process, they developed a deep bond.

The Growing Affection

AS DAVID RECOVERED, he and Claire spent hours talking about their hopes and dreams. David admired Claire's bravery and dedication, while Claire was captivated by David's strength and kindness. Their affection for each other grew with each passing day.

One evening, as they sat by the fire, David took Claire's hand and said, "Claire, I don't know what the future holds, but I know that I love you."

Claire's heart raced as she replied, "And I love you, David. But how can we be together when the world is at war?"

The First Kiss

IN A MOMENT OF PASSION and hope, David leaned in and kissed Claire. It was a kiss filled with longing and determination, a promise that their love would endure despite the challenges they faced.

The Struggle for Survival

THEIR LOVE FACED NUMEROUS obstacles. The constant threat of danger, the uncertainty of the war, and the distance that separated them when David returned to the front lines. But their love only grew stronger in the face of adversity.

They exchanged letters filled with words of love and hope, keeping their connection alive. Claire's letters gave David the strength to continue fighting, while David's letters gave Claire the courage to keep going.

A Love That Endures

AFTER THE WAR ENDED, David returned to France to be with Claire. They built a life together, filled with love and happiness. Their story became a symbol of hope and resilience, a reminder that love can endure even in the darkest of times.

Story 5: The Ancient Lovers

The Roman Empire

IN THE BUSTLING CITY of Rome during the height of the Roman Empire, love was a complicated and often dangerous affair. Marcus, a respected Roman senator, and Livia, a beautiful and intelligent courtesan, found themselves drawn to each other despite the societal norms that kept them apart.

The Forbidden Love

MARCUS WAS CAPTIVATED by Livia's beauty and intellect, while Livia admired Marcus's strength and honor. They began meeting in secret, their love growing stronger with each stolen moment. But their relationship was forbidden, and they faced the constant threat of discovery.

The Growing Bond

AS THEIR LOVE DEEPENED, Marcus and Livia dreamed of a future where they could be together openly. They knew their love was dangerous, but they were willing to risk everything for each other.

One evening, as they walked through the gardens of Livia's villa, Marcus took her hand and said, "Livia, I know our love is forbidden, but I cannot live without you. I love you."

Tears welled up in Livia's eyes as she replied, "And I love you, Marcus. But how can we be together in a world that will never accept us?"

The First Kiss

IN A MOMENT OF PASSION and defiance, Marcus kissed Livia. It was a kiss filled with longing and desperation, a moment of pure connection amidst the constraints of their society.

The Struggle for Freedom

THEIR LOVE FACED NUMEROUS obstacles. Marcus's political career was at risk, and Livia faced the constant threat of losing everything if their relationship was discovered. But their love only grew stronger in the face of adversity.

Determined to be together, Marcus and Livia devised a plan to escape Rome and start a new life where they could love freely. They faced many challenges along the way, but their love and determination kept them going.

A Love That Endures

IN A DISTANT LAND, far from the constraints of Rome, Marcus and Livia built a life together filled with love and happiness. They proved that love could transcend societal boundaries and bring about a new beginning. Their story became a symbol of hope and defiance, a reminder that true love knows no limits.

Story 6: The Medieval Lovers

The Medieval Period

IN THE HEART OF MEDIEVAL Scotland, amidst the towering castles and rugged landscapes, lived Lady Margaret, the daughter of a powerful laird. Margaret was known for her beauty and grace, but she was also fiercely independent and intelligent. She had grown up in a world where marriages were arranged for political alliances rather than love.

The Forbidden Love

SIR WILLIAM WAS A KNIGHT of humble origins, known for his bravery and honor. He had risen through the ranks of the laird's army due to his valor on the battlefield. When he was appointed to guard the castle where Lady Margaret resided, he never expected to find love.

Margaret and William's paths crossed during a summer festival. The moment their eyes met, they felt an inexplicable connection. They began to steal moments together, meeting in secret to talk about their dreams and fears. Their love grew in the shadows, forbidden by the societal boundaries that separated them.

The First Kiss

ONE EVENING, UNDER the cover of darkness, William and Margaret met in the castle gardens. The moonlight cast a soft glow on Margaret's face as William took her hand. "My lady," he whispered, "I cannot deny my feelings any longer. I love you."

Tears welled up in Margaret's eyes as she replied, "And I love you, Sir William." Their first kiss was tender and filled with promise, a moment of pure magic amidst the constraints of their world.

The Battle for Love

THEIR LOVE, HOWEVER, was discovered by Margaret's father, who was furious at the thought of his daughter with a common knight. He ordered William to leave the castle and never return. But Margaret and William were determined to be together. They planned to escape and start a new life where they could love freely.

On the night of their planned escape, the castle was attacked by a rival clan. William fought valiantly to protect Margaret and the people of the castle. In the chaos, Margaret's father saw the true bravery and honor of William. After the battle was won, he gave his blessing to their union, realizing that true love was more powerful than societal boundaries.

A Love That Transcends Time**

MARGARET AND WILLIAM'S love story became a legend, a testament to the power of love to transcend time and societal norms. They lived a long and happy life together, their love growing stronger with each passing year.

Story 7: The Renaissance Artists

The Renaissance Period

IN THE VIBRANT CITY of Venice during the Renaissance, art and culture flourished. It was a time of great intellectual and artistic achievement. Among the bustling streets and grand palaces lived Isabella, a talented painter who defied the conventions of her time. Women were not often allowed to pursue careers, but Isabella's talent could not be ignored.

The Unexpected Meeting

LEONARDO WAS A WEALTHY merchant, known for his patronage of the arts. He had commissioned many works from the most renowned artists of the time. One day, while visiting an art studio, he saw Isabella's work and was captivated by her talent. He requested a portrait, not realizing that his heart would soon be captivated by more than just her art.

The Blossoming Romance

AS ISABELLA WORKED on Leonardo's portrait, they spent hours together, talking about art, philosophy, and their dreams. Leonardo was enchanted by Isabella's intelligence and passion, while Isabella found in Leonardo a kindred spirit who appreciated her for who she was, not just her beauty or her art.

One evening, as they walked through the streets of Venice, Leonardo took Isabella's hand and said, "Isabella, your art has touched my soul, but it is you who has captured my heart. I love you."

Isabella's heart raced as she replied, "And I love you, Leonardo. But how can we be together when society does not approve of our union?"

The First Kiss

UNDER THE MOONLIT SKY, Leonardo leaned in and kissed Isabella. It was a kiss filled with hope and defiance, a promise that their love would overcome any obstacle.

The Struggle Against Society

THEIR LOVE FACED MANY challenges. Isabella's family disapproved of her relationship with a wealthy merchant, fearing it would ruin her reputation. Leonardo's peers looked down upon his association with a female artist. But their love only grew stronger in the face of adversity.

Leonardo decided to use his influence to support Isabella's career, commissioning her to paint for the most prestigious clients in Venice. Her work gained acclaim, and she became one of the most celebrated artists of her time.

A Love That Endures

ISABELLA AND LEONARDO'S love story was one of passion and resilience. They proved that love could transcend societal boundaries and bring about positive change. Their story became an inspiration to many, a reminder that true love knows no limits.

Story 8: The Victorian Romance

The Victorian Era

IN THE ELEGANT YET restrictive society of Victorian England, social class dictated every aspect of life, including love. Lady Catherine was the daughter of a wealthy nobleman, destined to marry someone of equal standing. But her heart had other plans.

The Secret Love

James was a humble but intelligent scholar who worked as a tutor for Lady Catherine's younger brother. From the moment they met, there was an undeniable connection between Catherine and James. They shared a love of literature and spent hours discussing their favorite books and poets.

The Growing Bond

AS THEIR FRIENDSHIP deepened, so did their feelings for each other. Catherine admired James's intellect and kindness, while James was captivated by Catherine's beauty and spirit. They knew their love was forbidden, but they could not help their growing affection.

One rainy afternoon, as they read poetry in the library, Catherine turned to James and said, "James, I know our love is impossible, but I cannot deny my feelings any longer. I love you."

James's heart soared as he replied, "And I love you, Catherine. But how can we be together in a world that will never accept us?"

The First Kiss

IN A MOMENT OF PASSION and defiance, James kissed Catherine. It was a kiss filled with longing and desperation, a moment of pure connection amidst the constraints of their society.

The Struggle for Acceptance

THEIR LOVE FACED NUMEROUS obstacles. Catherine's family forbade her from seeing James, threatening to disown her if she continued the relationship. James faced ridicule and scorn from his peers. But their love only grew stronger in the face of adversity.

Determined to be together, Catherine and James devised a plan to escape to America, where they could build a life together away from the strict societal norms of England. They faced many challenges along the way, but their love and determination kept them going.

A New Beginning

In America, Catherine and James built a life together filled with love and happiness. They proved that love could transcend societal boundaries and bring about a new beginning. Their story became a symbol of hope and defiance, a reminder that true love knows no limits.

Story 9: The World War II Romance

The War-Torn Era

DURING THE CHAOS AND uncertainty of World War II, love was a beacon of hope amidst the darkness. In a small village in France, Claire, a brave and compassionate nurse, worked tirelessly to care for the wounded soldiers. Her life changed forever when she met David, an American pilot whose plane had been shot down.

The Unexpected Meeting

DAVID WAS BROUGHT TO the makeshift hospital where Claire worked, injured but determined to continue the fight. From the moment their eyes met, Claire felt an inexplicable connection. She nursed him back to health, and in the process, they developed a deep bond.

The Growing Affection

AS DAVID RECOVERED, he and Claire spent hours talking about their hopes and dreams. David admired Claire's bravery and dedication, while Claire was captivated by David's strength and kindness. Their affection for each other grew with each passing day.

One evening, as they sat by the fire, David took Claire's hand and said, "Claire, I don't know what the future holds, but I know that I love you."

Claire's heart raced as she replied, "And I love you, David. But how can we be together when the world is at war?"

The First Kiss

IN A MOMENT OF PASSION and hope, David leaned in and kissed Claire. It was a kiss filled with longing and determination, a promise that their love would endure despite the challenges they faced.

The Struggle for Survival

THEIR LOVE FACED NUMEROUS obstacles. The constant threat of danger, the uncertainty of the war, and the distance that separated them when David returned to the front lines. But their love only grew stronger in the face of adversity.

They exchanged letters filled with words of love and hope, keeping their connection alive. Claire's letters gave David the strength to continue fighting, while David's letters gave Claire the courage to keep going.

A Love That Endures

AFTER THE WAR ENDED, David returned to France to be with Claire. They built a life together, filled with love and happiness. Their story became a symbol of hope and resilience, a reminder that love can endure even in the darkest of times.

Story 10: The Ancient Lovers

The Roman Empire

IN THE BUSTLING CITY of Rome during the height of the Roman Empire, love was a complicated and often dangerous affair. Marcus, a respected Roman senator, and Livia, a beautiful and intelligent courtesan, found themselves drawn to each other despite the societal norms that kept them apart.

The Forbidden Love

MARCUS WAS CAPTIVATED by Livia's beauty and intellect, while Livia admired Marcus's strength and honor. They began meeting in secret, their love growing stronger with each stolen moment. But their relationship was forbidden, and they faced the constant threat of discovery.

The Growing Bond

AS THEIR LOVE DEEPENED, Marcus and Livia dreamed of a future where they could be together openly. They knew their love was dangerous, but they were willing to risk everything for each other.

One evening, as they walked through the gardens of Livia's villa, Marcus took her hand and said, "Livia, I know our love is forbidden, but I cannot live without you. I love you."

Tears welled up in Livia's eyes as she replied, "And I love you, Marcus. But how can we be together in a world that will never accept us?"

The First Kiss

IN A MOMENT OF PASSION and defiance, Marcus kissed Livia. It was a kiss filled with longing and desperation, a moment of pure connection amidst the constraints of their society.

The Struggle for Freedom

THEIR LOVE FACED NUMEROUS obstacles. Marcus's political career was at risk, and Livia faced the constant threat of losing everything if their relationship was discovered. But their love only grew stronger in the face of adversity.

Determined to be together, Marcus and Livia devised a plan to escape Rome and start a new life where they could love freely. They faced many challenges along the way, but their love and determination kept them going.

A Love That Endures

IN A DISTANT LAND, far from the constraints of Rome, Marcus and Livia built a life together filled with love and happiness. They proved that love could transcend societal boundaries and bring about a new beginning. Their story became a symbol of hope and defiance, a reminder that true love knows no limits.

The Themes of Love Transcending Time and Societal Boundaries

LOVE IS A POWERFUL force that can transcend time and societal boundaries. These stories demonstrate the resilience of the human heart and the transformative power of love. They remind us that love knows no limits and can overcome any obstacle.

In each of these stories, the characters face numerous challenges, from societal norms and expectations to war and political turmoil. But their love remains strong, defying the constraints of their time and proving that true love can withstand the test of time.

These tales are a celebration of love's ability to transcend time and societal boundaries. They are a testament to the power of love to bring about positive change and inspire hope. As you read through these stories of love across time, may you be reminded of the timeless nature of love and the strength of the human heart.

Chapter 5: Urban Fairy Tales

Introduction to Urban Fairy Tales

In a world where the hustle and bustle of everyday life often overshadow the magic of romance, urban fairy tales breathe enchantment into the mundane. These modern-day love stories, with a fairy tale twist, remind us that extraordinary love can be found in the most ordinary places. With elements of magical realism woven into contemporary settings, these tales captivate the heart and ignite the imagination. Join us as we explore the lives of ordinary people who discover extraordinary love, where the fantastical becomes a part of everyday reality.

Story 1: The Magical Bookstore

The Ordinary Life

EMMA HAD ALWAYS BEEN a bookworm. She spent her days working at a quaint little bookstore in the heart of the city. Surrounded by the scent of old pages and the quiet rustle of paper, Emma found solace in her books. She had long since given up on finding love, content with the company of her literary heroes and heroines.

The Enchanted Encounter

ONE RAINY AFTERNOON, as Emma was sorting through a pile of old books, she discovered a beautifully bound volume she had never seen before. The cover was intricately designed with gold filigree, and the title read "The Enchanted Heart." Curious, she opened the book and was immediately transported into a magical world.

As she wandered through the pages, she met Alex, a charming and adventurous soul who seemed to have stepped right out of a fairy tale. They spent hours talking, laughing, and exploring the enchanted world within the book. Emma felt a connection with Alex that she had never felt with anyone before.

The Real-World Connection

TO HER SURPRISE, EMMA discovered that Alex was not just a character in the book. He was a real person, living in the same city, who had also found his way into the magical bookstore. They decided to meet in the real world, and when they did, the connection between them was undeniable.

The First Kiss

ONE EVENING, AS THEY walked through the city, Alex took Emma's hand and led her to a quiet park. Under the soft glow of the streetlights, he leaned in and kissed her. It was a kiss filled with magic and promise, a moment that felt like it was straight out of a fairy tale.

The Enchanted Love

EMMA AND ALEX'S LOVE story was a beautiful blend of the ordinary and the extraordinary. They continued to explore the magical world within the book, sharing adventures and deepening their bond. Their love transcended the boundaries of reality and fantasy, proving that extraordinary love can be found in the most unexpected places.

Story 2: The Clockmaker's Daughter

The Ordinary Life

LILA LIVED A QUIET life, working as an apprentice to her father, a skilled clockmaker. Their shop, filled with the ticking of clocks and the smell of polished wood, was a haven of precision and artistry. Lila loved the intricacies of clockwork, but she longed for something more in her life.

The Magical Clock

ONE DAY, WHILE CLEANING out the attic, Lila discovered an old, ornate clock that her father had never shown her. The clock was unlike any she had ever seen, with a face that seemed to shimmer with an otherworldly light. Curious, she wound the clock and set it ticking.

The Time Traveler

TO HER ASTONISHMENT, the clock opened a portal, and out stepped Daniel, a handsome and mysterious man from another time. Daniel explained that he was a time traveler, trapped in the past, and the clock was his only way back to his own time. Lila was captivated by his story and agreed to help him.

The Growing Connection

AS THEY WORKED TOGETHER to repair the clock, Lila and Daniel grew closer. They shared stories of their lives, dreams, and fears. Lila was drawn to Daniel's adventurous spirit, while Daniel admired Lila's intelligence and kindness.

One evening, as they stood in the workshop, Daniel took Lila's hand and said, "Lila, I don't know how much time we have, but I know that I love you."

Tears welled up in Lila's eyes as she replied, "And I love you, Daniel. But how can we be together when time separates us?"

The First Kiss

IN A MOMENT OF PASSION and hope, Daniel leaned in and kissed Lila. It was a kiss filled with longing and determination, a promise that their love would endure despite the challenges they faced.

The Struggle Against Time

THEIR LOVE FACED NUMEROUS obstacles. The clock needed a rare and powerful gem to function properly, and they had to embark on a dangerous journey to find it. Along the way, they faced trials that tested their courage and commitment.

A Love That Defies Time

IN THE END, THEY FOUND the gem and repaired the clock, but Daniel chose to stay with Lila rather than return to his own time. Their love had transcended the boundaries of time, proving that true love can defy even the most impossible odds. They built a life together, filled with love and adventure, and the magical clock became a symbol of their extraordinary love.

Story 3: The Artist's Muse

The Ordinary Life

MAYA WAS A TALENTED artist living in a bustling city, but she struggled to find inspiration. She spent her days painting landscapes and portraits, but her heart yearned for something more. Her life changed forever when she stumbled upon an old, abandoned building on the outskirts of town.

The Enchanted Studio

INSIDE THE BUILDING, Maya discovered a hidden studio filled with beautiful, unfinished paintings. The air seemed to hum with magic, and Maya felt an overwhelming urge to pick up a brush. As she painted, the figures on the canvas came to life, and she found herself face-to-face with Leo, a handsome and enigmatic man.

The Magical Connection

LEO EXPLAINED THAT he was an artist who had been trapped in the paintings for centuries, cursed by a jealous rival. Maya was the only one who could break the curse by completing the unfinished paintings. They began working together, and as they painted, their connection grew stronger.

One evening, as they stood in the enchanted studio, Leo took Maya's hand and said, "Maya, your art has given me life, but it is your heart that has captured mine. I love you."

Maya's heart raced as she replied, "And I love you, Leo. But how can we be together when a curse separates us?"

The First Kiss

IN A MOMENT OF PASSION and hope, Leo leaned in and kissed Maya. It was a kiss filled with magic and promise, a moment that felt like it was straight out of a fairy tale.

The Struggle Against the Curse

THEIR LOVE FACED NUMEROUS obstacles. The curse was powerful, and they had to find a way to break it before Leo could be free. They embarked on a journey to find the original spellbook, facing trials that tested their courage and commitment.

A Love That Breaks the Curse

IN THE END, THEY FOUND the spellbook and broke the curse, freeing Leo from the paintings. Their love had transcended the boundaries of magic, proving that true love can break even the most powerful curses. They built a life together, filled with art and passion, and the enchanted studio became a symbol of their extraordinary love.

Story 4: The Modern-Day Cinderella

The Ordinary Life

ELLA LIVED A HUMBLE life, working as a waitress in a busy diner. She had dreams of becoming a fashion designer, but her responsibilities at home kept her from pursuing her passion. Her life changed forever when she met Jake, a successful businessman, at a charity event.

The Fairy Godmother

Ella's friend, Sarah, who had always believed in Ella's talent, decided to play the role of a fairy godmother. She used her connections to get Ella an invitation to the city's most prestigious fashion show. Sarah also helped Ella design a stunning dress that showcased her talent.

The Enchanted Evening

AT THE FASHION SHOW, Ella's dress caught the eye of everyone, including Jake. He was captivated by her beauty and grace, and they spent the evening talking and dancing. Ella felt like she was living in a fairy tale, but she knew that midnight would bring an end to the magic.

The Growing Connection

AS THE EVENING CAME to an end, Jake took Ella's hand and said, "Ella, I don't know who you are, but I feel a connection with you that I've never felt with anyone else. I want to know more about you."

Tears welled up in Ella's eyes as she replied, "I feel the same way, Jake. But my life is far from glamorous. I'm just a waitress with dreams."

The First Kiss

IN A MOMENT OF PASSION and hope, Jake leaned in and kissed Ella. It was a kiss filled with magic and promise, a moment that felt like it was straight out of a fairy tale.

The Struggle for Dreams

THEIR LOVE FACED NUMEROUS obstacles. Ella's responsibilities at home and Jake's demanding career made it difficult for them to spend time together. But their love only grew stronger in the face of adversity.

Determined to support Ella's dreams, Jake used his influence to help her get an internship with a renowned fashion designer. Ella's talent soon gained recognition, and she began to build a career in the fashion industry.

A Love That Transcends Boundaries

ELLA AND JAKE'S LOVE story was a beautiful blend of the ordinary and the extraordinary. They proved that love could transcend societal boundaries and bring about positive change. Their story became an inspiration to many, a reminder that true love knows no limits.

Story 5: The Enchanted Garden

The Ordinary Life

LILY LIVED A QUIET life, tending to her family's garden in the heart of the city. The garden was a lush, green oasis amidst the concrete jungle, and Lily found solace in the beauty of nature. She had always felt a deep connection to the garden, but she never imagined it held magical secrets.

The Magical Garden

ONE EVENING, AS LILY was tending to the flowers, she discovered a hidden path that led to a secluded part of the garden she had never seen before. The air was filled with the scent of blooming flowers, and the moonlight cast a soft glow on the scene. In the center of the garden stood a tall, handsome man named Gabriel.

The Enchanted Encounter

GABRIEL EXPLAINED THAT he was a guardian of the enchanted garden, a place where magic and nature intertwined. He had been watching over the garden for centuries, waiting for someone with a pure heart to discover its secrets. Lily was captivated by Gabriel's story and felt an inexplicable connection to him.

The Growing Connection

AS THEY SPENT MORE time together, Lily and Gabriel's bond grew stronger. They shared stories of their lives, dreams, and fears. Lily was drawn to Gabriel's wisdom and kindness, while Gabriel admired Lily's passion for nature and her gentle spirit.

One evening, as they walked through the enchanted garden, Gabriel took Lily's hand and said, "Lily, your love for this garden has given it new life, but it is your heart that has captured mine. I love you."

Tears welled up in Lily's eyes as she replied, "And I love you, Gabriel. But how can we be together when magic separates us?"

The First Kiss

IN A MOMENT OF PASSION and hope, Gabriel leaned in and kissed Lily. It was a kiss filled with magic and promise, a moment that felt like it was straight out of a fairy tale.

The Struggle Against Magic

THEIR LOVE FACED NUMEROUS obstacles. The enchanted garden held powerful magic that required Gabriel to stay as its guardian. They had to find a way to break the magical bonds that kept them apart. Together, they embarked on a journey to discover the source of the garden's magic and find a way to be together.

A Love That Breaks the Bonds

IN THE END, THEY DISCOVERED that the magic of the garden was tied to the love and care it received. By nurturing the garden and spreading its beauty, they were able to break the magical bonds that kept Gabriel bound to it. Their love had transcended the boundaries of magic, proving that true love can break even the most powerful spells. They built a life together, filled with love and nature, and the enchanted garden became a symbol of their extraordinary love.

Story 6: The Musician's Melody

The Ordinary Life

SOPHIE WAS A TALENTED musician, playing her violin in the busy streets of the city. Her music brought joy to passersby, but she struggled to make a living. Her life changed forever when she met Max, a successful composer, at a small concert where she was performing.

The Enchanted Violin

MAX WAS CAPTIVATED by Sophie's talent and offered her a chance to play with his orchestra. He also gifted her an old, beautifully crafted violin, saying it had been passed down through generations of musicians. Little did they know, the violin held a magical secret.

The Magical Melody

AS SOPHIE PLAYED THE violin, she discovered that its music had the power to enchant and heal. Her performances became legendary, drawing large crowds and touching the hearts of everyone who heard her play. Max and Sophie grew closer as they worked together, their connection deepening with each note.

One evening, after a particularly moving performance, Max took Sophie's hand and said, "Sophie, your music has touched my soul, but it is your heart that has captured mine. I love you."

Sophie's heart raced as she replied, "And I love you, Max. But how can we be together when our worlds are so different?"

The First Kiss

IN A MOMENT OF PASSION and hope, Max leaned in and kissed Sophie. It was a kiss filled with magic and promise, a moment that felt like it was straight out of a fairy tale.

The Struggle for Harmony

THEIR LOVE FACED NUMEROUS obstacles. Sophie's humble background and Max's high-profile career made it difficult for them to be together. But their love only grew stronger in the face of adversity.

Determined to support Sophie's talent, Max used his influence to help her gain recognition in the music world. Sophie's magical violin and her enchanting performances soon made her a celebrated musician.

A Love That Harmonizes

SOPHIE AND MAX'S LOVE story was a beautiful blend of the ordinary and the extraordinary. They proved that love could transcend societal boundaries and bring about positive change. Their story became an inspiration to many, a reminder that true love knows no limits.

Story 7: The Modern-Day Mermaid

The Ordinary Life

MARINA LIVED A QUIET life by the sea, working as a marine biologist. She had always felt a deep connection to the ocean, but she never imagined it held magical secrets. Her life changed forever when she discovered a hidden underwater cave.

The Enchanted Encounter

INSIDE THE CAVE, MARINA found a beautiful, magical pendant. As she touched it, she was transformed into a mermaid. In her new form, she met Finn, a handsome and mysterious merman who explained that the pendant had chosen her to protect the ocean.

The Magical Connection

Marina and Finn spent their days exploring the underwater world, discovering its beauty and secrets. Their connection grew stronger with each adventure. Marina was drawn to Finn's strength and kindness, while Finn admired Marina's intelligence and passion for the ocean.

One evening, as they swam under the moonlit waves, Finn took Marina's hand and said, "Marina, your love for the ocean has given it new life, but it is your heart that has captured mine. I love you."

Tears welled up in Marina's eyes as she replied, "And I love you, Finn. But how can we be together when magic separates us?"

The First Kiss

IN A MOMENT OF PASSION and hope, Finn leaned in and kissed Marina. It was a kiss filled with magic and promise, a moment that felt like it was straight out of a fairy tale.

The Struggle Against Magic

THEIR LOVE FACED NUMEROUS obstacles. The magical pendant required Marina to spend part of her life as a mermaid and part as a human. They had to find a way to balance their two worlds. Together, they embarked on a journey to discover the true power of the pendant and find a way to be together.

A Love That Transcends Worlds

IN THE END, THEY DISCOVERED that the pendant's magic was tied to the love and care they showed for the ocean. By protecting and nurturing the underwater world, they were able to find a way to be together in both forms. Their love had transcended the boundaries of magic, proving that true love can break even the most powerful spells. They built a life together, filled with love and adventure, and the magical pendant became a symbol of their extraordinary love.

Story 8: The Urban Enchanter

The Ordinary Life

LUCAS WAS A TALENTED magician, performing street magic in the busy city. His tricks amazed and delighted passersby, but he struggled to make a living. His life changed forever when he met Isabelle, a successful businesswoman, at a corporate event where he was hired to perform.

The Enchanted Encounter

ISABELLE WAS CAPTIVATED by Lucas's talent and offered him a chance to perform at her company's events. She also gifted him an old, beautifully crafted magician's hat, saying it had been passed down through generations of magicians. Little did they know, the hat held a magical secret.

The Magical Connection

AS LUCAS PERFORMED with the hat, he discovered that it had the power to make his tricks truly magical. His performances became legendary, drawing large crowds and touching the hearts of everyone who saw him perform. Lucas and Isabelle grew closer as they worked together, their connection deepening with each performance.

One evening, after a particularly moving performance, Lucas took Isabelle's hand and said, "Isabelle, your belief in me has given me new life, but it is your heart that has captured mine. I love you."

Isabelle's heart raced as she replied, "And I love you, Lucas. But how can we be together when our worlds are so different?"

The First Kiss

IN A MOMENT OF PASSION and hope, Lucas leaned in and kissed Isabelle. It was a kiss filled with magic and promise, a moment that felt like it was straight out of a fairy tale.

The Struggle for Magic

THEIR LOVE FACED NUMEROUS obstacles. Lucas's humble background and Isabelle's high-profile career made it difficult for them to be together. But their love only grew stronger in the face of adversity.

Determined to support Lucas's talent, Isabelle used her influence to help him gain recognition in the magic world. Lucas's magical hat and his enchanting performances soon made him a celebrated magician.

A Love That Enchants

LUCAS AND ISABELLE'S love story was a beautiful blend of the ordinary and the extraordinary. They proved that love could transcend societal boundaries and bring about positive change. Their story became an inspiration to many, a reminder that true love knows no limits.

Story 9: The Enchanted Café

The Ordinary Life

SOPHIA LIVED A QUIET life, running a small café in the heart of the city. The café was a cozy haven, filled with the scent of fresh coffee and the sound of soft music. Sophia loved her work, but she longed for something more in her life.

The Magical Café

ONE DAY, WHILE CLEANING out the storeroom, Sophia discovered an old, beautifully crafted coffee grinder. As she used it to grind coffee beans, she noticed that the coffee had a magical quality. It seemed to bring people together, creating an atmosphere of warmth and connection.

The Enchanted Encounter

ONE RAINY AFTERNOON, a handsome and mysterious man named Ethan walked into the café. He was drawn to the magical atmosphere and struck up a conversation with Sophia. They discovered they had a lot in common and felt an instant connection.

The Growing Connection

AS THEY SPENT MORE time together, Sophia and Ethan's bond grew stronger. They shared stories of their lives, dreams, and fears. Sophia was drawn to Ethan's wisdom and kindness, while Ethan admired Sophia's passion for her café and her gentle spirit.

One evening, as they sat by the fire, Ethan took Sophia's hand and said, "Sophia, your love for this café has given it new life, but it is your heart that has captured mine. I love you."

Tears welled up in Sophia's eyes as she replied, "And I love you, Ethan. But how can we be together when magic separates us?"

The First Kiss

IN A MOMENT OF PASSION and hope, Ethan leaned in and kissed Sophia. It was a kiss filled with magic and promise, a moment that felt like it was straight out of a fairy tale.

The Struggle for Connection

THEIR LOVE FACED NUMEROUS obstacles. Ethan had a mysterious past, and Sophia's responsibilities at the café made it difficult for them to spend time together. But their love only grew stronger in the face of adversity.

Determined to support Sophia's dream, Ethan used his skills to help her expand the café. The magical coffee and the enchanting atmosphere soon made the café a beloved spot in the city.

A Love That Brews

SOPHIA AND ETHAN'S love story was a beautiful blend of the ordinary and the extraordinary. They proved that love could transcend societal boundaries and bring about positive change. Their story became an inspiration to many, a reminder that true love knows no limits.

Story 10: The Modern-Day Fairy Godmother

The Ordinary Life

MIA LIVED A QUIET LIFE, working as a social worker in a busy city. She had always felt a deep connection to helping others, but she never imagined she had a magical gift. Her life changed forever when she discovered an old, beautifully crafted wand hidden in her grandmother's attic.

The Enchanted Encounter

AS MIA HELD THE WAND, she felt a surge of magic. She realized that she had the power to grant wishes and help people in extraordinary ways. Her first task was to help a young couple, Lily and Jack, who were struggling to make ends meet.

The Magical Connection

MIA USED HER MAGIC to help Lily and Jack find good jobs and a cozy apartment. She also helped them rekindle their love, which had been strained by their difficult circumstances. As she worked her magic, Mia discovered that her own heart was drawn to a kind and handsome man named Ben, who volunteered at the shelter where she worked.

The Growing Connection

AS THEY SPENT MORE time together, Mia and Ben's bond grew stronger. They shared stories of their lives, dreams, and fears. Mia was drawn to Ben's compassion and dedication, while Ben admired Mia's kindness and her magical gift.

One evening, as they walked through the city, Ben took Mia's hand and said, "Mia, your magic has brought so much joy to others, but it is your heart that has captured mine. I love you."

Mia's heart raced as she replied, "And I love you, Ben. But how can we be together when magic separates us?"

The First Kiss

IN A MOMENT OF PASSION and hope, Ben leaned in and kissed Mia. It was a kiss filled with magic and promise, a moment that felt like it was straight out of a fairy tale.

The Struggle for Magic

THEIR LOVE FACED NUMEROUS obstacles. Mia's responsibilities as a social worker and her magical gift made it difficult for them to be together. But their love only grew stronger in the face of adversity.

Determined to support Mia's dream, Ben used his skills to help her create a magical community center where people could come for help and support. The enchanted atmosphere and Mia's magical gift soon made the center a beloved spot in the city.

A Love That Grants Wishes

MIA AND BEN'S LOVE story was a beautiful blend of the ordinary and the extraordinary. They proved that love could transcend societal boundaries and bring about positive change. Their story became an inspiration to many, a reminder that true love knows no limits.

Conclusion

Urban fairy tales remind us that love can be found in the most ordinary places, and that magic exists all around us if we only know where to look. These stories of ordinary people finding extraordinary love, set against the backdrop of contemporary settings with a touch of magical realism, capture the imagination and warm the heart. They celebrate the power of love to transcend societal boundaries, time, and even magic itself.

As you read through these urban fairy tales, may you be inspired to look for the magic in your own life and to believe in the extraordinary power of love. These tales are a testament to the timeless nature of love and the strength of the human heart.

Chapter 6: Love in Unlikely Places

Introduction to Love in Unlikely Places

Love often appears when we least expect it, transforming ordinary moments into extraordinary experiences. Whether in the workplace, during a travel adventure, or through a chance encounter, love has a way of finding us in the most unexpected settings. This chapter explores stories of romance blossoming in such unlikely places, highlighting the serendipity of love and the magic it brings into our lives.

Story 1: Love in the Office

The Mundane Routine

JESSICA HAD BEEN WORKING at the same marketing firm for five years. Her days were filled with meetings, deadlines, and the humdrum of office life. She enjoyed her job but often found herself yearning for something more, both professionally and personally.

The New Hire

EVERYTHING CHANGED when Daniel joined the team as the new creative director. Daniel was charming, talented, and had an infectious enthusiasm that quickly spread through the office. From the moment Jessica met him, she felt an undeniable connection.

The Unexpected Bond

AS THEY COLLABORATED on various projects, Jessica and Daniel discovered they had much in common. They shared a love for travel, a passion for cooking, and a similar sense of humor. Their professional relationship soon evolved into a deep friendship.

One evening, after a particularly successful campaign, they decided to celebrate with a few colleagues at a nearby bar. As the night wore on, the group dwindled until it was just Jessica and Daniel. They talked for hours, sharing their dreams and fears.

The First Kiss

AS THEY WALKED BACK to the office to retrieve their cars, Daniel took Jessica's hand. "Jess, I know we work together, but I can't ignore my feelings any longer. I think I'm falling for you."

Jessica's heart raced as she replied, "I feel the same way, Daniel."

Under the soft glow of the streetlights, Daniel leaned in and kissed her. It was a tender, electrifying kiss that marked the beginning of their romantic journey.

Navigating Office Romance

THEIR RELATIONSHIP faced challenges, primarily the need to maintain professionalism at work. They agreed to keep their romance private, enjoying stolen moments during lunch breaks and after work.

Despite the challenges, their love grew stronger. Their colleagues eventually noticed the change in their dynamic, but rather than causing issues, it became a source of inspiration for others.

A Love That Thrives

JESSICA AND DANIEL'S love story is a testament to finding romance in the most unexpected places. They navigated the complexities of office romance with grace and found that love can blossom even amidst deadlines and board meetings. Their journey serves as a reminder that love often finds us when we least expect it, turning the mundane into something magical.

Story 2: The Serendipity of Travel

The Routine Getaway

EMILY WAS A SEASONED traveler who loved exploring new destinations. She often traveled alone, enjoying the freedom and adventure it brought. Her latest trip was to a small coastal town in Italy, a place she had longed to visit for its scenic beauty and rich history.

The Chance Encounter

ON HER FIRST DAY IN the town, Emily decided to visit a local café known for its incredible views of the ocean. As she settled at a table, she noticed a man sketching the coastline. Intrigued by his talent, she struck up a conversation.

The man, Alex, was a travel artist who captured the essence of his journeys through his sketches. They spent hours talking about their travels, art, and life. There was an instant connection, and they decided to explore the town together.

The Growing Affection

OVER THE NEXT FEW DAYS, Emily and Alex visited historical sites, tasted local cuisine, and shared countless stories. They discovered they had a shared love for adventure and a deep appreciation for the beauty of life.

One evening, as they watched the sunset over the ocean, Alex turned to Emily and said, "Emily, I've never felt this way before. Traveling with you has been an incredible experience, and I think I'm falling for you."

Emily's heart swelled with emotion as she replied, "I feel the same way, Alex. This trip has been magical because of you."

The First Kiss

UNDER THE FADING LIGHT of the sunset, Alex leaned in and kissed Emily. It was a kiss filled with promise and the thrill of new love. Their serendipitous meeting had turned into a beautiful romance.

Navigating Long-Distance Love

AS THEIR TRIP CAME to an end, they faced the reality of their lives back home. Emily was from New York, while Alex lived in London. They promised to stay in touch and find a way to be together despite the distance.

Their love faced challenges, but their shared experiences and deep connection kept them close. They visited each other frequently, exploring new destinations together and making the most of their time apart.

A Love That Travels

EMILY AND ALEX'S LOVE story is a testament to the serendipity of travel. Their chance encounter in a small coastal town turned into a lifelong adventure of love and exploration. They proved that love can blossom in the most unexpected places, and that distance is no barrier to a strong, enduring connection.

Story 3: Love at the Library

The Ordinary Routine

SAMANTHA WAS A LIBRARIAN who loved her job. She found joy in the quiet of the library, surrounded by books and the scent of old paper. Her life was peaceful, but she often dreamed of finding someone who shared her love for literature.

The Unexpected Patron

ONE RAINY AFTERNOON, a man named James walked into the library, soaked from the downpour. Samantha noticed him immediately, as he seemed out of place among the usual patrons. He approached the counter, asking for a book on local history.

The Shared Interest

SAMANTHA HELPED JAMES find the book, and they struck up a conversation. She discovered that James was a writer working on a historical novel. They spent hours discussing their favorite books and authors, finding a kindred spirit in each other.

The Growing Connection

JAMES BEGAN VISITING the library regularly, and their conversations became the highlight of Samantha's day. They shared recommendations, debated literary themes, and gradually, their connection deepened.

One evening, as they sat in a cozy corner of the library, James turned to Samantha and said, "Samantha, I've been coming here not just for the books, but because I enjoy spending time with you. I think I'm falling for you."

Samantha's heart raced as she replied, "I feel the same way, James."

The First Kiss

IN THE QUIET OF THE library, surrounded by their favorite books, James leaned in and kissed Samantha. It was a kiss filled with warmth and the promise of a new chapter in their lives.

Navigating Love in the Library

THEIR RELATIONSHIP faced challenges, primarily the need to maintain professionalism in the library. They agreed to keep their romance private, enjoying stolen moments among the stacks and after closing time.

Despite the challenges, their love grew stronger. Their colleagues eventually noticed the change in their dynamic, but rather than causing issues, it became a source of inspiration for others.

A Love That Reads

SAMANTHA AND JAMES'S love story is a testament to finding romance in the most unexpected places. They navigated the complexities of a workplace romance with grace and found that love can blossom even among the quiet shelves of a library. Their journey serves as a reminder that love often finds us when we least expect it, turning the ordinary into something magical.

Story 4: The Unexpected Adventure

The Ordinary Life

DAVID WAS AN AVID HIKER and adventurer who loved exploring the great outdoors. He often embarked on solo trips to escape the hustle and bustle of city life. His latest adventure took him to a remote mountain range, known for its breathtaking views and challenging trails.

The Chance Encounter

DURING HIS HIKE, DAVID stumbled upon a fellow hiker named Lily, who had sprained her ankle and was struggling to continue. David offered to help, and they decided to finish the hike together. They shared stories of their lives and adventures, discovering a mutual love for nature and exploration.

The Growing Connection

As they navigated the rugged terrain, David and Lily's bond grew stronger. They shared moments of awe at the beauty around them and found comfort in each other's company. By the time they reached the summit, they felt a deep connection.

One evening, as they sat by a campfire under the stars, David turned to Lily and said, "Lily, this adventure has been incredible because of you. I think I'm falling for you."

Lily's heart swelled with emotion as she replied, "I feel the same way, David. This has been a magical journey."

The First Kiss

UNDER THE STARRY SKY, David leaned in and kissed Lily. It was a kiss filled with promise and the thrill of new love. Their chance encounter on the mountain had turned into a beautiful romance.

Navigating Love and Adventure

AS THEIR HIKE CAME to an end, they faced the reality of their lives back home. David lived in the city, while Lily was from a small town. They promised to stay in touch and find a way to continue their adventures together.

Their love faced challenges, but their shared passion for nature and exploration kept them close. They planned regular trips together, exploring new destinations and making the most of their time apart.

A Love That Ventures

DAVID AND LILY'S LOVE story is a testament to the serendipity of adventure. Their chance encounter on a remote mountain turned into a lifelong journey of love and exploration. They proved that love can blossom in the most unexpected places and that shared passions can create a strong, enduring connection.

Story 5: Love on the Train

The Routine Commute

MEGAN HAD BEEN TAKING the same train to work for years. Her daily commute was a time to catch up on reading and enjoy a few moments of peace before the busy workday began. She never expected that her routine journey would lead to a life-changing encounter.

The Serendipitous Meeting

ONE MORNING, AS MEGAN boarded the train, she found herself sitting next to a man named Ryan. They exchanged polite greetings, and Megan returned to her book. However, a sudden jolt caused her to drop it, and Ryan picked it up for her.

The Shared Interest

AS THEY TALKED ABOUT the book, Megan discovered that Ryan shared her love for literature. They spent the rest of the journey discussing their favorite authors and genres. There was an instant connection, and they exchanged contact information before parting ways.

The Growing Affection

MEGAN AND RYAN BEGAN meeting regularly on the train, and their conversations soon became the highlight of their day. They shared recommendations, debated literary themes, and gradually, their connection deepened.

One evening, after a particularly engaging discussion, Ryan turned to Megan and said, "Megan, I've been looking forward to our train rides not just for the books, but because I enjoy spending time with you. I think I'm falling for you."

Megan's heart raced as she replied, "I feel the same way, Ryan."

The First Kiss

IN THE QUIET OF THE train station, as they waited for their respective trains, Ryan leaned in and kissed Megan. It was a tender, electrifying kiss that marked the beginning of their romantic journey.

Navigating Love on the Train

THEIR RELATIONSHIP faced challenges, primarily the need to maintain their individual routines. They agreed to meet regularly on the train, enjoying stolen moments during their commute and planning weekend dates.

Despite the challenges, their love grew stronger. Their fellow commuters eventually noticed the change in their dynamic, but rather than causing issues, it became a source of inspiration for others.

A Love That Travels

MEGAN AND RYAN'S LOVE story is a testament to finding romance in the most unexpected places. They navigated the complexities of a commuter romance with grace and found that love can blossom even amidst the daily grind of a routine commute. Their journey serves as a reminder that love often finds us when we least expect it, turning the ordinary into something magical.

Story 6: Love at the Farmers' Market

The Weekend Routine

OLIVIA LOVED VISITING the local farmers' market every weekend. It was her favorite place to find fresh produce, homemade goods, and unique crafts. She enjoyed the vibrant atmosphere and the sense of community.

The Chance Encounter

ONE SATURDAY, WHILE browsing a stall of handmade candles, Olivia struck up a conversation with the vendor, a man named Ethan. They bonded over their shared love for the market and spent the morning exploring the various stalls together.

The Growing Connection

As they wandered through the market, Olivia and Ethan's bond grew stronger. They shared stories of their lives, dreams, and fears. Olivia was drawn to Ethan's passion for his craft, while Ethan admired Olivia's enthusiasm for life.

One evening, as they sat on a bench overlooking the market, Ethan turned to Olivia and said, "Olivia, this market has always been special to me, but it has become even more so because of you. I think I'm falling for you."

Olivia's heart swelled with emotion as she replied, "I feel the same way, Ethan."

The First Kiss

UNDER THE SOFT GLOW of the market lights, Ethan leaned in and kissed Olivia. It was a kiss filled with promise and the thrill of new love. Their chance encounter at the market had turned into a beautiful romance.

Navigating Love at the Market

THEIR RELATIONSHIP faced challenges, primarily the need to balance their individual lives and commitments. They agreed to meet regularly at the market, enjoying their shared passion and planning weekend dates.

Despite the challenges, their love grew stronger. Their fellow market-goers eventually noticed the change in their dynamic, but rather than causing issues, it became a source of inspiration for others.

A Love That Blooms

OLIVIA AND ETHAN'S love story is a testament to finding romance in the most unexpected places. They navigated the complexities of a market romance with grace and found that love can blossom even amidst the hustle and bustle of a busy marketplace. Their journey serves as a reminder that love often finds us when we least expect it, turning the ordinary into something magical.

Story 7: The Café Connection

THE DAILY ROUTINE

Laura was a regular at her neighborhood café, where she would spend her mornings sipping coffee and working on her laptop. The café was her sanctuary, a place where she could focus and relax before starting her day.

The Serendipitous Meeting

ONE MORNING, AS LAURA was working on a particularly challenging project, a man named Jack sat down at the table next to hers. They exchanged polite greetings, and Laura returned to her work. However, a spilled coffee led to a conversation, and they quickly discovered a shared love for writing.

The Growing Affection

JACK WAS A FREELANCE writer, and they spent hours discussing their favorite books, authors, and writing techniques. There was an instant connection, and they began meeting regularly at the café to work together.

One evening, as they sat in the cozy corner of the café, Jack turned to Laura and said, "Laura, I've been looking forward to our café meetings not just for the work, but because I enjoy spending time with you. I think I'm falling for you."

Laura's heart raced as she replied, "I feel the same way, Jack."

The First Kiss

IN THE QUIET OF THE café, surrounded by the scent of coffee and the soft hum of conversation, Jack leaned in and kissed Laura. It was a tender, electrifying kiss that marked the beginning of their romantic journey.

Navigating Love in the Café

THEIR RELATIONSHIP faced challenges, primarily the need to balance their individual work routines. They agreed to meet regularly at the café, enjoying their shared passion for writing and planning weekend dates.

Despite the challenges, their love grew stronger. Their fellow café-goers eventually noticed the change in their dynamic, but rather than causing issues, it became a source of inspiration for others.

A Love That Brews

LAURA AND JACK'S LOVE story is a testament to finding romance in the most unexpected places. They navigated the complexities of a café romance with grace and found that love can blossom even amidst the daily grind of a routine. Their journey serves as a reminder that love often finds us when we least expect it, turning the ordinary into something magical.

Story 8: Love on the Airplane

The Routine Flight

SARAH WAS A FREQUENT flyer, traveling often for her job as a marketing executive. She had grown accustomed to the monotony of airport lounges and in-flight meals. On one particular flight, she found herself seated next to a man named Tom.

The Serendipitous Meeting

TOM WAS A TRAVEL WRITER, and they quickly struck up a conversation about their respective journeys. They shared travel stories, laughed over the quirks of frequent flying, and discovered a mutual love for adventure.

The Growing Connection

AS THE FLIGHT PROGRESSED, Sarah and Tom's bond grew stronger. They shared stories of their lives, dreams, and fears. Sarah was drawn to Tom's passion for travel, while Tom admired Sarah's adventurous spirit.

One evening, as they watched the sunset from the airplane window, Tom turned to Sarah and said, "Sarah, this flight has been incredible because of you. I think I'm falling for you."

Sarah's heart swelled with emotion as she replied, "I feel the same way, Tom."

The First Kiss

IN THE DIMLY LIT CABIN, as the plane soared above the clouds, Tom leaned in and kissed Sarah. It was a kiss filled with promise and the thrill of new love. Their serendipitous meeting on the airplane had turned into a beautiful romance.

Navigating Love in the Air

THEIR RELATIONSHIP faced challenges, primarily the need to balance their individual travel schedules. They agreed to stay in touch and plan trips together, exploring new destinations and making the most of their time apart.

Despite the challenges, their love grew stronger. Their fellow travelers eventually noticed the change in their dynamic, but rather than causing issues, it became a source of inspiration for others.

A Love That Soars

SARAH AND TOM'S LOVE story is a testament to finding romance in the most unexpected places. They navigated the complexities of a long-distance romance with grace and found that love can blossom even amidst the frequent flyers' routine. Their journey serves as a reminder that love often finds us when we least expect it, turning the ordinary into something magical.

Story 9: The Festival Encounter

The Annual Event

EVERY YEAR, MIA ATTENDED the local music festival with her friends. It was a weekend filled with great music, food, and fun. She loved the vibrant atmosphere and the chance to discover new bands.

The Chance Encounter

DURING ONE OF THE PERFORMANCES, Mia found herself standing next to a man named Ben. They struck up a conversation about the band playing on stage and quickly discovered a shared love for music.

The Growing Affection

AS THEY SPENT THE WEEKEND together, Mia and Ben's bond grew stronger. They attended concerts, explored the festival grounds, and shared stories of their favorite bands and musical experiences.

One evening, as they watched a fireworks display, Ben turned to Mia and said, "Mia, this festival has been incredible because of you. I think I'm falling for you."

Mia's heart swelled with emotion as she replied, "I feel the same way, Ben."

The First Kiss

UNDER THE COLORFUL explosion of fireworks, Ben leaned in and kissed Mia. It was a kiss filled with promise and the thrill of new love. Their chance encounter at the music festival had turned into a beautiful romance.

Navigating Love at the Festival

THEIR RELATIONSHIP faced challenges, primarily the need to balance their individual lives and commitments. They agreed to stay in touch and plan trips to other music festivals, making the most of their shared passion for music.

Despite the challenges, their love grew stronger. Their fellow festival-goers eventually noticed the change in their dynamic, but rather than causing issues, it became a source of inspiration for others.

A Love That Grooves

MIA AND BEN'S LOVE story is a testament to finding romance in the most unexpected places. They navigated the complexities of a festival romance with grace and found that love can blossom even amidst the hustle and bustle of a crowded event. Their journey serves as a reminder that love often finds us when we least expect it, turning the ordinary into something magical.

Story 10: The Unexpected Reunion

The Ordinary Life

ALEX AND EMMA HAD BEEN best friends in college but had lost touch after graduation. They both went on to build successful careers, with Alex becoming a lawyer and Emma a journalist. Neither of them expected to cross paths again.

The Serendipitous Meeting

ONE DAY, WHILE COVERING a high-profile case, Emma found herself in the courtroom where Alex was the lead attorney. They recognized each other immediately and were thrilled to reconnect.

The Growing Connection

AS THEY CAUGHT UP OVER coffee, Alex and Emma discovered that their bond was as strong as ever. They reminisced about their college days and shared stories of their lives since then. There was an undeniable spark between them.

One evening, as they walked through the city, Alex turned to Emma and said, "Emma, reconnecting with you has been incredible. I think I'm falling for you."

Emma's heart swelled with emotion as she replied, "I feel the same way, Alex."

The First Kiss

Under the soft glow of the streetlights, Alex leaned in and kissed Emma. It was a kiss filled with promise and the thrill of new love. Their serendipitous meeting had turned into a beautiful romance.

Navigating Love in the City

THEIR RELATIONSHIP faced challenges, primarily the need to balance their demanding careers. They agreed to make time for each other, planning regular dates and weekend getaways.

Despite the challenges, their love grew stronger. Their colleagues eventually noticed the change in their dynamic, but rather than causing issues, it became a source of inspiration for others.

A Love That Reconnects

ALEX AND EMMA'S LOVE story is a testament to finding romance in the most unexpected places. They navigated the complexities of a city romance with grace and found that love can blossom even amidst the hustle and bustle of urban life. Their journey serves as a reminder that love often finds us when we least expect it, turning the ordinary into something magical.

CONCLUSION

Love in unlikely places reminds us that romance can blossom in the most unexpected settings. Whether in the workplace, during a travel adventure, or through a chance encounter, these stories highlight the serendipity of love and the magic it brings into our lives. They celebrate the power of love to transform ordinary moments into extraordinary experiences, proving that true love often finds us when we least expect it. As you read through these stories, may you be inspired to look for love in unexpected places and believe in the magic of serendipity.

Chapter 7: Forbidden Passions

Introduction to Forbidden Passions

Forbidden love has always been a compelling theme in literature and life. It encapsulates the allure of the unattainable and the intensity of emotions heightened by obstacles. Tales of forbidden love delve deep into the challenges posed by societal and familial constraints, exploring the raw, passionate, and often tumultuous journeys of those who dare to love against the odds. This chapter unveils the depth and complexity of secret romances, where love flourishes in the shadows, defying conventions and expectations.

Story 1: The Aristocrat and the Servant

The Aristocratic Life

IN THE GRAND ESTATE of the Blackwell family, life was a series of opulent parties, strict etiquette, and clear societal boundaries. Lady Isabella Blackwell, the daughter of the Earl, was accustomed to a life of privilege and duty. Despite her luxurious surroundings, Isabella often felt confined by the rigid expectations placed upon her.

The Forbidden Attraction

JAMES WAS A YOUNG SERVANT who worked in the stables, known for his kindness and skill with horses. He had always admired

Isabella from afar, captivated by her beauty and grace. Their paths rarely crossed until one fateful afternoon when Isabella ventured into the stables, seeking solace from the pressures of her life.

The Blossoming Romance

Their initial conversations were brief and cautious, but a mutual respect and curiosity quickly developed. Isabella found in James a confidant and a friend, someone who saw her as a person rather than a title. James, in turn, admired Isabella's intelligence and spirit. As their bond deepened, so did their feelings for each other.

One evening, as they stood in the dimly lit stables, James took Isabella's hand and said, "Lady Isabella, I know our love is impossible, but I cannot deny my feelings any longer. I love you."

Tears welled up in Isabella's eyes as she replied, "I love you too, James. But how can we be together when society will never accept us?"

The First Kiss

IN A MOMENT OF PASSION and defiance, James leaned in and kissed Isabella. It was a tender, electrifying kiss that marked the beginning of their secret romance.

The Struggle Against Societal Constraints

THEIR LOVE FACED NUMEROUS obstacles. They had to keep their relationship hidden from Isabella's family and the other servants. The constant threat of discovery loomed over them, adding an intensity to their stolen moments.

Despite the challenges, their love only grew stronger. They found creative ways to communicate and meet, cherishing every minute they spent together. Their love was a refuge from the rigid expectations of their world.

The Ultimate Sacrifice

THEIR SECRET COULD not remain hidden forever. When Isabella's father discovered their relationship, he was furious and demanded that James leave the estate immediately. Faced with the choice between her family and her love, Isabella made the painful decision to leave with James.

They fled to a distant village where they could build a life together, free from the constraints of society. Though they faced hardships, their love provided the strength to endure. They proved that true love can defy even the most rigid societal boundaries, turning their forbidden passion into a lasting bond.

Story 2: The Student and the Professor

The Academic World

SOPHIE WAS A BRILLIANT and ambitious student at one of the most prestigious universities in the country. She had always been passionate about literature and was thrilled to be studying under Professor Michael Turner, a renowned scholar in the field. Michael was known for his intellect and dedication to his students, but he kept a strict professional distance.

The Intellectual Connection

FROM THE MOMENT SOPHIE attended Michael's first lecture, she felt a profound connection to his teaching. His passion for literature mirrored her own, and she admired his insight and depth of knowledge. Michael, in turn, recognized Sophie's talent and dedication, finding himself increasingly drawn to her intellect and spirit.

The Growing Affection

THEIR PROFESSIONAL relationship soon evolved into a deep intellectual bond. They spent hours discussing literature, sharing ideas, and challenging each other's perspectives. As their connection deepened, so did their feelings for each other.

One evening, after a particularly intense discussion, Michael turned to Sophie and said, "Sophie, our connection goes beyond the classroom. I think I'm falling for you."

Sophie's heart raced as she replied, "I feel the same way, Michael. But how can we be together when our relationship is forbidden?"

The First Kiss

IN THE QUIET OF MICHAEL'S office, surrounded by books and the scent of old paper, Michael leaned in and kissed Sophie. It was a tender, electrifying kiss that marked the beginning of their secret romance.

The Struggle Against Institutional Rules

THEIR LOVE FACED NUMEROUS obstacles. They had to keep their relationship hidden from the university, knowing that discovery could jeopardize both of their futures. The constant threat of exposure added an intensity to their stolen moments.

Despite the challenges, their love only grew stronger. They found creative ways to communicate and meet, cherishing every minute they spent together. Their love was a refuge from the rigid rules of their world.

The Ultimate Sacrifice

THEIR SECRET COULD not remain hidden forever. When the university discovered their relationship, they were both summoned before the administration. Faced with the choice between their careers and their love, Michael chose to resign, while Sophie decided to transfer to another institution.

They moved to a different city where they could build a life together, free from the constraints of the academic world. Though they faced hardships, their love provided the strength to endure. They proved that true love can defy even the most rigid institutional rules, turning their forbidden passion into a lasting bond.

Story 3: The Officer and the Rebel

The Divided Society

IN A NATION TORN APART by civil unrest, Alex was a loyal officer in the government forces, while Elena was a passionate leader of the rebel movement. They came from different worlds, each committed to their cause and believing in the righteousness of their actions.

The Unexpected Encounter

THEIR PATHS CROSSED during a clandestine meeting aimed at negotiating a temporary ceasefire. Despite their opposing beliefs, Alex and Elena felt an immediate connection, drawn to each other's courage and conviction.

The Growing Affection

THEIR INITIAL CONVERSATIONS were filled with tension and debate, but a mutual respect and understanding soon developed. They began to see each other not as enemies, but as individuals with shared humanity. As their bond deepened, so did their feelings for each other.

One evening, after a particularly heated discussion, Alex turned to Elena and said, "Elena, despite everything, I cannot deny my feelings for you. I think I'm falling for you."

Elena's heart raced as she replied, "I feel the same way, Alex. But how can we be together when our worlds are at war?"

The First Kiss

IN THE DIMLY LIT ROOM, surrounded by maps and strategies, Alex leaned in and kissed Elena. It was a tender, electrifying kiss that marked the beginning of their secret romance.

The Struggle Against Political Boundaries

THEIR LOVE FACED NUMEROUS obstacles. They had to keep their relationship hidden from their respective factions, knowing that discovery could have dire consequences. The constant threat of exposure added an intensity to their stolen moments.

Despite the challenges, their love only grew stronger. They found creative ways to communicate and meet, cherishing every minute they spent together. Their love was a refuge from the rigid boundaries of their world.

The Ultimate Sacrifice

THEIR SECRET COULD not remain hidden forever. When their relationship was discovered, they were both captured and brought before their leaders. Faced with the choice between their loyalty to their causes and their love, they chose to defect and seek asylum in a neutral territory.

They fled to a distant country where they could build a life together, free from the constraints of their divided nation. Though they faced hardships, their love provided the strength to endure. They proved that true love can defy even the most rigid political boundaries, turning their forbidden passion into a lasting bond.

Story 4: The Heir and the Commoner

The Royal Life

IN A SMALL, PICTURESQUE kingdom, Prince Edward was the heir to the throne. His life was filled with royal duties, public appearances, and the weight of his family's expectations. Despite his privileged position, Edward often felt isolated and yearned for genuine connections.

The Forbidden Attraction

AMELIA WAS A COMMONER who worked as a gardener in the royal palace. She had always admired the beauty of the gardens and took pride in her work. Her paths rarely crossed with the royals until one fateful day when Edward visited the gardens seeking solitude.

The Blossoming Romance

THEIR INITIAL CONVERSATIONS were brief and cautious, but a mutual respect and curiosity quickly developed. Edward found in Amelia a confidant and a friend, someone who saw him as a person rather than a prince. Amelia, in turn, admired Edward's kindness and humility. As their bond deepened, so did their feelings for each other.

One evening, as they walked through the moonlit gardens, Edward took Amelia's hand and said, "Amelia, I know our love is impossible, but I cannot deny my feelings any longer. I love you."

Tears welled up in Amelia's eyes as she replied, "I love you too, Edward. But how can we be together when society will never accept us?"

The First Kiss

IN A MOMENT OF PASSION and defiance, Edward leaned in and kissed Amelia. It was a tender, electrifying kiss that marked the beginning of their secret romance.

The Struggle Against Royal Expectations

THEIR LOVE FACED NUMEROUS obstacles. They had to keep their relationship hidden from Edward's family and the royal court. The constant threat of discovery loomed over them, adding an intensity to their stolen moments.

Despite the challenges, their love only grew stronger. They found creative ways to communicate and meet, cherishing every minute they spent together. Their love was a refuge from the rigid expectations of their world.

The Ultimate Sacrifice

THEIR SECRET COULD not remain hidden forever. When Edward's parents discovered their relationship, they were furious and demanded that Amelia leave the palace immediately. Faced with the choice between his family and his love, Edward made the painful decision to abdicate the throne.

They fled to a distant land where they could build a life together, free from the constraints of royalty. Though they faced hardships, their love provided the strength to endure. They proved that true love can defy even the most rigid royal expectations, turning their forbidden passion into a lasting bond.

Story 5: The Married Woman and the Artist

The Confined Life

ANNA WAS TRAPPED IN an unhappy marriage with a wealthy but controlling husband. Her life was filled with luxury, but she felt suffocated by the lack of freedom and genuine affection. She found solace in her art, painting in secret to express her true self.

The Forbidden Attraction

LIAM WAS A TALENTED artist who had recently moved to the town. He was known for his passionate and unconventional style. When Anna attended one of his art exhibitions, she was captivated by his work and felt an instant connection.

The Blossoming Romance

THEIR INITIAL CONVERSATIONS were brief and cautious, but a mutual respect and curiosity quickly developed. Anna found in Liam a confidant and a friend, someone who appreciated her art and saw her as an individual. Liam, in turn, admired Anna's talent and spirit. As their bond deepened, so did their feelings for each other.

One evening, as they worked on a painting together in Liam's studio, he took her hand and said, "Anna, I know our love is impossible, but I cannot deny my feelings any longer. I love you."

Tears welled up in Anna's eyes as she replied, "I love you too, Liam. But how can we be together when society will never accept us?"

The First Kiss

IN A MOMENT OF PASSION and defiance, Liam leaned in and kissed Anna. It was a tender, electrifying kiss that marked the beginning of their secret romance.

The Struggle Against Marital Constraints

THEIR LOVE FACED NUMEROUS obstacles. They had to keep their relationship hidden from Anna's husband and the town. The constant threat of discovery loomed over them, adding an intensity to their stolen moments.

Despite the challenges, their love only grew stronger. They found creative ways to communicate and meet, cherishing every minute they spent together. Their love was a refuge from the rigid constraints of Anna's marriage.

The Ultimate Sacrifice

THEIR SECRET COULD not remain hidden forever. When Anna's husband discovered their relationship, he was furious and demanded that she end it immediately. Faced with the choice between her marriage and her love, Anna made the painful decision to leave her husband.

They fled to a distant town where they could build a life together, free from the constraints of her marriage. Though they faced hardships, their love provided the strength to endure. They proved that true love can defy even the most rigid marital constraints, turning their forbidden passion into a lasting bond.

Story 6: The Priest and the Parishioner

The Devout Life

FATHER THOMAS WAS A dedicated priest in a small, close-knit community. He had devoted his life to his faith and his parishioners, finding fulfillment in his spiritual duties. Despite his commitment, he often felt a deep sense of loneliness and longing for human connection.

The Forbidden Attraction

CLARA WAS A DEVOUT parishioner who had recently moved to the town. She was known for her kindness and dedication to helping others. When she attended Father Thomas's sermons, she felt a profound connection to his words and his spirit.

The Blossoming Romance

THEIR INITIAL CONVERSATIONS were brief and cautious, but a mutual respect and curiosity quickly developed. Clara found in Father Thomas a confidant and a friend, someone who understood her struggles and shared her values. Father Thomas, in turn, admired Clara's compassion and strength. As their bond deepened, so did their feelings for each other.

One evening, as they worked together in the church garden, Father Thomas took Clara's hand and said, "Clara, I know our love is impossible, but I cannot deny my feelings any longer. I love you."

Tears welled up in Clara's eyes as she replied, "I love you too, Father Thomas. But how can we be together when our love is forbidden by the church?"

The First Kiss

IN A MOMENT OF PASSION and defiance, Father Thomas leaned in and kissed Clara. It was a tender, electrifying kiss that marked the beginning of their secret romance.

The Struggle Against Religious Constraints

THEIR LOVE FACED NUMEROUS obstacles. They had to keep their relationship hidden from the church and the community. The constant threat of discovery loomed over them, adding an intensity to their stolen moments.

Despite the challenges, their love only grew stronger. They found creative ways to communicate and meet, cherishing every minute they spent together. Their love was a refuge from the rigid constraints of their faith.

The Ultimate Sacrifice

THEIR SECRET COULD not remain hidden forever. When the church discovered their relationship, Father Thomas was faced with an ultimatum: end the relationship or leave the priesthood. Faced with the choice between his vocation and his love, Father Thomas made the painful decision to leave the priesthood.

They moved to a distant town where they could build a life together, free from the constraints of the church. Though they faced hardships, their love provided the strength to endure. They proved that true love can defy even the most rigid religious constraints, turning their forbidden passion into a lasting bond.

Story 7: The Rival Families

The Feuding Families

IN A SMALL, RURAL TOWN, the Johnsons and the Andersons had been feuding for generations. Their animosity was deeply ingrained, with both families holding grudges over past wrongs. Despite the hostility, life in the town continued, with everyone knowing to keep their distance from the rival family.

The Forbidden Attraction

LILA JOHNSON AND JACK Anderson had grown up knowing they were supposed to hate each other. Yet, a chance encounter at the town's annual fair led to an unexpected connection. They discovered they shared common interests and values, and their mutual curiosity turned into something deeper.

The Blossoming Romance

THEIR INITIAL CONVERSATIONS were brief and cautious, hidden from the prying eyes of their families. Lila found in Jack a confidant and a friend, someone who understood her frustrations with the family feud. Jack, in turn, admired Lila's courage and spirit. As their bond deepened, so did their feelings for each other.

One evening, as they met in a secluded spot by the river, Jack took Lila's hand and said, "Lila, I know our love is impossible, but I cannot deny my feelings any longer. I love you."

Tears welled up in Lila's eyes as she replied, "I love you too, Jack. But how can we be together when our families will never accept us?"

The First Kiss

IN A MOMENT OF PASSION and defiance, Jack leaned in and kissed Lila. It was a tender, electrifying kiss that marked the beginning of their secret romance.

The Struggle Against Familial Constraints

THEIR LOVE FACED NUMEROUS obstacles. They had to keep their relationship hidden from both families, knowing that discovery could reignite the feud. The constant threat of exposure loomed over them, adding an intensity to their stolen moments.

Despite the challenges, their love only grew stronger. They found creative ways to communicate and meet, cherishing every minute they spent together. Their love was a refuge from the rigid constraints of their families.

The Ultimate Sacrifice

THEIR SECRET COULD not remain hidden forever. When their families discovered the relationship, they were furious and demanded that Lila and Jack end it immediately. Faced with the choice between their families and their love, Lila and Jack made the painful decision to leave the town together.

They moved to a distant city where they could build a life together, free from the constraints of their feuding families. Though they faced hardships, their love provided the strength to endure. They proved that true love can defy even the most rigid familial constraints, turning their forbidden passion into a lasting bond.

Story 8: The Teacher and the Parent

The School Life

GRACE WAS A DEDICATED and passionate teacher at a small elementary school. She loved her job and took pride in helping her students learn and grow. Despite her fulfillment in her work, Grace often felt isolated and longed for a deeper connection.

The Forbidden Attraction

DAVID WAS A SINGLE father whose son, Ethan, was in Grace's class. He admired Grace's dedication and the positive impact she had on Ethan. When they first met during a parent-teacher conference, there was an instant connection.

The Blossoming Romance

THEIR INITIAL CONVERSATIONS were brief and cautious, centered around Ethan's progress. However, as they continued to interact, Grace and David discovered they shared similar values and aspirations. Their mutual respect quickly turned into something deeper.

One evening, after a school event, David took Grace's hand and said, "Grace, I know our love is impossible, but I cannot deny my feelings any longer. I love you."

Tears welled up in Grace's eyes as she replied, "I love you too, David. But how can we be together when our relationship is forbidden by the school?"

The First Kiss

IN A MOMENT OF PASSION and defiance, David leaned in and kissed Grace. It was a tender, electrifying kiss that marked the beginning of their secret romance.

The Struggle Against Professional Constraints

THEIR LOVE FACED NUMEROUS obstacles. They had to keep their relationship hidden from the school administration and other parents, knowing that discovery could jeopardize Grace's career. The constant threat of exposure loomed over them, adding an intensity to their stolen moments.

Despite the challenges, their love only grew stronger. They found creative ways to communicate and meet, cherishing every minute they spent together. Their love was a refuge from the rigid constraints of their professional lives.

The Ultimate Sacrifice

THEIR SECRET COULD not remain hidden forever. When the school discovered their relationship, Grace was faced with an ultimatum: end the relationship or leave her job. Faced with the choice between her career and her love, Grace made the painful decision to resign.

They moved to a different town where Grace could find a new teaching position, free from the constraints of their previous life. Though they faced hardships, their love provided the strength to endure. They proved that true love can defy even the most rigid professional constraints, turning their forbidden passion into a lasting bond.

Story 9: The Political Rivals

The Political Landscape

IN A BUSTLING CITY, Sarah and John were rising stars in their respective political parties. They were known for their passion, intelligence, and dedication to their causes. Despite their mutual respect, they often found themselves on opposite sides of the political spectrum, clashing in debates and policy discussions.

The Forbidden Attraction

THEIR INITIAL ENCOUNTERS were filled with heated arguments and intense debates. However, over time, they developed a mutual admiration for each other's intellect and conviction. A chance meeting at a charity event led to a more personal conversation, revealing shared values and dreams beyond politics.

The Blossoming Romance

THEIR INITIAL CONVERSATIONS were brief and cautious, hidden from the public eye. Sarah found in John a confidant and a friend, someone who understood her struggles and shared her passion for making a difference. John, in turn, admired Sarah's courage and determination. As their bond deepened, so did their feelings for each other.

One evening, after a particularly intense debate, John took Sarah's hand and said, "Sarah, I know our love is impossible, but I cannot deny my feelings any longer. I love you."

Tears welled up in Sarah's eyes as she replied, "I love you too, John. But how can we be together when our relationship is forbidden by our parties?"

The First Kiss

IN A MOMENT OF PASSION and defiance, John leaned in and kissed Sarah. It was a tender, electrifying kiss that marked the beginning of their secret romance.

The Struggle Against Political Constraints

THEIR LOVE FACED NUMEROUS obstacles. They had to keep their relationship hidden from their parties and the public, knowing that discovery could jeopardize their political careers. The constant threat of exposure loomed over them, adding an intensity to their stolen moments.

Despite the challenges, their love only grew stronger. They found creative ways to communicate and meet, cherishing every minute they spent together. Their love was a refuge from the rigid constraints of their political lives.

The Ultimate Sacrifice

THEIR SECRET COULD not remain hidden forever. When their parties discovered the relationship, Sarah and John were faced with an ultimatum: end the relationship or leave politics. Faced with the choice between their careers and their love, they made the painful decision to resign from their respective parties.

They moved to a different city where they could build a life together, free from the constraints of their political careers. Though they faced hardships, their love provided the strength to endure. They proved that true love can defy even the most rigid political constraints, turning their forbidden passion into a lasting bond.

Story 10: The Scientist and the Environmentalist

The Conflicting Worlds

IN A WORLD WHERE SCIENTIFIC progress often clashed with environmental preservation, Dr. Emily Foster was a renowned scientist working on advanced technological solutions, while Mark Hayes was a passionate environmentalist advocating for sustainable practices. Their worlds were frequently at odds, each believing in the importance of their work.

The Forbidden Attraction

THEIR INITIAL ENCOUNTERS were marked by intense debates and ideological clashes. However, a mutual respect for each other's dedication slowly emerged. During a joint panel discussion at a global conference, their interactions took on a more personal tone.

The Blossoming Romance

THEIR INITIAL CONVERSATIONS were brief and cautious, hidden from their respective organizations. Emily found in Mark a confidant and a friend, someone who understood her struggles and shared her passion for making a difference. Mark, in turn, admired Emily's intelligence and dedication. As their bond deepened, so did their feelings for each other.

One evening, after a particularly intense discussion, Mark took Emily's hand and said, "Emily, I know our love is impossible, but I cannot deny my feelings any longer. I love you."

Tears welled up in Emily's eyes as she replied, "I love you too, Mark. But how can we be together when our relationship is forbidden by our organizations?"

The First Kiss

IN A MOMENT OF PASSION and defiance, Mark leaned in and kissed Emily. It was a tender, electrifying kiss that marked the beginning of their secret romance.

The Struggle Against Ideological Constraints

THEIR LOVE FACED NUMEROUS obstacles. They had to keep their relationship hidden from their respective organizations, knowing that discovery could jeopardize their work and reputations. The constant threat of exposure loomed over them, adding an intensity to their stolen moments.

Despite the challenges, their love only grew stronger. They found creative ways to communicate and meet, cherishing every minute they spent together. Their love was a refuge from the rigid constraints of their professional lives.

The Ultimate Sacrifice

THEIR SECRET COULD not remain hidden forever. When their organizations discovered the relationship, Emily and Mark were faced with an ultimatum: end the relationship or leave their respective causes. Faced with the choice between their careers and their love, they made the painful decision to resign from their positions.

They moved to a different country where they could build a life together, free from the constraints of their professional worlds. Though they faced hardships, their love provided the strength to endure. They proved that true love can defy even the most rigid ideological constraints, turning their forbidden passion into a lasting bond.

CONCLUSION

Forbidden passions delve into the depths of love's resilience against societal, familial, and ideological constraints. These stories explore the intensity and challenges of secret romances, where love flourishes despite the obstacles. They highlight the raw, passionate, and often tumultuous journeys of those who dare to love against the odds. As you read through these tales of forbidden love, may you be inspired by the power of love to transcend boundaries and defy conventions, proving that true love knows no limits.

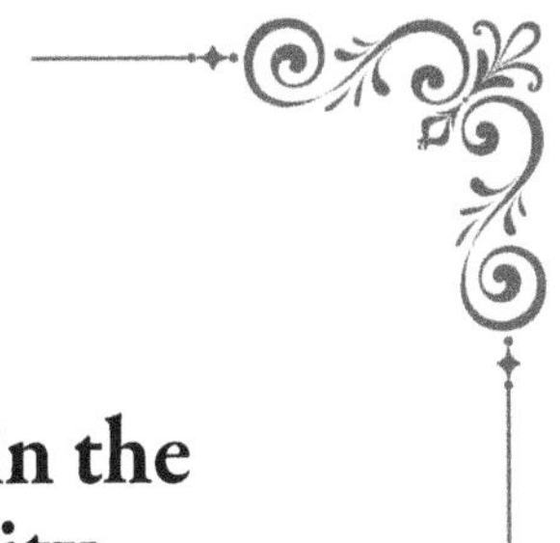

Chapter 8: Love in the Face of Adversity

Introduction to Love in the Face of Adversity

Love that endures and flourishes despite significant obstacles is often the most inspiring. These stories demonstrate the power of resilience, commitment, and the unwavering strength of the human spirit. This chapter explores tales of couples who faced and conquered both personal and external challenges, proving that true love can triumph over adversity.

Story 1: The Long-Distance Relationship

The Separation

EMMA AND JACK HAD BEEN inseparable during their time in university. Their love was deep and genuine, filled with shared dreams and mutual support. However, after graduation, life took them in different directions. Emma secured a prestigious job in New York, while Jack was offered an incredible opportunity in London. The prospect of maintaining their relationship across an ocean was daunting.

The Commitment to Love

DESPITE THE DISTANCE, they were determined to make their relationship work. They scheduled regular video calls, sent each other heartfelt letters and emails, and visited as often as their schedules and finances allowed. Each reunion was filled with joy, but each departure was a new heartbreak.

One evening, during a particularly challenging week, Emma expressed her fears. "Jack, I'm worried that the distance will eventually wear us down. How can we keep going like this?"

Jack, ever the optimist, replied, "Emma, our love is stronger than any distance. We just have to keep believing in us and work through the tough times."

Overcoming External Challenges

THEIR LOVE FACED NUMEROUS challenges beyond the physical distance. Time zone differences, career demands, and the longing for physical closeness were constant hurdles. However, they found creative ways to stay connected. They would watch movies together over video calls, read the same books, and even cooked the same meals to share a virtual dinner date.

The Proposal

After two years of maintaining their long-distance relationship, Jack planned a surprise visit to New York. He arranged a romantic evening and proposed to Emma at the spot where they had their first date. Tears of joy filled Emma's eyes as she said, "Yes, Jack. A thousand times yes!"

Building a Future Together

THEY DECIDED TO CLOSE the distance by moving to a city where both could pursue their careers. They faced new challenges of adjusting to a new place and building their lives together, but their commitment and love only grew stronger. Their story became a testament to the resilience and strength of love, proving that distance is no match for true commitment.

Story 2: The Illness

THE DIAGNOSIS

Sophia and Daniel had been married for five years when Daniel was diagnosed with a rare and aggressive form of cancer. The diagnosis was a devastating blow, shattering their dreams and plunging them into a world of uncertainty and fear.

The Commitment to Fight

DESPITE THE GRIM PROGNOSIS, Sophia and Daniel were determined to fight the illness together. They researched treatments, sought out the best doctors, and leaned on each other for support. Sophia became Daniel's primary caregiver, balancing her job and their household responsibilities with his medical appointments and treatments.

One night, as Daniel lay in bed after a particularly grueling chemotherapy session, he whispered, "Sophia, I don't want you to have to go through this. It's too much."

Sophia, holding back tears, replied, "We're in this together, Daniel. I love you, and I will fight for you every step of the way."

Facing the Struggles Together

THEIR JOURNEY WAS FRAUGHT with challenges. The physical and emotional toll of the illness, financial strain, and the fear of an uncertain future tested their relationship. But through it all, their love remained steadfast. They found moments of joy in the midst of pain, celebrating small victories and cherishing their time together.

The Turning Point

AFTER MONTHS OF TREATMENT, Daniel's condition began to improve. The tumor shrank, and his doctors were cautiously optimistic.

The road to recovery was still long, but there was hope. Sophia and Daniel's love and resilience had carried them through the darkest times.

A New Beginning

AS DANIEL'S HEALTH continued to improve, they renewed their vows in a small, intimate ceremony, surrounded by close friends and family. Their journey through illness had strengthened their bond and deepened their appreciation for each other. They emerged stronger and more committed, proving that love can conquer even the most daunting adversities.

Story 3: The Financial Struggles

The Unexpected Crisis

MIA AND ETHAN WERE living a comfortable life with their two children when Ethan lost his job due to company downsizing. Their financial security was suddenly at risk, and the stress of their new reality weighed heavily on both of them.

The Commitment to Overcome

Despite the financial strain, Mia and Ethan were determined to face the crisis together. They reevaluated their budget, cut unnecessary expenses, and found creative ways to make ends meet. Ethan took on freelance work while searching for a new full-time position, and Mia picked up extra shifts at her job.

One evening, as they sat at the kitchen table reviewing their finances, Ethan said, "Mia, I feel like I've let you and the kids down. I'm so sorry."

Mia took his hand and replied, "Ethan, we're a team. We'll get through this together. Our love and our family are stronger than any financial struggle."

Facing the Challenges

THEIR JOURNEY WAS FILLED with sacrifices and difficult decisions. They had to move to a smaller apartment, sell their second car, and delay plans for vacations and other luxuries. However, they found strength in their love and their commitment to each other and their family.

Finding Strength in Love

THROUGH THEIR STRUGGLES, Mia and Ethan discovered new depths of their relationship. They supported each other emotionally, finding solace in their shared determination to overcome their financial difficulties. Their children, too, learned valuable lessons about resilience and the importance of family.

A New Opportunity

After months of searching, Ethan finally secured a new job. Their financial situation gradually improved, and they were able to rebuild their savings and regain their stability. Their journey through financial adversity had brought them closer and made them appreciate the true value of their love and family.

A Stronger Bond

MIA AND ETHAN'S STORY became an inspiration to others facing financial struggles. They proved that love, resilience, and commitment could conquer even the most challenging economic hardships. Their bond emerged stronger, and their love continued to thrive in the face of adversity.

Story 4: The Family Opposition

The Forbidden Love

AISHA AND JOHN CAME from different cultural backgrounds. Their families held deep-seated prejudices and disapproved of their relationship. Despite the opposition, Aisha and John's love for each other was undeniable, and they were determined to be together.

The Commitment to Love

FACING STRONG FAMILY opposition, Aisha and John decided to continue their relationship in secret. They knew their love was worth fighting for, even if it meant going against their families' wishes. They found ways to meet and communicate without their families knowing, building their relationship on trust and mutual respect.

One night, as they sat under the stars, John said, "Aisha, I can't imagine my life without you. We'll find a way to make this work, no matter what."

Aisha, holding his hand, replied, "John, our love is stronger than any prejudice. We'll face whatever comes our way together."

Facing the Opposition

THEIR JOURNEY WAS FILLED with challenges. They had to navigate the hurtful comments and actions from their families, the fear of being discovered, and the pain of not having their relationship accepted. However, their love only grew stronger in the face of adversity.

Finding Allies

OVER TIME, AISHA AND John found allies among their friends and some family members who supported their love. These allies provided emotional support and helped them navigate the complexities of their situation. They encouraged Aisha and John to stay true to their love and fight for their happiness.

The Turning Point

AFTER YEARS OF PERSEVERANCE, Aisha and John decided to take a bold step. They invited both families to a meeting, hoping to bridge the gap and find a path to acceptance. The meeting was tense, but Aisha and John spoke from their hearts, sharing their love story and their desire for unity.

A New Beginning

THEIR HONESTY AND COURAGE touched their families. While it took time for full acceptance, both families gradually began to see the strength and sincerity of Aisha and John's love. They started to build new relationships, learning to appreciate and respect each other's cultures.

A Stronger Bond

AISHA AND JOHN'S STORY became a symbol of love conquering prejudice and adversity. Their resilience and commitment proved that love can overcome even the most deep-rooted opposition. They built a life together, filled with love, respect, and a newfound appreciation for their cultural heritage.

Story 5: The Disability

THE DIAGNOSIS

Lena and Mark had been married for three years when Mark was diagnosed with multiple sclerosis, a chronic illness that affects the central nervous system. The diagnosis was a devastating blow, bringing fear and uncertainty into their lives.

The Commitment to Fight

DESPITE THE CHALLENGES, Lena and Mark were determined to face the illness together. They researched treatments, joined support groups, and adapted their lifestyle to accommodate Mark's changing needs. Lena became Mark's primary caregiver, balancing her job with his medical appointments and daily care.

One evening, as they sat on the porch, Mark said, "Lena, I hate that you have to go through this because of me. I feel like I'm a burden."

Lena, holding back tears, replied, "Mark, you're not a burden. We're in this together. Our love is stronger than any illness, and we'll face whatever comes our way."

Facing the Daily Challenges

THEIR JOURNEY WAS FILLED with daily challenges. The physical and emotional toll of the illness, financial strain, and the fear of an uncertain future tested their relationship. But through it all, their love remained steadfast. They found moments of joy in the midst of pain, celebrating small victories and cherishing their time together.

The Turning Point

AFTER MONTHS OF ADJUSTING to their new reality, they found a treatment plan that helped manage Mark's symptoms. While the illness was still a part of their lives, they learned to navigate it with resilience and hope. Lena and Mark's love and commitment had carried them through the darkest times.

A New Beginning

AS THEY ADAPTED TO their new normal, they renewed their vows in a small, intimate ceremony, surrounded by close friends and family. Their journey through illness had strengthened their bond and deepened their appreciation for each other. They emerged stronger and more committed, proving that love can conquer even the most daunting adversities.

Story 6: The Natural Disaster

THE CATASTROPHE

Lucy and Tom had built a beautiful life together in their coastal town. They had a cozy home, fulfilling jobs, and a close-knit community. However, their world was turned upside down when a devastating hurricane struck, destroying their home and much of their town.

The Commitment to Rebuild

DESPITE THE DESTRUCTION, Lucy and Tom were determined to rebuild their lives. They found temporary shelter and immediately began working with their community to clean up and repair the damage. Their resilience and commitment to each other and their town kept them going through the toughest times.

One night, as they sat in their temporary shelter, Tom said, "Lucy, it feels like we've lost everything. How can we rebuild our lives from scratch?"

Lucy, holding his hand, replied, "Tom, as long as we have each other, we can rebuild anything. Our love and our community will get us through this."

Facing the Challenges

THEIR JOURNEY WAS FILLED with challenges. They had to navigate the emotional trauma of losing their home, the financial strain of rebuilding, and the logistical difficulties of living in temporary conditions. However, their love only grew stronger in the face of adversity.

Finding Strength in Community

LUCY AND TOM FOUND strength in their community. Neighbors came together to support each other, sharing resources, and providing emotional support. This sense of unity and collective resilience helped them navigate the difficult times.

The Turning Point

AFTER MONTHS OF HARD work and determination, Lucy and Tom were able to rebuild their home. It wasn't the same as before, but it was filled with new memories and a renewed sense of hope. Their journey through the natural disaster had brought them closer and deepened their appreciation for each other and their community.

A New Beginning

As they settled into their rebuilt home, they hosted a community gathering to celebrate their collective resilience and commitment. Lucy and Tom's story became a symbol of hope and inspiration, proving that love can conquer even the most devastating adversities. They emerged stronger and more committed, ready to face whatever the future held.

Story 7: The Mental Health Struggles

The Silent Battle

RACHEL AND CHRIS HAD been married for two years when Rachel started experiencing severe anxiety and depression. The mental health struggles took a toll on their relationship, bringing feelings of isolation, fear, and helplessness into their lives.

The Commitment to Support

DESPITE THE CHALLENGES, Chris was determined to support Rachel through her struggles. He researched treatments, encouraged her to seek professional help, and provided emotional support. Rachel, in turn, was committed to working through her mental health issues for herself and their relationship.

One evening, as they sat on the couch, Rachel said, "Chris, I feel like I'm dragging you down with me. Maybe you'd be better off without me."

Chris, holding her hand, replied, "Rachel, we're in this together. Your struggles are our struggles, and I'm here for you no matter what. Our love is stronger than any illness."

Facing the Daily Challenges

THEIR JOURNEY WAS FILLED with daily challenges. The emotional toll of Rachel's mental health struggles, the financial strain of therapy and medication, and the fear of an uncertain future tested their relationship. But through it all, their love remained steadfast. They found moments of joy in the midst of pain, celebrating small victories and cherishing their time together.

The Turning Point

AFTER MONTHS OF THERAPY and treatment, Rachel's mental health began to improve. While she still had difficult days, she learned to manage her anxiety and depression with the support of Chris and her healthcare providers. Their love and commitment had carried them through the darkest times.

A New Beginning

AS RACHEL'S MENTAL health stabilized, they renewed their vows in a small, intimate ceremony, surrounded by close friends and family. Their journey through mental health struggles had strengthened their bond and deepened their appreciation for each other. They emerged stronger and more committed, proving that love can conquer even the most daunting adversities.

Story 8: The Addiction

The Hidden Struggle

JAKE AND EMILY HAD been married for five years when Jake's addiction to alcohol began to spiral out of control. The addiction took a toll on their relationship, bringing feelings of betrayal, fear, and helplessness into their lives.

The Commitment to Recovery

DESPITE THE CHALLENGES, Emily was determined to support Jake through his addiction. She encouraged him to seek professional help, attended support groups with him, and provided emotional support. Jake, in turn, was committed to working through his addiction for himself and their relationship.

One evening, as they sat on the porch, Jake said, "Emily, I'm so sorry for everything I've put you through. I don't deserve your love."

Emily, holding his hand, replied, "Jake, we're in this together. Your struggles are our struggles, and I'm here for you no matter what. Our love is stronger than any addiction."

Facing the Daily Challenges

THEIR JOURNEY WAS FILLED with daily challenges. The emotional toll of Jake's addiction, the financial strain of therapy and treatment, and the fear of relapse tested their relationship. But through it all, their love remained steadfast. They found moments of joy in the midst of pain, celebrating small victories and cherishing their time together.

The Turning Point

AFTER MONTHS OF THERAPY and treatment, Jake's addiction began to improve. While he still had difficult days, he learned to manage his addiction with the support of Emily and his healthcare providers. Their love and commitment had carried them through the darkest times.

A New Beginning

AS JAKE'S RECOVERY stabilized, they renewed their vows in a small, intimate ceremony, surrounded by close friends and family. Their journey through addiction had strengthened their bond and deepened their appreciation for each other. They emerged stronger and more committed, proving that love can conquer even the most daunting adversities.

Story 9: The Cultural Differences

The Different Worlds

MARIA AND DAVID CAME from vastly different cultural backgrounds. Maria was from a traditional Hispanic family, while David was from a conservative Jewish family. Their love for each other was strong, but their cultural differences created numerous challenges.

The Commitment to Understand

DESPITE THE CHALLENGES, Maria and David were determined to make their relationship work. They took the time to learn about each other's cultures, attending family gatherings, and participating in cultural traditions. They found ways to blend their cultures, creating a unique and harmonious relationship.

One evening, as they sat by the fire, David said, "Maria, I love you, but sometimes our cultural differences feel overwhelming. How can we make this work?"

Maria, holding his hand, replied, "David, our love is stronger than any cultural differences. We'll find a way to blend our cultures and build a life together."

Facing the Challenges

THEIR JOURNEY WAS FILLED with challenges. They had to navigate the expectations and prejudices of their families, the fear of not being accepted, and the complexities of blending their cultures. However, their love only grew stronger in the face of adversity.

Finding Strength in Love

THROUGH THEIR STRUGGLES, Maria and David discovered new depths of their relationship. They supported each other emotionally, finding solace in their shared determination to overcome their cultural differences. Their families, too, learned to appreciate and respect their love, gradually accepting their relationship.

A New Beginning

As their families began to accept their relationship, Maria and David decided to get married. They blended their cultural traditions in a beautiful and unique wedding ceremony, surrounded by their loved ones. Their journey through cultural differences had strengthened their bond and deepened their appreciation for each other's heritage.

A Stronger Bond

MARIA AND DAVID'S STORY became an inspiration to others facing cultural differences. They proved that love, resilience, and commitment could conquer even the most challenging cultural obstacles. Their bond emerged stronger, and their love continued to thrive in the face of adversity.

Story 10: The Age Difference

The Unconventional Love

CAROLINE AND MICHAEL had a significant age difference, with Caroline being fifteen years older than Michael. Despite their age gap, they shared a deep and genuine love for each other. Their relationship faced skepticism and criticism from friends, family, and society.

The Commitment to Each Other

DESPITE THE EXTERNAL judgments, Caroline and Michael were determined to build a life together. They focused on their shared values, interests, and goals, finding strength in their love and commitment to each other.

One evening, as they sat on the porch, Michael said, "Caroline, I know people judge us because of our age difference. How can we make them see our love is real?"

Caroline, holding his hand, replied, "Michael, our love is stronger than any societal judgment. We'll prove that love knows no age."

Facing the Challenges

Their journey was filled with challenges. They had to navigate the prejudices of society, the fear of not being accepted, and the complexities of their different life stages. However, their love only grew stronger in the face of adversity.

Finding Strength in Love

THROUGH THEIR STRUGGLES, Caroline and Michael discovered new depths of their relationship. They supported each other emotionally, finding solace in their shared determination to overcome the judgments of society. Their families, too, learned to appreciate and respect their love, gradually accepting their relationship.

A New Beginning

As their families and friends began to accept their relationship, Caroline and Michael decided to get married. They celebrated their love in a beautiful and intimate ceremony, surrounded by their loved ones. Their journey through societal judgments had strengthened their bond and deepened their appreciation for each other.

A Stronger Bond

CAROLINE AND MICHAEL'S story became an inspiration to others facing societal judgments. They proved that love, resilience, and commitment could conquer even the most challenging obstacles. Their bond emerged stronger, and their love continued to thrive in the face of adversity.

CONCLUSION

Love in the face of adversity highlights the strength and resilience of the human spirit. These stories of couples overcoming obstacles and facing challenges together demonstrate the power of commitment and the unwavering strength of true love. As you read through these tales of love conquering adversity, may you be inspired by the depth and beauty of love that endures and flourishes, proving that love can triumph over any challenge.

Chapter 9: Whispers of Fantasy

Introduction to Whispers of Fantasy

Fantasy worlds offer an escape into realms where magic, mythical creatures, and enchantments are the norms. Within these settings, love stories transcend the ordinary, weaving together the ethereal and the profound. This chapter explores romantic tales set in fantastical landscapes, where love flourishes amidst enchanted realms and mystical challenges.

Story 1: The Enchanted Forest

The Mysterious Realm

IN THE HEART OF THE Enchanted Forest, where ancient trees whispered secrets and magical creatures roamed, lived Elara, a guardian of the forest. Her duty was to protect the forest's magic from those who would misuse it. Elara was a powerful enchantress, but her heart yearned for companionship amidst the solitude of her duty.

The Forbidden Entrance

ONE DAY, A BRAVE AND curious warrior named Thane entered the forest, seeking a legendary artifact said to grant immense power. Thane had heard tales of the Enchanted Forest and its guardian, but he was determined to find the artifact to protect his homeland from an impending war.

The Unexpected Encounter

AS THANE VENTURED DEEPER into the forest, he encountered Elara. Their initial meeting was tense, as Elara was wary of intruders. However, Thane's noble intentions and genuine respect for the forest's magic intrigued her. She decided to guide him, testing his character along the way.

The Blossoming Romance

THEIR JOURNEY THROUGH the forest brought them closer. They faced trials that tested their courage and revealed their deepest fears and desires. Thane admired Elara's strength and wisdom, while Elara was drawn to Thane's bravery and honor. As their bond deepened, so did their feelings for each other.

One evening, as they sat by a magical spring, Thane turned to Elara and said, "Elara, I know I came here seeking power, but what I've found is far more valuable. I think I'm falling for you."

Elara's heart raced as she replied, "And I for you, Thane. But how can we be together when our worlds are so different?"

The First Kiss

IN A MOMENT OF PASSION and hope, Thane leaned in and kissed Elara. It was a kiss filled with magic and promise, marking the beginning of their love story.

The Struggle Against Dark Forces

THEIR LOVE FACED NUMEROUS obstacles. Dark forces, drawn to the power of the artifact, threatened the forest and their bond. Thane and Elara had to combine their strengths to protect the forest and each other. The trials they faced only strengthened their love, proving that together, they could overcome any challenge.

A Love That Transcends Realms

IN THE END, THANE CHOSE to stay with Elara in the Enchanted Forest. Their love became a legend, a testament to the power of love to transcend realms and conquer darkness. They ruled the forest together, their bond a beacon of hope and magic.

Story 2: The Dragon and the Sorceress

The Mystical Kingdom

IN THE MYSTICAL KINGDOM of Eldoria, dragons and humans lived in uneasy harmony. Dragons, powerful and majestic, were revered and feared. Among them was Draken, a noble dragon with a fierce but lonely heart. Draken guarded the kingdom's treasures and maintained the balance of magic.

The Sorceress's Quest

SERAPHINA, A YOUNG and talented sorceress, sought a way to harness the dragons' magic to heal her dying village. She ventured into the dragons' territory, determined to plead for their aid. Her bravery and determination caught Draken's attention.

The Unlikely Alliance

DRAKEN, INTRIGUED BY Seraphina's courage, agreed to help her but insisted she prove her intentions. Seraphina accepted the challenge, and they embarked on a journey to gather rare magical ingredients needed to create the healing potion.

The Growing Affection

AS THEY TRAVELED TOGETHER, Seraphina and Draken's bond grew stronger. Seraphina admired Draken's strength and wisdom, while Draken was captivated by Seraphina's kindness and intelligence. Their adventures brought them closer, revealing their vulnerabilities and deepening their connection.

One evening, as they rested by a shimmering lake, Seraphina turned to Draken and said, "Draken, I came here seeking your magic, but what I've found is so much more. I think I'm falling for you."

Draken's heart, long hardened by solitude, softened as he replied, "And I for you, Seraphina. But how can we be together when our worlds are so different?"

The First Kiss

IN A MOMENT OF PASSION and hope, Draken, in his human form, leaned in and kissed Seraphina. It was a kiss filled with magic and promise, marking the beginning of their love story.

The Struggle Against Prejudice

THEIR LOVE FACED NUMEROUS obstacles. The prejudices and fears of both dragons and humans threatened to tear them apart. They had to prove their love to their respective communities, showing that unity and understanding could overcome fear and hatred.

A Love That Heals

IN THE END, SERAPHINA and Draken's love became a symbol of hope and healing. Their bond brought peace to Eldoria, proving that love could bridge even the widest chasms. Together, they ruled the kingdom, their love a beacon of unity and magic.

Story 3: The Elven Prince and the Human

Maiden

The Enchanted Elven Realm

IN THE ENCHANTED REALM of Arvandor, elves and humans rarely interacted. The elves, with their ethereal beauty and long lives, kept to their mystical forests, while humans lived in bustling towns and villages. Among the elves was Prince Aerandir, known for his grace and wisdom.

The Forbidden Love

LILA, A HUMAN MAIDEN, stumbled into the elven realm while seeking a cure for her ailing father. Her presence caused a stir among the elves, who viewed humans with suspicion. Prince Aerandir, however, was captivated by Lila's bravery and determination.

The Blossoming Romance

AERANDIR DECIDED TO help Lila, guiding her through the enchanted forests to find the rare herb needed for her father's cure. Their journey brought them closer, revealing their similarities despite their differences. Aerandir admired Lila's strength and compassion, while Lila was enchanted by Aerandir's grace and wisdom.

One evening, as they stood beneath the glowing blossoms of an ancient tree, Aerandir turned to Lila and said, "Lila, I know our love is forbidden, but I cannot deny my feelings any longer. I think I'm falling for you."

Lila's heart raced as she replied, "And I for you, Aerandir. But how can we be together when our worlds are so different?"

The First Kiss

In a moment of passion and hope, Aerandir leaned in and kissed Lila. It was a kiss filled with magic and promise, marking the beginning of their love story.

The Struggle Against Elven Traditions

THEIR LOVE FACED NUMEROUS obstacles. Elven traditions and prejudices against humans threatened to tear them apart. They had to prove their love to the elven council, showing that unity and understanding could overcome fear and hatred.

A Love That Unites

IN THE END, AERANDIR and Lila's love became a symbol of hope and unity. Their bond brought peace to Arvandor, proving that love could bridge even the widest chasms. Together, they ruled the realm, their love a beacon of unity and magic.

Story 4: The Warrior and the Enchantress

The War-Torn Land

IN THE WAR-TORN LAND of Valtoria, magic and might clashed in a struggle for power. Aric, a fierce warrior, fought to protect his homeland from invaders. His strength and courage were legendary, but his heart carried the scars of battle.

The Enchantress's Gift

ELYSIA, A POWERFUL enchantress, lived in the heart of the Whispering Woods. She possessed ancient magic that could turn the tide of war, but she remained neutral, fearing the consequences of her power. When Aric sought her help, she was hesitant but intrigued by his noble spirit.

The Unlikely Alliance

ARIC AND ELYSIA FORMED an alliance to protect Valtoria. Their journey to gather allies and resources was fraught with danger and magic. Aric admired Elysia's wisdom and compassion, while Elysia was drawn to Aric's bravery and honor. As their bond deepened, so did their feelings for each other.

One evening, as they camped by a mystical river, Aric turned to Elysia and said, "Elysia, I know we come from different worlds, but I cannot deny my feelings any longer. I think I'm falling for you."

Elysia's heart raced as she replied, "And I for you, Aric. But how can we be together when our paths are so different?"

The First Kiss

IN A MOMENT OF PASSION and hope, Aric leaned in and kissed Elysia. It was a kiss filled with magic and promise, marking the beginning of their love story.

The Struggle Against War

THEIR LOVE FACED NUMEROUS obstacles. The ongoing war and the prejudices of their respective communities threatened to tear them apart. They had to prove their love to their people, showing that unity and understanding could overcome fear and hatred.

A Love That Triumphs

IN THE END, ARIC AND Elysia's love became a symbol of hope and peace. Their bond brought an end to the war, proving that love could conquer even the darkest forces. Together, they ruled Valtoria, their love a beacon of unity and magic.

Story 5: The Mermaid and the Sailor

The Enchanted Ocean

IN THE DEPTHS OF THE enchanted ocean, mermaids and humans rarely interacted. Mermaids, with their ethereal beauty and magical abilities, kept to their underwater kingdoms, while humans sailed the seas above. Among the mermaids was Seraphina, known for her grace and curiosity about the human world.

The Forbidden Love

CAPTAIN LIAM, A BRAVE sailor, had always been fascinated by tales of mermaids. During a storm, his ship was wrecked, and he found himself rescued by Seraphina. Their worlds collided in that moment, sparking a connection that defied their differences.

The Blossoming Romance

SERAPHINA DECIDED TO help Liam return to his ship, guiding him through the underwater realms. Their journey brought them closer, revealing their similarities despite their differences. Liam admired Seraphina's strength and compassion, while Seraphina was enchanted by Liam's bravery and honor.

One evening, as they floated beneath the moonlit waves, Liam turned to Seraphina and said, "Seraphina, I know our love is forbidden, but I cannot deny my feelings any longer. I think I'm falling for you."

Seraphina's heart raced as she replied, "And I for you, Liam. But how can we be together when our worlds are so different?"

The First Kiss

IN A MOMENT OF PASSION and hope, Liam leaned in and kissed Seraphina. It was a kiss filled with magic and promise, marking the beginning of their love story.

The Struggle Against Ocean Boundaries

THEIR LOVE FACED NUMEROUS obstacles. The prejudices and fears of both mermaids and humans threatened to tear them apart.

They had to prove their love to their respective communities, showing that unity and understanding could overcome fear and hatred.

A Love That Bridges Realms

IN THE END, SERAPHINA and Liam's love became a symbol of hope and unity. Their bond brought peace to the seas, proving that love could bridge even the widest chasms. Together, they ruled both land and sea, their love a beacon of unity and magic.

Story 6: The Phoenix and the Witch

THE FIERY REBIRTH

In the mystical land of Pyra, where flames of magic burned bright, lived Ashara, a powerful witch with control over fire. Her heart, however, was as cold as the ashes of the past, scarred by betrayal and loss.

The Phoenix's Descent

ELIOR, A MAJESTIC PHOENIX, descended to Pyra in search of a legendary artifact that could bring eternal peace to his realm. His fiery spirit and unwavering determination caught Ashara's attention.

The Unlikely Partnership

Ashara and Elior formed a partnership to find the artifact, navigating through fiery trials and ancient magic. Ashara admired Elior's strength and resilience, while Elior was captivated by Ashara's wisdom and compassion. Their journey brought them closer, revealing their vulnerabilities and deepening their connection.

One evening, as they stood amidst the glowing embers of an ancient ruin, Elior turned to Ashara and said, "Ashara, I know we come from different worlds, but I cannot deny my feelings any longer. I think I'm falling for you."

Ashara's heart, long hardened by loss, softened as she replied, "And I for you, Elior. But how can we be together when our paths are so different?"

The First Kiss

IN A MOMENT OF PASSION and hope, Elior, in his human form, leaned in and kissed Ashara. It was a kiss filled with magic and promise, marking the beginning of their love story.

The Struggle Against Elemental Forces

THEIR LOVE FACED NUMEROUS obstacles. The elemental forces and ancient curses that guarded the artifact threatened to tear them apart. They had to prove their love to the elemental guardians, showing that unity and understanding could overcome fear and hatred.

A Love That Burns Bright

IN THE END, ASHARA and Elior's love became a symbol of hope and unity. Their bond brought peace to Pyra, proving that love could conquer even the fiercest flames. Together, they ruled the land, their love a beacon of unity and magic.

Story 7: The Unicorn and the Sorcerer

The Mystical Glade

IN THE MYSTICAL GLADE of Eldoria, where unicorns roamed freely and magic filled the air, lived Lyra, a unicorn with a heart as pure as the moonlight. Her beauty and grace were unparalleled, but her heart longed for a companion who understood her soul.

The Sorcerer's Quest

KIERAN, A POWERFUL sorcerer, ventured into the glade seeking the Unicorn's Tear, a magical gem said to grant immense power. He had heard tales of the glade and its guardian but was determined to find the gem to protect his realm from dark forces.

The Unexpected Encounter

AS KIERAN VENTURED deeper into the glade, he encountered Lyra. Their initial meeting was tense, as Lyra was wary of intruders. However, Kieran's noble intentions and genuine respect for the glade's magic intrigued her. She decided to guide him, testing his character along the way.

The Blossoming Romance

THEIR JOURNEY THROUGH the glade brought them closer. They faced trials that tested their courage and revealed their deepest fears and desires. Kieran admired Lyra's strength and wisdom, while Lyra was drawn to Kieran's bravery and honor. As their bond deepened, so did their feelings for each other.

One evening, as they stood beneath the glowing blossoms of an ancient tree, Kieran turned to Lyra and said, "Lyra, I know I came here seeking power, but what I've found is far more valuable. I think I'm falling for you."

Lyra's heart raced as she replied, "And I for you, Kieran. But how can we be together when our worlds are so different?"

The First Kiss

IN A MOMENT OF PASSION and hope, Kieran leaned in and kissed Lyra. It was a kiss filled with magic and promise, marking the beginning of their love story.

The Struggle Against Dark Forces

THEIR LOVE FACED NUMEROUS obstacles. Dark forces, drawn to the power of the Unicorn's Tear, threatened the glade and their bond. Kieran and Lyra had to combine their strengths to protect the glade and each other. The trials they faced only strengthened their love, proving that together, they could overcome any challenge.

A Love That Transcends Realms

IN THE END, KIERAN chose to stay with Lyra in the mystical glade. Their love became a legend, a testament to the power of love to transcend realms and conquer darkness. They ruled the glade together, their bond a beacon of hope and magic.

Story 8: The Fairy and the Knight

The Enchanted Meadow

IN THE ENCHANTED MEADOW of Lyria, where fairies danced among the flowers and magic filled the air, lived Aeliana, a fairy with a heart as light as the morning dew. Her beauty and grace were unmatched, but her heart longed for a companion who understood her spirit.

The Knight's Quest

SIR CEDRIC, A BRAVE knight, ventured into the meadow seeking a magical flower said to grant immense power. He had heard tales of the meadow and its guardian, but he was determined to find the flower to protect his kingdom from an impending threat.

The Unexpected Encounter

AS CEDRIC VENTURED deeper into the meadow, he encountered Aeliana. Their initial meeting was tense, as Aeliana was wary of intruders. However, Cedric's noble intentions and genuine respect for the meadow's magic intrigued her. She decided to guide him, testing his character along the way.

The Blossoming Romance

THEIR JOURNEY THROUGH the meadow brought them closer. They faced trials that tested their courage and revealed their deepest fears and desires. Cedric admired Aeliana's strength and wisdom, while Aeliana was drawn to Cedric's bravery and honor. As their bond deepened, so did their feelings for each other.

One evening, as they stood beneath the glowing blossoms of an ancient tree, Cedric turned to Aeliana and said, "Aeliana, I know I came here seeking power, but what I've found is far more valuable. I think I'm falling for you."

Aeliana's heart raced as she replied, "And I for you, Cedric. But how can we be together when our worlds are so different?"

The First Kiss

IN A MOMENT OF PASSION and hope, Cedric leaned in and kissed Aeliana. It was a kiss filled with magic and promise, marking the beginning of their love story.

The Struggle Against Dark Forces

THEIR LOVE FACED NUMEROUS obstacles. Dark forces, drawn to the power of the magical flower, threatened the meadow and their bond. Cedric and Aeliana had to combine their strengths to protect the meadow and each other. The trials they faced only strengthened their love, proving that together, they could overcome any challenge.

A Love That Transcends Realms

IN THE END, CEDRIC chose to stay with Aeliana in the enchanted meadow. Their love became a legend, a testament to the power of love to transcend realms and conquer darkness. They ruled the meadow together, their bond a beacon of hope and magic.

Story 9: The Werewolf and the Witch

The Moonlit Forest

IN THE MOONLIT FOREST of Lunaria, where werewolves roamed and magic filled the air, lived Aria, a witch with a heart as wild as the night sky. Her beauty and power were unmatched, but her heart longed for a companion who understood her spirit.

The Werewolf's Journey

RONAN, A NOBLE WEREWOLF, ventured into the forest seeking a powerful artifact said to grant immense power. He had heard tales of the forest and its guardian, but he was determined to find the artifact to protect his pack from an impending threat.

The Unexpected Encounter

AS RONAN VENTURED DEEPER into the forest, he encountered Aria. Their initial meeting was tense, as Aria was wary of intruders. However, Ronan's noble intentions and genuine respect for the forest's magic intrigued her. She decided to guide him, testing his character along the way.

The Blossoming Romance

THEIR JOURNEY THROUGH the forest brought them closer. They faced trials that tested their courage and revealed their deepest fears and desires. Ronan admired Aria's strength and wisdom, while Aria was drawn to Ronan's bravery and honor. As their bond deepened, so did their feelings for each other.

One evening, as they stood beneath the glowing blossoms of an ancient tree, Ronan turned to Aria and said, "Aria, I know I came here seeking power, but what I've found is far more valuable. I think I'm falling for you."

Aria's heart raced as she replied, "And I for you, Ronan. But how can we be together when our worlds are so different?"

The First Kiss

IN A MOMENT OF PASSION and hope, Ronan leaned in and kissed Aria. It was a kiss filled with magic and promise, marking the beginning of their love story.

The Struggle Against Dark Forces

THEIR LOVE FACED NUMEROUS obstacles. Dark forces, drawn to the power of the artifact, threatened the forest and their bond. Ronan and Aria had to combine their strengths to protect the forest and each other. The trials they faced only strengthened their love, proving that together, they could overcome any challenge.

A Love That Transcends Realms**

IN THE END, RONAN CHOSE to stay with Aria in the moonlit forest. Their love became a legend, a testament to the power of love to transcend realms and conquer darkness. They ruled the forest together, their bond a beacon of hope and magic.

Story 10: The Ghost and the Mortal

The Haunted Manor**

IN THE HAUNTED MANOR of Ravenswood, where spirits lingered and magic filled the air, lived Evelyn, a ghost with a heart as restless as the night wind. Her beauty and grace were ethereal, but her heart longed for a companion who understood her spirit.

The Mortal's Search

ALEXANDER, A BRAVE mortal, ventured into the manor seeking answers to the mysteries that surrounded his family. He had heard tales of the manor and its guardian, but he was determined to uncover the truth and protect his loved ones from an impending threat.

The Unexpected Encounter

AS ALEXANDER VENTURED deeper into the manor, he encountered Evelyn. Their initial meeting was tense, as Evelyn was wary of intruders. However, Alexander's noble intentions and genuine respect for the manor's magic intrigued her. She decided to guide him, testing his character along the way.

The Blossoming Romance

THEIR JOURNEY THROUGH the manor brought them closer. They faced trials that tested their courage and revealed their deepest fears and desires. Alexander admired Evelyn's strength and wisdom, while Evelyn was drawn to Alexander's bravery and honor. As their bond deepened, so did their feelings for each other.

One evening, as they stood beneath the glowing chandeliers of an ancient hall, Alexander turned to Evelyn and said, "Evelyn, I know I came here seeking answers, but what I’ve found is far more valuable. I think I’m falling for you."

Evelyn's heart, long hardened by solitude, softened as she replied, "And I for you, Alexander. But how can we be together when our worlds are so different?"

The First Kiss

IN A MOMENT OF PASSION and hope, Alexander leaned in and kissed Evelyn. It was a kiss filled with magic and promise, marking the beginning of their love story.

The Struggle Against Dark Forces

THEIR LOVE FACED NUMEROUS obstacles. Dark forces, drawn to the power of the manor, threatened their bond. Alexander and Evelyn had to combine their strengths to protect the manor and each other. The trials they faced only strengthened their love, proving that together, they could overcome any challenge.

A Love That Transcends Realms

IN THE END, ALEXANDER chose to stay with Evelyn in the haunted manor. Their love became a legend, a testament to the power of love to transcend realms and conquer darkness. They ruled the manor together, their bond a beacon of hope and magic.

CONCLUSION

Whispers of fantasy transport us to realms where love transcends the ordinary, flourishing amidst magic, mythical creatures, and enchanted landscapes. These stories of romantic adventures in fantastical settings remind us of the boundless possibilities of love and the magic it can bring into our lives. As you read through these tales, may you be inspired by the ethereal beauty and profound depth of love that knows no bounds, proving that true love can thrive even in the most enchanted realms.

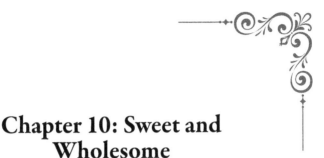

Chapter 10: Sweet and Wholesome

Introduction to Sweet and Wholesome

In a world filled with complexity and turmoil, sweet and wholesome romances offer a refreshing escape into stories of pure, heartfelt connections. These gentle and heartwarming tales focus on emotional bonds and innocent love, suitable for readers of all ages. This chapter presents a collection of such romances, where the beauty of love shines through simplicity and sincerity.

Story 1: The Bookshop Romance

THE QUAINT BOOKSHOP

Lila owned a charming little bookshop in a small town. Nestled on a quiet street, the shop was a haven for book lovers, filled with the scent of old paper and the soft rustle of turning pages. Lila's love for books was evident in every corner of the store, from the carefully curated collections to the cozy reading nooks.

The Regular Customer

HENRY, A SHY AND KIND-hearted schoolteacher, was a regular customer at Lila's bookshop. He visited every Saturday, browsing the shelves for new finds and often leaving with a stack of books. Over time, he and Lila developed a friendly rapport, sharing recommendations and discussing their favorite authors.

The Growing Connection

AS THEIR CONVERSATIONS grew longer and more frequent, Lila and Henry discovered they had much in common beyond their love for books. They both enjoyed quiet walks in the park, a good cup of tea, and the simple joys of life. Their bond deepened, each finding comfort and joy in the other's company.

One Saturday, as they chatted by the counter, Henry shyly asked, "Lila, would you like to join me for tea sometime?"

Lila's heart fluttered as she replied, "I'd love to, Henry."

The First Date

THEIR FIRST DATE WAS as simple and sweet as their budding romance. They met at a cozy café, enjoying tea and pastries while talking about their lives and dreams. The conversation flowed effortlessly, and both felt a sense of rightness being together.

The Blossoming Love

OVER THE FOLLOWING months, Lila and Henry spent more time together. They went on picnics, attended local events, and continued their tea dates. Their love grew in the warmth of shared experiences and quiet moments of understanding.

A Love That Heals

Henry confided in Lila about his past heartbreak, and she shared her fears of loneliness. Through their honest conversations and gentle support, they healed old wounds and built a relationship based on trust and affection.

A Sweet Proposal

One evening, in the soft glow of the bookshop, Henry proposed. He had written a poem for Lila, expressing his love and asking her to be his forever. With tears of joy, Lila said yes, her heart full of love for the man who had become her best friend and soulmate.

A Wholesome Future

LILA AND HENRY'S STORY is a testament to the power of simple, wholesome love. Their gentle romance, built on emotional connection and pure affection, proves that true love doesn't need grand gestures or dramatic events. Sometimes, the sweetest love stories are those that unfold in the quiet moments of everyday life.

Story 2: The Farmer and the Baker

The Small Town Life

IN THE PICTURESQUE town of Willow Creek, life moved at a gentle pace. Everyone knew each other, and community bonds were strong. Emma, a talented baker, owned a small bakery known for its delicious pastries and warm, welcoming atmosphere. Her days were filled with the comforting routines of baking and serving her beloved customers.

The Neighboring Farmer

SAM, A KIND AND HARDWORKING farmer, lived on a farm just outside town. He supplied fresh produce to the local market and was known for his generosity and dedication. Every week, he delivered fresh ingredients to Emma's bakery, always enjoying their friendly chats.

The Unspoken Attraction

EMMA AND SAM HAD ALWAYS felt a quiet attraction towards each other, but both were too shy to express their feelings. They found comfort in their weekly interactions, sharing stories and laughter amidst the bustle of the market.

One day, as Sam delivered a basket of fresh strawberries, he said, "Emma, these are the best strawberries we've ever grown. I saved the best for you."

Emma's heart warmed at his thoughtfulness. "Thank you, Sam. You always bring the best."

The Sweet Gesture

INSPIRED BY SAM'S KINDNESS, Emma decided to bake a special strawberry tart and deliver it to his farm. When she arrived, she found Sam working in the fields, his face lighting up at the sight of her.

"I made this for you," Emma said, handing him the tart. "Thank you for always bringing me the freshest ingredients."

Sam took the tart, touched by her gesture. "Thank you, Emma. This means a lot to me."

The First Date

THEIR MUTUAL ACTS OF kindness sparked the courage to take the next step. Sam invited Emma to a local fair, and she gladly accepted. They spent the day enjoying the simple pleasures of the fair—rides, games, and delicious food. Their laughter and easy conversation made the day unforgettable.

The Blossoming Love

AS THE MONTHS PASSED, Emma and Sam grew closer. They shared more dates, from picnics in the fields to quiet evenings at the bakery. Their love blossomed in the warmth of shared moments and mutual support.

A Love That Nourishes

SAM CONFIDED IN EMMA about his dreams of expanding the farm, and she shared her vision for the bakery. Together, they encouraged and supported each other's dreams, their love providing strength and inspiration.

A Wholesome Proposal

ONE EVENING, UNDER the stars at the farm, Sam proposed. With a heart full of love, he asked Emma to marry him and build a future together. Emma, tears of joy in her eyes, said yes, knowing she had found her partner in life and love.

A Sweet Future

EMMA AND SAM'S STORY is a beautiful example of wholesome, nurturing love. Their gentle romance, built on kindness, support, and shared dreams, proves that true love can flourish in the simple joys of everyday life. Their sweet and wholesome love story is a reminder that the most meaningful connections often grow from the smallest acts of kindness.

Story 3: The Music Teacher and the Librarian

The Heart of the Community

IN THE HEART OF A BUSTLING town, the local library and music school were hubs of activity and learning. Grace, a dedicated librarian, loved her job and the joy of connecting people with books. Her days were filled with the quiet rhythm of the library and the satisfaction of helping others.

The Music Teacher's Passion

ETHAN, A PASSIONATE music teacher, worked at the nearby music school. He taught children and adults alike, sharing his love for music and helping his students discover their own talents. His enthusiasm and kindness made him a beloved figure in the community.

The Library Concert

ONE SUMMER, THE LIBRARY and music school collaborated on a community concert. Grace and Ethan worked together to organize the event, their shared commitment to enriching the community bringing them closer. As they planned and prepared, they found themselves enjoying each other's company more than they expected.

The Growing Affection

THEIR COLLABORATION led to frequent meetings and long conversations about their passions and dreams. Grace admired Ethan's dedication to his students and his gentle nature, while Ethan was drawn to Grace's intelligence and warmth.

One evening, after a particularly successful planning session, Ethan said, "Grace, I've really enjoyed working with you. Would you like to have dinner sometime?"

Grace's heart skipped a beat as she replied, "I'd love to, Ethan."

The First Date

THEIR FIRST DATE WAS simple and delightful. They dined at a cozy restaurant, sharing stories and laughter over delicious food. The connection they felt during their work together blossomed into something deeper, and both felt a sense of rightness being together.

The Blossoming Love

OVER THE FOLLOWING months, Grace and Ethan spent more time together. They attended concerts, visited museums, and enjoyed quiet evenings at the library and music school. Their love grew in the warmth of shared experiences and deep conversations.

A Love That Inspires

Ethan confided in Grace about his dream of composing a symphony, and she shared her vision for expanding the library's community programs. Together, they encouraged and supported each other's dreams, their love providing strength and inspiration.

A Wholesome Proposal

ONE EVENING, AFTER a beautiful concert, Ethan proposed. He had composed a piece of music for Grace, expressing his love and asking her to be his forever. With tears of joy, Grace said yes, her heart full of love for the man who had become her best friend and soulmate.

A Sweet Future

Grace and Ethan's story is a testament to the power of simple, wholesome love. Their gentle romance, built on emotional connection and pure affection, proves that true love doesn't need grand gestures or dramatic events. Sometimes, the sweetest love stories are those that unfold in the quiet moments of everyday life.

Story 4: The Childhood Friends

The Small Town Memories

IN THE SMALL TOWN OF Maplewood, everyone knew each other, and childhood friendships often lasted a lifetime. Lily and Ben had been best friends since kindergarten. They grew up together, sharing adventures, secrets, and dreams.

The Unspoken Love

AS THEY GREW OLDER, their friendship deepened, but unspoken feelings of love began to stir in both their hearts. Neither wanted to risk their cherished friendship, so they kept their feelings hidden, content with the bond they shared.

The Reunion

After college, both returned to Maplewood to start their careers. Lily became a teacher at the local elementary school, while Ben opened a small café. Their friendship picked up right where it left off, but the unspoken feelings remained just beneath the surface.

The Gentle Realization

ONE SUMMER EVENING, during the town's annual fair, Lily and Ben found themselves alone on a Ferris wheel. As they looked out over the town, memories of their shared past filled their hearts. Ben turned to Lily and said, "Lily, I've always cherished our friendship, but I need to tell you something. I think I've loved you for as long as I can remember."

Lily's heart soared as she replied, "Ben, I've felt the same way. I was just too afraid to say it."

The First Kiss

IN THE SOFT GLOW OF the Ferris wheel lights, Ben leaned in and kissed Lily. It was a tender, gentle kiss, filled with the promise of a love that had been years in the making.

The Blossoming Romance

THEIR LOVE STORY BLOSSOMED in the familiar surroundings of Maplewood. They spent their days building their careers and their evenings reliving old memories and creating new ones. Their love, built on a foundation of deep friendship, grew stronger with each passing day.

A Love That Endures

BEN CONFIDED IN LILY about his dreams of expanding the café, and she shared her vision for innovative teaching methods. Together, they encouraged and supported each other's dreams, their love providing strength and inspiration.

A Wholesome Proposal

ONE EVENING, UNDER the stars at the town's annual picnic, Ben proposed. With a heart full of love, he asked Lily to marry him and build a future together. Lily, tears of joy in her eyes, said yes, knowing she had found her partner in life and love.

A Sweet Future

LILY AND BEN'S STORY is a beautiful example of wholesome, enduring love. Their gentle romance, built on a lifelong friendship and pure affection, proves that true love can grow from the simplest and most cherished connections. Their sweet and wholesome love story is a reminder that the most meaningful relationships are often those that have been nurtured over time.

Story 5: The Flower Shop Romance

The Charming Flower Shop

SOPHIE OWNED A CHARMING flower shop in the heart of the city. Her days were filled with the vibrant colors and delicate scents of flowers, each arrangement crafted with love and care. Sophie's warm and friendly nature made her shop a beloved spot for locals.

The Loyal Customer

James, a kind and thoughtful architect, was a regular customer at Sophie's flower shop. He often bought flowers for his clients, friends, and family, always enjoying the brief interactions with Sophie.

The Growing Affection

OVER TIME, SOPHIE AND James developed a friendly rapport. They shared conversations about their lives, dreams, and the simple joys of life. Their bond deepened, each finding comfort and joy in the other's company.

One day, as James picked up a bouquet, he said, "Sophie, I've always admired your passion for flowers. Would you like to join me for a walk in the park this weekend?"

Sophie's heart fluttered as she replied, "I'd love to, James."

The First Date

THEIR FIRST DATE WAS as simple and sweet as their budding romance. They met at a nearby park, enjoying a leisurely walk among the blooming flowers and lush greenery. The conversation flowed effortlessly, and both felt a sense of rightness being together.

The Blossoming Love

OVER THE FOLLOWING months, Sophie and James spent more time together. They went on picnics, attended local events, and enjoyed quiet evenings at the flower shop. Their love grew in the warmth of shared experiences and quiet moments of understanding.

A Love That Grows

JAMES CONFIDED IN SOPHIE about his dream of designing a community garden, and she shared her vision for expanding the flower shop. Together, they encouraged and supported each other's dreams, their love providing strength and inspiration.

A Wholesome Proposal

ONE EVENING, IN THE soft glow of the flower shop, James proposed. He had designed a beautiful arrangement of flowers, spelling out "Will you marry me?" With tears of joy, Sophie said yes, her heart full of love for the man who had become her best friend and soulmate.

A Sweet Future

Sophie and James's story is a testament to the power of simple, wholesome love. Their gentle romance, built on emotional connection and pure affection, proves that true love doesn't need grand gestures or dramatic events. Sometimes, the sweetest love stories are those that unfold in the quiet moments of everyday life.

Story 6: The Café Connection

The Cozy Café*

MIA OWNED A COZY CAFÉ on a quiet street corner. Her love for baking and creating a welcoming atmosphere made the café a popular spot for locals. The scent of fresh coffee and homemade pastries filled the air, creating a warm and inviting space.

The Regular Patron

ETHAN, A KIND AND GENTLE writer, was a regular patron at Mia's café. He spent his mornings writing at a corner table, savoring Mia's delicious pastries and enjoying the peaceful ambiance. Over time, Mia and Ethan developed a friendly rapport, sharing conversations about their lives and dreams.

The Growing Affection

AS THEIR CONVERSATIONS grew longer and more frequent, Mia and Ethan discovered they had much in common beyond their love for coffee and pastries. They both enjoyed quiet walks in the park, a good book, and the simple joys of life. Their bond deepened, each finding comfort and joy in the other's company.

One morning, as they chatted over coffee, Ethan shyly asked, "Mia, would you like to join me for a walk this weekend?"

Mia's heart fluttered as she replied, "I'd love to, Ethan."

The First Date

THEIR FIRST DATE WAS as simple and sweet as their budding romance. They met at the café and walked to a nearby park, enjoying the fresh air and the beauty of nature. The conversation flowed effortlessly, and both felt a sense of rightness being together.

The Blossoming Love

OVER THE FOLLOWING months, Mia and Ethan spent more time together. They went on picnics, attended local events, and enjoyed quiet evenings at the café. Their love grew in the warmth of shared experiences and quiet moments of understanding.

A Love That Inspires

ETHAN CONFIDED IN MIA about his dream of publishing a novel, and she shared her vision for expanding the café. Together, they encouraged and supported each other's dreams, their love providing strength and inspiration.

A Wholesome Proposal

ONE EVENING, IN THE soft glow of the café, Ethan proposed. He had written a short story for Mia, expressing his love and asking her to be his forever. With tears of joy, Mia said yes, her heart full of love for the man who had become her best friend and soulmate.

A Sweet Future

MIA AND ETHAN'S STORY is a testament to the power of simple, wholesome love. Their gentle romance, built on emotional connection and pure affection, proves that true love doesn't need grand gestures or dramatic events. Sometimes, the sweetest love stories are those that unfold in the quiet moments of everyday life.

Story 7: The Garden Romance

The Community Garden

IN A BUSTLING CITY, a hidden gem thrived in the form of a community garden. This green oasis was a sanctuary for residents seeking a respite from urban life. Among the dedicated gardeners was Olivia, a horticulturist with a passion for nature and a heart full of dreams.

The New Gardener

Leo, a quiet and thoughtful artist, moved into the neighborhood and joined the community garden to find inspiration and tranquility. His gentle nature and love for plants quickly made him a beloved member of the gardening community.

The Growing Connection

OLIVIA AND LEO OFTEN found themselves working side by side, their conversations blossoming amidst the flowers and greenery. They shared stories, laughter, and a mutual appreciation for the simple beauty of nature. Their bond deepened, each finding comfort and joy in the other's company.

One afternoon, as they tended to a bed of roses, Leo said, "Olivia, I've really enjoyed our time together in the garden. Would you like to have dinner with me sometime?"

Olivia's heart fluttered as she replied, "I'd love to, Leo."

The First Date

Their first date was simple and delightful. They dined at a small, charming restaurant, sharing stories and laughter over delicious food. The connection they felt in the garden blossomed into something deeper, and both felt a sense of rightness being together.

The Blossoming Love

OVER THE FOLLOWING months, Olivia and Leo spent more time together. They attended art exhibits, explored new parks, and enjoyed quiet evenings in the garden. Their love grew in the warmth of shared experiences and deep conversations.

A Love That Inspires

LEO CONFIDED IN OLIVIA about his dream of creating a botanical art series, and she shared her vision for expanding the community garden. Together, they encouraged and supported each other's dreams, their love providing strength and inspiration.

A Wholesome Proposal

ONE EVENING, UNDER the stars in the garden, Leo proposed. He had painted a beautiful scene of the garden, with a heartwarming message asking Olivia to be his forever. With tears of joy, Olivia said yes, her heart full of love for the man who had become her best friend and soulmate.

A Sweet Future

OLIVIA AND LEO'S STORY is a testament to the power of simple, wholesome love. Their gentle romance, built on emotional connection and pure affection, proves that true love doesn't need grand gestures or dramatic events. Sometimes, the sweetest love stories are those that unfold in the quiet moments of everyday life.

Story 8: The Teacher and the Veterinarian

The Elementary School

IN A SMALL TOWN, THE elementary school was a hub of activity and learning. Grace, a dedicated and passionate teacher, loved her job and the joy of connecting with her students. Her days were filled with the quiet rhythm of the classroom and the satisfaction of helping others.

The Local Veterinarian

LUKE, A KIND AND GENTLE veterinarian, worked at the local animal clinic. His love for animals and his gentle nature made him a beloved figure in the community. He often visited the school to teach the children about animals and how to care for them.

The Growing Affection

OVER TIME, GRACE AND Luke developed a friendly rapport.

They shared conversations about their lives, dreams, and the simple joys of life. Their bond deepened, each finding comfort and joy in the other's company.

One afternoon, as they chatted after a school visit, Luke said, "Grace, I've really enjoyed our conversations. Would you like to join me for a walk this weekend?"

Grace's heart fluttered as she replied, "I'd love to, Luke."

The First Date

Their first date was simple and delightful. They met at a nearby park, enjoying a leisurely walk among the blooming flowers and lush greenery. The conversation flowed effortlessly, and both felt a sense of rightness being together.

The Blossoming Love

OVER THE FOLLOWING months, Grace and Luke spent more time together. They attended local events, volunteered at animal shelters, and enjoyed quiet evenings at the school and clinic. Their love grew in the warmth of shared experiences and quiet moments of understanding.

A Love That Inspires

LUKE CONFIDED IN GRACE about his dream of opening a wildlife sanctuary, and she shared her vision for innovative teaching methods. Together, they encouraged and supported each other's dreams, their love providing strength and inspiration.

A Wholesome Proposal

ONE EVENING, IN THE soft glow of the clinic, Luke proposed. He had arranged a beautiful display of flowers and a heartfelt message asking Grace to be his forever. With tears of joy, Grace said yes, her heart full of love for the man who had become her best friend and soulmate.

A Sweet Future

GRACE AND LUKE'S STORY is a testament to the power of simple, wholesome love. Their gentle romance, built on emotional connection and pure affection, proves that true love doesn't need grand gestures or dramatic events. Sometimes, the sweetest love stories are those that unfold in the quiet moments of everyday life.

Story 9: The Ice Cream Shop Romance

The Charming Ice Cream Shop

SOPHIE OWNED A CHARMING ice cream shop in a small town. Her love for creating unique and delicious flavors made the shop a popular spot for locals. The scent of freshly made waffle cones and the sound of laughter filled the air, creating a warm and inviting space.

The Loyal Customer

BEN, A KIND AND THOUGHTFUL engineer, was a regular customer at Sophie's ice cream shop. He often brought his nieces and nephews for a sweet treat, always enjoying the brief interactions with Sophie.

The Growing Affection

OVER TIME, SOPHIE AND Ben developed a friendly rapport. They shared conversations about their lives, dreams, and the simple joys of life. Their bond deepened, each finding comfort and joy in the other's company.

One evening, as Ben picked up an ice cream order, he said, "Sophie, I've always admired your passion for ice cream. Would you like to join me for dinner sometime?"

Sophie's heart fluttered as she replied, "I'd love to, Ben."

The First Date

THEIR FIRST DATE WAS as simple and sweet as their budding romance. They met at a cozy restaurant, sharing stories and laughter over delicious food. The connection they felt during their work together blossomed into something deeper, and both felt a sense of rightness being together.

The Blossoming Love

OVER THE FOLLOWING months, Sophie and Ben spent more time together. They attended local events, explored new parks, and enjoyed quiet evenings at the ice cream shop. Their love grew in the warmth of shared experiences and quiet moments of understanding.

A Love That Inspires

BEN CONFIDED IN SOPHIE about his dream of designing a community playground, and she shared her vision for expanding the ice cream shop. Together, they encouraged and supported each other's dreams, their love providing strength and inspiration.

A Wholesome Proposal

ONE EVENING, IN THE soft glow of the ice cream shop, Ben proposed. He had arranged a beautiful display of ice cream cones, spelling out "Will you marry me?" With tears of joy, Sophie said yes, her heart full of love for the man who had become her best friend and soulmate.

A Sweet Future

SOPHIE AND BEN'S STORY is a testament to the power of simple, wholesome love. Their gentle romance, built on emotional connection and pure affection, proves that true love doesn't need grand gestures or dramatic events. Sometimes, the sweetest love stories are those that unfold in the quiet moments of everyday life.

Story 10: The Book Club Romance

The Cozy Book Club

IN A COZY CORNER OF the town's library, a book club met every week to discuss their latest reads. Among the dedicated members was Clara, a book lover with a passion for storytelling. Her enthusiasm and warmth made her a beloved figure in the book club.

The New Member

Jack, a kind and thoughtful writer, joined the book club to find inspiration and connect with fellow readers. His gentle nature and love for books quickly made him a cherished member of the group.

The Growing Connection

CLARA AND JACK OFTEN found themselves engrossed in deep conversations about their favorite books and authors. They shared stories, laughter, and a mutual appreciation for the power of storytelling. Their bond deepened, each finding comfort and joy in the other's company.

One evening, after a particularly engaging book club meeting, Jack said, "Clara, I've really enjoyed our conversations. Would you like to have dinner with me sometime?"

Clara's heart fluttered as she replied, "I'd love to, Jack."

The First Date

THEIR FIRST DATE WAS simple and delightful. They dined at a small, charming restaurant, sharing stories and laughter over delicious food. The connection they felt in the book club blossomed into something deeper, and both felt a sense of rightness being together.

The Blossoming Love

OVER THE FOLLOWING months, Clara and Jack spent more time together. They attended book signings, visited literary festivals, and enjoyed quiet evenings discussing their latest reads. Their love grew in the warmth of shared experiences and deep conversations.

A Love That Inspires

JACK CONFIDED IN CLARA about his dream of publishing a novel, and she shared her vision for expanding the book club's outreach programs. Together, they encouraged and supported each other's dreams, their love providing strength and inspiration.

A Wholesome Proposal

ONE EVENING, IN THE soft glow of the library, Jack proposed. He had written a short story for Clara, expressing his love and asking her to be his forever. With tears of joy, Clara said yes, her heart full of love for the man who had become her best friend and soulmate.

A Sweet Future

CLARA AND JACK'S STORY is a testament to the power of simple, wholesome love. Their gentle romance, built on emotional connection and pure affection, proves that true love doesn't need grand gestures or dramatic events. Sometimes, the sweetest love stories are those that unfold in the quiet moments of everyday life.

CONCLUSION

Sweet and wholesome romances offer a heartwarming escape into stories of pure, heartfelt connections. These gentle tales focus on emotional bonds and innocent love, suitable for readers of all ages. As you read through these stories, may you be inspired by the beauty of love that shines through simplicity and sincerity, proving that true love can thrive in the quiet moments of everyday life.

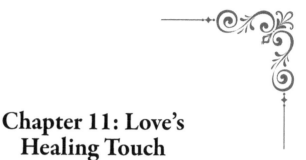

Chapter 11: Love's Healing Touch

Introduction to Love's Healing Touch

Love has an incredible ability to heal wounds, mend broken hearts, and redeem souls lost in darkness. This chapter delves into romance stories with themes of healing and redemption, where characters find love while overcoming personal traumas. These tales explore the therapeutic power of love and its capacity to transform lives.

Story 1: The War Veteran and the Therapist

The Battle Scars

JAKE WAS A WAR VETERAN haunted by the traumas of his past. The battles he fought overseas left him with deep emotional scars, and the transition back to civilian life was fraught with challenges. Nightmares and flashbacks plagued his days and nights, making it difficult for him to find peace.

The Compassionate Therapist

EMMA WAS A COMPASSIONATE therapist specializing in helping veterans. Her dedication to her work stemmed from a personal loss—her brother, also a soldier, had struggled with PTSD before his untimely death. Emma was determined to make a difference in the lives of those who served.

The First Meeting

JAKE WAS INITIALLY resistant to therapy, but his family convinced him to give it a try. He walked into Emma's office, guarded and wary. Emma, with her gentle demeanor and understanding eyes, immediately put him at ease.

Their first sessions were tough. Jake was reluctant to open up, and Emma had to gently coax him into sharing his experiences. She used creative therapies like art and music to help him express his emotions.

The Growing Connection

OVER TIME, A BOND FORMED between Jake and Emma. Jake began to trust Emma and opened up about his deepest fears and traumas. Emma admired Jake's courage and resilience, while Jake appreciated Emma's patience and dedication.

One afternoon, after a particularly emotional session, Jake said, "Emma, you've done more for me than anyone ever has. I don't know how to thank you."

Emma, touched by his words, replied, "Jake, your progress is the best thanks I could ever receive."

The Blossoming Love

THEIR PROFESSIONAL relationship gradually evolved into a deep friendship. They started spending time together outside of therapy sessions, enjoying simple activities like hiking and visiting art galleries. Their shared experiences brought them closer, and they found solace in each other's company.

A Love That Heals

JAKE CONFIDED IN EMMA about his struggles with guilt and self-worth, and Emma shared her own grief over her brother's death. Through their honest conversations and mutual support, they began to heal old wounds.

The First Kiss

ONE EVENING, AS THEY walked through a peaceful park, Jake turned to Emma and said, "Emma, I don't think I could have come this far without you. I think I'm falling in love with you."

Emma's heart swelled with emotion as she replied, "Jake, I feel the same way."

In a moment of vulnerability and hope, Jake leaned in and kissed Emma. It was a tender, healing kiss that marked the beginning of their romantic journey.

A Future Together

JAKE AND EMMA CONTINUED to support each other through their healing process. Their love grew stronger, rooted in their shared experiences and mutual understanding. They proved that love has the power to heal even the deepest wounds, and their story became a testament to the therapeutic power of love.

Story 2: The Artist and the Survivor

The Hidden Pain

LILA WAS AN ARTIST with a talent for capturing emotions on canvas. However, her own life was marked by hidden pain. She had survived an abusive relationship that left her with deep emotional scars. Despite her outward success, Lila struggled with trust and vulnerability.

The Gentle Soul

ETHAN WAS A GENTLE soul who worked as a counselor at a local support center. His empathetic nature and kind heart made him a beacon of hope for those seeking help. Ethan had his own history of loss, having lost his mother to illness when he was young.

The First Encounter

Lila and Ethan first met at a charity art auction where Lila's paintings were being showcased. Ethan was captivated by her work, sensing the depth of emotion behind each piece. He approached her, and they struck up a conversation about art and healing.

The Growing Connection

Their initial conversations turned into regular meetings at the support center, where Lila volunteered her time to teach art therapy classes. Ethan admired Lila's resilience and strength, while Lila appreciated Ethan's gentle support and understanding.

One afternoon, as they painted together, Ethan said, "Lila, your art speaks volumes. It's incredibly powerful."

Lila smiled, touched by his words. "Thank you, Ethan. It means a lot coming from you."

The Blossoming Love

AS THEY SPENT MORE time together, Lila and Ethan's bond deepened. They shared their stories of pain and loss, finding comfort in their mutual understanding. Their friendship slowly blossomed into love, built on trust and emotional connection.

A Love That Redeems

Ethan confided in Lila about his struggles with grief and guilt, and Lila shared her fears of never being able to trust again. Through their honest conversations and mutual support, they began to heal old wounds and rediscover the joy of life.

The First Kiss

ONE EVENING, AS THEY walked along the beach, Ethan turned to Lila and said, "Lila, you've brought so much light into my life. I think I'm falling in love with you."

Lila's heart swelled with emotion as she replied, "Ethan, I feel the same way."

In a moment of vulnerability and hope, Ethan leaned in and kissed Lila. It was a tender, healing kiss that marked the beginning of their romantic journey.

A Future Together

Lila and Ethan continued to support each other through their healing process. Their love grew stronger, rooted in their shared experiences and mutual understanding. They proved that love has the power to redeem even the most broken souls, and their story became a testament to the therapeutic power of love.

Story 3: The Single Mother and the Doctor

The Struggle for Stability

MAYA WAS A SINGLE MOTHER raising her young daughter, Lily, on her own. After escaping an abusive marriage, Maya struggled to provide stability for her child while managing her own emotional wounds. Despite the challenges, she was determined to build a better life for Lily.

The Caring Doctor

DR. ALEX WAS A COMPASSIONATE pediatrician who had dedicated his life to helping children. His own childhood had been marked by loss, having lost his father at a young age. Alex's empathy and dedication made him a beloved figure in the community.

The First Meeting

Maya and Alex first met when Maya brought Lily to the clinic for a routine check-up. Alex's gentle demeanor immediately put Maya at ease, and Lily quickly warmed up to him. Over time, their paths crossed frequently as Maya sought medical care for Lily.

The Growing Connection

THEIR INITIAL INTERACTIONS turned into regular conversations about parenting, life, and the challenges they faced. Alex admired Maya's strength and resilience, while Maya appreciated Alex's kindness and support.

One afternoon, after a particularly difficult day, Maya confided in Alex, "Sometimes I feel like I'm failing Lily. It's so hard to do this alone."

Alex gently replied, "Maya, you're an incredible mother. You're doing the best you can, and that's more than enough."

The Blossoming Love

AS THEY SPENT MORE time together, Maya and Alex's bond deepened. They shared their stories of pain and loss, finding comfort in their mutual understanding. Their friendship slowly blossomed into love, built on trust and emotional connection.

A Love That Heals

ALEX CONFIDED IN MAYA about his struggles with grief and guilt, and Maya shared her fears of never being able to trust again. Through their honest conversations and mutual support, they began to heal old wounds and rediscover the joy of life.

The First Kiss

One evening, as they walked through a peaceful park, Alex turned to Maya and said, "Maya, you've brought so much light into my life. I think I'm falling in love with you."

Maya's heart swelled with emotion as she replied, "Alex, I feel the same way."

In a moment of vulnerability and hope, Alex leaned in and kissed Maya. It was a tender, healing kiss that marked the beginning of their romantic journey.

A Future Together

Maya and Alex continued to support each other through their healing process. Their love grew stronger, rooted in their shared experiences and mutual understanding. They proved that love has the power to heal even the deepest wounds, and their story became a testament to the therapeutic power of love.

Story 4: The Widow and the Carpenter

The Weight of Grief

ANNA WAS A WIDOW STRUGGLING to move on after the sudden death of her husband. The loss left her with a heavy heart and a sense of emptiness. She found solace in her garden, where she spent hours tending to her plants and flowers.

The Compassionate Carpenter

MICHAEL WAS A COMPASSIONATE carpenter who had experienced his own share of loss. He had lost his wife to illness and understood the depths of grief. Michael channeled his pain into his work, creating beautiful pieces of furniture that brought comfort to others.

The First Encounter

Anna and Michael first met when Michael was hired to build a new garden shed for Anna. Their initial interactions were polite and professional, but they quickly discovered a shared understanding of loss and grief.

The Growing Connection

THEIR CONVERSATIONS grew longer and more personal as they worked together on the shed. Michael admired Anna's strength and resilience, while Anna appreciated Michael's kindness and support.

One afternoon, as they took a break from their work, Michael said, "Anna, your garden is beautiful. It must bring you a lot of peace."

Anna smiled softly, "It does. It's my sanctuary."

The Blossoming Love

AS THEY SPENT MORE time together, Anna and Michael's bond deepened. They shared their stories of pain and loss, finding comfort in their mutual understanding. Their friendship slowly blossomed into love, built on trust and emotional connection.

A Love That Heals

MICHAEL CONFIDED IN Anna about his struggles with grief and guilt, and Anna shared her fears of never being able to love again. Through their honest conversations and mutual support, they began to heal old wounds and rediscover the joy of life.

The First Kiss

ONE EVENING, AS THEY stood in the glow of the garden lights, Michael turned to Anna and said, "Anna, you've brought so much light into my life. I think I'm falling in love with you."

Anna's heart swelled with emotion as she replied, "Michael, I feel the same way."

In a moment of vulnerability and hope, Michael leaned in and kissed Anna. It was a tender, healing kiss that marked the beginning of their romantic journey.

A Future Together

ANNA AND MICHAEL CONTINUED to support each other through their healing process. Their love grew stronger, rooted in their shared experiences and mutual understanding. They proved that love has the power to heal even the deepest wounds, and their story became a testament to the therapeutic power of love.

Story 5: The Teacher and the Firefighter

The Pain of Loss

SAMANTHA WAS A DEDICATED teacher who had recently lost her fiancé in a tragic accident. The pain of his loss was a constant ache in her heart, and she struggled to find joy in her once-fulfilling career. Her students, however, gave her a sense of purpose and a reason to keep going.

The Brave Firefighter

Dylan was a brave firefighter who had experienced his own share of loss. He had lost his best friend in a fire and carried the weight of survivor's guilt. Dylan found solace in his work, dedicating himself to saving lives and helping others.

The First Meeting

SAMANTHA AND DYLAN first met at a community fundraiser for the local fire department. Their initial interactions were polite and friendly, but they quickly discovered a shared understanding of loss and grief.

The Growing Connection

THEIR CONVERSATIONS grew longer and more personal as they attended more community events together. Dylan admired Samantha's strength and resilience, while Samantha appreciated Dylan's bravery and compassion.

One afternoon, as they volunteered at a local shelter, Dylan said, "Samantha, your dedication to your students is incredible. They must be lucky to have you."

Samantha smiled softly, "Thank you, Dylan. It's not always easy, but they give me a reason to keep going."

The Blossoming Love

AS THEY SPENT MORE time together, Samantha and Dylan's bond deepened. They shared their stories of pain and loss, finding comfort in their mutual understanding. Their friendship slowly blossomed into love, built on trust and emotional connection.

A Love That Heals

DYLAN CONFIDED IN SAMANTHA about his struggles with guilt and self-worth, and Samantha shared her fears of never being able to love again. Through their honest conversations and mutual support, they began to heal old wounds and rediscover the joy of life.

The First Kiss

ONE EVENING, AS THEY stood under the stars at a community picnic, Dylan turned to Samantha and said, "Samantha, you've brought so much light into my life. I think I'm falling in love with you."

Samantha's heart swelled with emotion as she replied, "Dylan, I feel the same way."

In a moment of vulnerability and hope, Dylan leaned in and kissed Samantha. It was a tender, healing kiss that marked the beginning of their romantic journey.

A Future Together

SAMANTHA AND DYLAN continued to support each other through their healing process. Their love grew stronger, rooted in their shared experiences and mutual understanding. They proved that love has the power to heal even the deepest wounds, and their story became a testament to the therapeutic power of love.

Story 6: The Musician and the Chef

The Broken Dream

CLAIRE WAS A TALENTED musician who had once dreamed of performing on the world's biggest stages. However, a devastating injury to her hand ended her dreams of being a concert pianist. Struggling to find a new purpose, Claire found solace in composing music and teaching others.

The Passionate Chef

LIAM WAS A PASSIONATE chef who had opened a small restaurant in the heart of the city. His love for cooking stemmed from his grandmother, who taught him the magic of creating delicious meals that brought people together. Liam's restaurant quickly became a beloved spot for locals.

The First Encounter

Claire and Liam first met when Claire dined at Liam's restaurant. The ambiance and the delicious food brought her a sense of peace she hadn't felt in a long time. Liam noticed her emotional reaction to the music playing in the background and approached her, sparking a conversation about music and food.

The Growing Connection

THEIR INITIAL CONVERSATIONS turned into regular meetings at the restaurant, where Claire played the piano in the evenings, and Liam prepared special meals for her. Liam admired Claire's resilience and talent, while Claire appreciated Liam's passion and kindness.

One evening, after a particularly heartfelt performance, Liam said, "Claire, your music is incredible. It's like it speaks directly to the soul."

Claire smiled softly, "Thank you, Liam. Your food does the same."

The Blossoming Love

AS THEY SPENT MORE time together, Claire and Liam's bond deepened. They shared their stories of pain and loss, finding comfort in their mutual understanding. Their friendship slowly blossomed into love, built on trust and emotional connection.

A Love That Heals

LIAM CONFIDED IN CLAIRE about his struggles with self-doubt and pressure, and Claire shared her fears of never being able to perform again. Through their honest conversations and mutual support, they began to heal old wounds and rediscover the joy of life.

The First Kiss

ONE EVENING, AFTER a beautiful dinner at the restaurant, Liam turned to Claire and said, "Claire, you've brought so much light into my life. I think I'm falling in love with you."

Claire's heart swelled with emotion as she replied, "Liam, I feel the same way."

In a moment of vulnerability and hope, Liam leaned in and kissed Claire. It was a tender, healing kiss that marked the beginning of their romantic journey.

A Future Together

Claire and Liam continued to support each other through their healing process. Their love grew stronger, rooted in their shared experiences and mutual understanding. They proved that love has the power to heal even the deepest wounds, and their story became a testament to the therapeutic power of love.

Story 7: The Writer and the Nurse

The Emotional Burnout

NORA WAS A DEDICATED nurse who had spent years caring for patients in a busy hospital. The emotional toll of her work left her feeling drained and disconnected from her own life. Despite her love for nursing, Nora struggled with burnout and a sense of emptiness.

The Broken Spirit

ETHAN WAS A WRITER who had lost his inspiration after a series of personal setbacks. His once-successful career was now marked by writer's block and self-doubt. Ethan retreated from the world, hoping to find solace in solitude but instead feeling isolated and lost.

The First Meeting

NORA AND ETHAN FIRST met at a support group for caregivers and creatives. Their initial interactions were polite and reserved, but they quickly discovered a shared understanding of emotional exhaustion and the need for healing.

The Growing Connection

THEIR CONVERSATIONS grew longer and more personal as they attended more support group meetings together. Ethan admired Nora's compassion and dedication, while Nora appreciated Ethan's sensitivity and introspection.

One evening, after a particularly challenging support group session, Ethan said, "Nora, your dedication to your patients is incredible. It must be hard to care so much."

Nora smiled softly, "Thank you, Ethan. It's not always easy, but it's worth it."

The Blossoming Love

AS THEY SPENT MORE time together, Nora and Ethan's bond deepened. They shared their stories of pain and loss, finding comfort in their mutual understanding. Their friendship slowly blossomed into love, built on trust and emotional connection.

A Love That Heals

ETHAN CONFIDED IN NORA about his struggles with writer's block and self-doubt, and Nora shared her fears of never being able to find balance in her life. Through their honest conversations and mutual support, they began to heal old wounds and rediscover the joy of life.

The First Kiss

ONE EVENING, AS THEY stood under the stars at a community event, Ethan turned to Nora and said, "Nora, you've brought so much light into my life. I think I'm falling in love with you."

Nora's heart swelled with emotion as she replied, "Ethan, I feel the same way."

In a moment of vulnerability and hope, Ethan leaned in and kissed Nora. It was a tender, healing kiss that marked the beginning of their romantic journey.

A Future Together

NORA AND ETHAN CONTINUED to support each other through their healing process. Their love grew stronger, rooted in their shared experiences and mutual understanding. They proved that love has the power to heal even the deepest wounds, and their story became a testament to the therapeutic power of love.

Story 8: The Photographer and the Florist

The Shattered Dream

ISABELLA WAS A TALENTED photographer who had once dreamed of capturing the world's beauty through her lens. However, a devastating car accident left her with physical scars and a shattered confidence. Struggling to find a new purpose, Isabella found solace in photographing flowers and nature.

The Passionate Florist

LIAM WAS A PASSIONATE florist who owned a small flower shop in the heart of the city. His love for flowers and creating beautiful arrangements stemmed from his grandmother, who taught him the magic of nature. Liam's shop quickly became a beloved spot for locals.

The First Encounter

Isabella and Liam first met when Isabella wandered into Liam's flower shop, captivated by the vibrant colors and delicate scents. Liam noticed her emotional reaction to the flowers and approached her, sparking a conversation about photography and nature.

The Growing Connection

THEIR INITIAL CONVERSATIONS turned into regular meetings at the flower shop, where Isabella photographed Liam's arrangements, and Liam created special bouquets for her. Liam admired Isabella's resilience and talent, while Isabella appreciated Liam's passion and kindness.

One afternoon, as they worked together on a floral photoshoot, Liam said, "Isabella, your photographs are incredible. It's like you capture the soul of each flower."

Isabella smiled softly, "Thank you, Liam. Your arrangements make it easy."

The Blossoming Love

AS THEY SPENT MORE time together, Isabella and Liam's bond deepened. They shared their stories of pain and loss, finding comfort in their mutual understanding. Their friendship slowly blossomed into love, built on trust and emotional connection.

A Love That Heals

LIAM CONFIDED IN ISABELLA about his struggles with self-doubt and pressure, and Isabella shared her fears of never being able to find her confidence again. Through their honest conversations and mutual support, they began to heal old wounds and rediscover the joy of life.

The First Kiss

ONE EVENING, AFTER a beautiful photoshoot in the flower shop, Liam turned to Isabella and said, "Isabella, you've brought so much light into my life. I think I'm falling in love with you."

Isabella's heart swelled with emotion as she replied, "Liam, I feel the same way."

In a moment of vulnerability and hope, Liam leaned in and kissed Isabella. It was a tender, healing kiss that marked the beginning of their romantic journey.

A Future Together

ISABELLA AND LIAM CONTINUED to support each other through their healing process. Their love grew stronger, rooted in their shared experiences and mutual understanding. They proved that love has the power to heal even the deepest wounds, and their story became a testament to the therapeutic power of love.

Story 9: The Dancer and the Poet

The Broken Dream

MIA WAS A TALENTED dancer who had once dreamed of performing on the world's biggest stages. However, a devastating injury to her leg ended her dreams of being a professional dancer. Struggling to find a new purpose, Mia found solace in teaching dance to children.

The Passionate Poet

RYAN WAS A PASSIONATE poet who had lost his inspiration after a series of personal setbacks. His once-successful career was now marked by writer's block and self-doubt. Ryan retreated from the world, hoping to find solace in solitude but instead feeling isolated and lost.

The First Encounter

Mia and Ryan first met at a local café where Mia was reading poetry to a group of children. Ryan was captivated by her passion and grace, and he approached her, sparking a conversation about dance and poetry.

The Growing Connection

THEIR INITIAL CONVERSATIONS turned into regular meetings at the café, where Mia taught dance to children, and Ryan read his poems. Ryan admired Mia's resilience and talent, while Mia appreciated Ryan's passion and sensitivity.

One afternoon, after a particularly heartfelt performance, Ryan said, "Mia, your dancing is incredible. It's like you speak directly to the soul."

Mia smiled softly, "Thank you, Ryan. Your poetry does the same."

The Blossoming Love

AS THEY SPENT MORE time together, Mia and Ryan's bond deepened. They shared their stories of pain and loss, finding comfort in their mutual understanding. Their friendship slowly blossomed into love, built on trust and emotional connection.

A Love That Heals

RYAN CONFIDED IN MIA about his struggles with writer's block and self-doubt, and Mia shared her fears of never being able to dance again. Through their honest conversations and mutual support, they began to heal old wounds and rediscover the joy of life.

The First Kiss

ONE EVENING, AFTER a beautiful performance at the café, Ryan turned to Mia and said, "Mia, you've brought so much light into my life. I think I'm falling in love with you."

Mia's heart swelled with emotion as she replied, "Ryan, I feel the same way."

In a moment of vulnerability and hope, Ryan leaned in and kissed Mia. It was a tender, healing kiss that marked the beginning of their romantic journey.

A Future Together

MIA AND RYAN CONTINUED to support each other through their healing process. Their love grew stronger, rooted in their shared experiences and mutual understanding. They proved that love has the power to heal even the deepest wounds, and their story became a testament to the therapeutic power of love.

Story 10: The Teacher and the Doctor

The Pain of Loss

GRACE WAS A DEDICATED teacher who had recently lost her husband in a tragic accident. The pain of his loss was a constant ache in her heart, and she struggled to find joy in her once-fulfilling career. Her students, however, gave her a sense of purpose and a reason to keep going.

The Caring Doctor

ALEX WAS A COMPASSIONATE doctor who had experienced his own share of loss. He had lost his best friend in a fire and carried the weight of survivor's guilt. Alex found solace in his work, dedicating himself to saving lives and helping others.

The First Meeting

Grace and Alex first met at a community fundraiser for the local hospital. Their initial interactions were polite and friendly, but they quickly discovered a shared understanding of loss and grief.

The Growing Connection

THEIR CONVERSATIONS grew longer and more personal as they attended more community events together. Alex admired Grace's strength and resilience, while Grace appreciated Alex's kindness and support.

One afternoon, as they volunteered at a local shelter, Alex said, "Grace, your dedication to your students is incredible. They must be lucky to have you."

Grace smiled softly, "Thank you, Alex. It's not always easy, but they give me a reason to keep going."

The Blossoming Love

AS THEY SPENT MORE time together, Grace and Alex's bond deepened. They shared their stories of pain and loss, finding comfort in their mutual understanding. Their friendship slowly blossomed into love, built on trust and emotional connection.

A Love That Heals

ALEX CONFIDED IN GRACE about his struggles with guilt and self-worth, and Grace shared her fears of never being able to love again. Through their honest conversations and mutual support, they began to heal old wounds and rediscover the joy of life.

The First Kiss

ONE EVENING, AS THEY stood under the stars at a community picnic, Alex turned to Grace and said, "Grace, you've brought so much light into my life. I think I'm falling in love with you."

Grace's heart swelled with emotion as she replied, "Alex, I feel the same way."

In a moment of vulnerability and hope, Alex leaned in and kissed Grace. It was a tender, healing kiss that marked the beginning of their romantic journey.

A Future Together

Grace and Alex continued to support each other through their healing process. Their love grew stronger, rooted in their shared experiences and mutual understanding. They proved that love has the power to heal even the deepest wounds, and their story became a testament to the therapeutic power of love.

CONCLUSION

Love's healing touch showcases the incredible power of love to mend broken hearts and redeem souls. These romance stories explore the themes of healing and redemption, where characters find love while overcoming personal traumas. As you read through these tales, may you be inspired by the transformative power of love and the hope it brings, proving that love can truly heal and renew even the most wounded hearts.

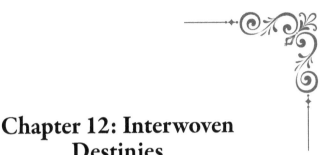

Chapter 12: Interwoven Destinies

Introduction to Interwoven Destinies

Life is a tapestry of interconnected threads, where seemingly separate lives often intertwine in unexpected ways. Love stories, too, are rarely isolated; they ripple out, impacting and shaping the lives around them. This chapter explores tales of interconnected lives and love stories, delving into how different romances influence one another and create a ripple effect of love.

Story 1: The Café Owner and the Baker

The Heart of the Community

IN A CHARMING NEIGHBORHOOD, a cozy café served as the heart of the community. Owned by Julia, a warm and friendly woman, the café was a place where locals gathered to enjoy coffee, pastries, and good company. Julia's best friend, Mia, owned the bakery next door, supplying the café with delicious treats.

The Budding Romance

JULIA HAD ALWAYS HARBORED a quiet affection for Ryan, a regular customer who visited the café every morning. Ryan, a talented artist, often sat by the window, sketching and sipping his coffee. Julia admired his creativity and kind spirit, but she was too shy to express her feelings.

The Friendly Baker

MIA, ON THE OTHER HAND, was more outgoing and noticed Julia's unspoken crush on Ryan. Determined to help her friend, Mia began to strike up conversations with Ryan whenever he visited the bakery. She soon discovered that Ryan was equally smitten with Julia but hesitant to make a move.

The Interwoven Plan

MIA DECIDED TO TAKE matters into her own hands. She invited both Julia and Ryan to a small gathering at her bakery, hoping to create an opportunity for them to connect. The evening was filled with laughter, delicious pastries, and heartfelt conversations. Julia and Ryan found themselves drawn to each other, their shared interests and mutual admiration blossoming into a deeper connection.

The Ripple Effect

AS JULIA AND RYAN'S relationship grew, their love began to impact the lives around them. The café and bakery became even more vibrant, filled with the warmth of their romance. Their friends and regular customers, inspired by their love story, found themselves more open to forming connections and pursuing their own dreams.

A Love That Inspires

JULIA AND RYAN'S LOVE not only strengthened their own lives but also brought the community closer together. They organized art and baking classes, fostering creativity and camaraderie among their neighbors. Their story became a testament to the ripple effect of love, proving that when hearts connect, they can create waves of positive change.

Story 2: The Doctor and the Musician

The Healing Melody

EMILY WAS A DEDICATED doctor who worked tirelessly at the local hospital. Her compassionate nature and commitment to her patients made her a beloved figure in the community. Despite her fulfilling career, Emily often felt the weight of her responsibilities and longed for a creative outlet.

The Soothing Tunes

DAVID WAS A TALENTED musician who performed at local venues and taught music classes. His soulful melodies had a way of touching hearts and bringing comfort to those who listened. David had experienced his own share of hardships, using music as a way to heal and express his emotions.

The First Encounter

EMILY AND DAVID FIRST met at a charity event organized by the hospital. David's performance captivated Emily, and she approached him afterward to express her admiration. Their conversation flowed effortlessly, and they discovered a shared passion for helping others.

The Growing Connection

THEIR INITIAL MEETING turned into regular interactions as they attended more community events together. Emily admired David's ability to bring joy and healing through music, while David appreciated Emily's dedication and compassion. Their bond deepened, each finding solace and inspiration in the other's presence.

The Interwoven Lives

AS EMILY AND DAVID'S relationship blossomed, their love began to ripple out, impacting the lives of those around them. Emily's patients found comfort in David's music, which she often played during her rounds. David's students, inspired by his love story, were encouraged to pursue their own passions with renewed vigor.

A Love That Heals

Emily and David's love not only enriched their own lives but also brought healing and hope to their community. They organized benefit concerts and health fairs, combining their talents to make a positive impact. Their story became a testament to the ripple effect of love, showing how interconnected lives can create waves of change and inspiration.

Story 3: The Teacher and the Librarian

The Beacon of Knowledge

SARAH WAS A DEDICATED teacher who loved inspiring her students with the wonders of literature and learning. Her classroom was a place of discovery, where young minds were encouraged to explore their passions and dreams. Despite her fulfilling career, Sarah often felt isolated, longing for a deeper connection.

The Keeper of Stories

ALEX WAS A KIND-HEARTED librarian who worked at the local library. His love for books and storytelling made him a beloved figure among patrons. Alex enjoyed helping others find the perfect book and often organized community events to foster a love for reading.

The Shared Passion

SARAH AND ALEX FIRST met at a book club meeting held at the library. Their mutual love for literature sparked an immediate connection, and they soon found themselves lost in deep conversations about their favorite authors and stories. Their shared passion for education and knowledge created a strong bond between them.

The Growing Affection

AS THEY SPENT MORE time together, Sarah and Alex's bond deepened. They collaborated on projects to promote literacy and learning in the community, organizing book drives and reading programs for children. Their friendship blossomed into love, built on a foundation of mutual respect and admiration.

The Interwoven Dreams

SARAH AND ALEX'S LOVE began to ripple out, impacting the lives of their students and library patrons. Their collaborative efforts brought new resources and opportunities to the community, inspiring others to pursue their own dreams and passions. The students, motivated by their teachers' love story, found new ways to express themselves and explore their interests.

A Love That Educates

SARAH AND ALEX'S LOVE not only enriched their own lives but also brought knowledge and inspiration to their community. Their story became a testament to the ripple effect of love, proving that when hearts connect, they can create waves of positive change in the lives around them.

Story 4: The Chef and the Gardener

The Culinary Artist

SOPHIE WAS A TALENTED chef who owned a small restaurant known for its farm-to-table approach. Her love for cooking and dedication to using fresh, local ingredients made her restaurant a favorite among food enthusiasts. Despite her success, Sophie often felt the pressures of running a business and longed for a deeper connection.

The Green Thumb

Liam was a passionate gardener who managed a community garden. His love for nature and commitment to sustainable practices made him a respected figure in the community. Liam enjoyed teaching others about gardening and often donated fresh produce to local food banks.

The First Meeting

SOPHIE AND LIAM FIRST met at a farmer's market where Liam was selling his garden's produce. Their shared passion for fresh, local ingredients sparked an immediate connection, and they soon found themselves lost in conversations about cooking and gardening.

The Growing Connection

THEIR INITIAL MEETING turned into regular interactions as they collaborated on farm-to-table events at Sophie's restaurant. Liam admired Sophie's culinary skills and dedication, while Sophie appreciated Liam's knowledge and passion for sustainable practices. Their bond deepened, each finding inspiration and joy in the other's presence.

The Interwoven Lives

AS SOPHIE AND LIAM'S relationship blossomed, their love began to ripple out, impacting the lives of those around them. The community garden and restaurant became hubs of activity, where people gathered to learn about sustainable living and enjoy delicious, fresh meals. Their friends and patrons, inspired by their love story, found new ways to connect with nature and each other.

A Love That Nourishes

SOPHIE AND LIAM'S LOVE not only enriched their own lives but also brought nourishment and sustainability to their community. They organized cooking classes and gardening workshops, fostering a sense of unity and purpose among their neighbors. Their story became a testament to the ripple effect of love, showing how interconnected lives can create waves of positive change and inspiration.

Story 5: The Single Father and the Nurse

The Struggles of Parenthood

DANIEL WAS A SINGLE father raising his young daughter, Lily, on his own. After the sudden loss of his wife, Daniel struggled to balance his career and responsibilities as a parent. Despite the challenges, he was determined to provide a loving and stable environment for Lily.

The Compassionate Nurse

EMILY WAS A COMPASSIONATE nurse who worked at the local clinic. Her dedication to her patients and her kind heart made her a beloved figure in the community. Emily had experienced her own share of loss, having lost her mother to illness when she was young.

The First Encounter

DANIEL AND EMILY FIRST met when Daniel brought Lily to the clinic for a check-up. Emily's gentle demeanor immediately put both father and daughter at ease, and they quickly formed a connection. Over time, their paths crossed frequently as Daniel sought medical care for Lily.

The Growing Connection

THEIR INITIAL INTERACTIONS turned into regular conversations about parenting, life, and the challenges they faced. Emily admired Daniel's strength and resilience, while Daniel appreciated Emily's kindness and support. Their bond deepened, each finding comfort and joy in the other's company.

The Interwoven Lives

AS DANIEL AND EMILY'S relationship blossomed, their love began to ripple out, impacting the lives of those around them. Emily became a trusted friend and mentor to Lily, helping her navigate the challenges of growing up without a mother. Daniel, inspired by Emily's dedication, found new ways to support his daughter and become a more attentive parent.

A Love That Heals

DANIEL AND EMILY'S love not only enriched their own lives but also brought healing and hope to their community. They organized health fairs and parenting workshops, combining their talents to make a positive impact. Their story became a testament to the ripple effect of love, showing how interconnected lives can create waves of change and inspiration.

Story 6: The Veterinarian and the Teacher

The Animal Lover

MIA WAS A DEDICATED veterinarian who loved caring for animals and educating their owners about proper pet care. Her compassionate nature and commitment to her work made her a beloved figure in the community. Despite her fulfilling career, Mia often felt isolated, longing for a deeper connection.

The Dedicated Teacher

JAMES WAS A DEDICATED teacher who loved inspiring his students with the wonders of science and nature. His classroom was a place of discovery, where young minds were encouraged to explore their passions and dreams. Despite his fulfilling career, James often felt the weight of his responsibilities and longed for a creative outlet.

The Shared Passion

MIA AND JAMES FIRST met at a community event focused on animal conservation. Their mutual love for animals and education sparked an immediate connection, and they soon found themselves lost in deep conversations about their work and passions. Their shared dedication to making a positive impact created a strong bond between them.

The Growing Affection

AS THEY SPENT MORE time together, Mia and James's bond deepened. They collaborated on projects to promote animal welfare and education in the community, organizing pet adoption events and science fairs for children. Their friendship blossomed into love, built on a foundation of mutual respect and admiration.

The Interwoven Dreams

MIA AND JAMES'S LOVE began to ripple out, impacting the lives of their students and pet owners. Their collaborative efforts brought new resources and opportunities to the community, inspiring others to pursue their own dreams and passions. The students, motivated by their teachers' love story, found new ways to express themselves and explore their interests.

A Love That Educates

MIA AND JAMES'S LOVE not only enriched their own lives but also brought knowledge and inspiration to their community. Their story became a testament to the ripple effect of love, proving that when hearts connect, they can create waves of positive change in the lives around them.

Story 7: The Architect and the Artist

The Visionary Designer

SAMANTHA WAS A TALENTED architect known for her innovative designs and sustainable practices. Her love for creating beautiful, functional spaces made her a respected figure in the community. Despite her success, Samantha often felt the pressures of her career and longed for a deeper connection.

The Creative Soul

ETHAN WAS A PASSIONATE artist who used his work to express his emotions and connect with others. His vibrant paintings and sculptures brought joy and inspiration to those who saw them. Ethan had experienced his own share of struggles, using art as a way to heal and express his feelings.

The First Encounter

Samantha and Ethan first met at an art exhibition where Ethan's work was being showcased. Samantha was captivated by his art, and they struck up a conversation about creativity and design. Their shared passion for creating beauty sparked an immediate connection.

The Growing Connection

THEIR INITIAL CONVERSATIONS turned into regular meetings at art galleries and design studios. Samantha admired Ethan's creativity and sensitivity, while Ethan appreciated Samantha's vision and dedication. Their bond deepened, each finding inspiration and joy in the other's presence.

The Interwoven Lives

AS SAMANTHA AND ETHAN'S relationship blossomed, their love began to ripple out, impacting the lives of those around them. They collaborated on projects that combined art and architecture, creating spaces that inspired and uplifted the community. Their friends and colleagues, inspired by their love story, found new ways to connect with their own creativity and passions.

A Love That Creates

SAMANTHA AND ETHAN'S love not only enriched their own lives but also brought beauty and inspiration to their community. They organized art and design workshops, fostering a sense of creativity and unity among their neighbors. Their story became a testament to the ripple effect of love, showing how interconnected lives can create waves of positive change and inspiration.

Story 8: The Entrepreneur and the Social Worker

THE DRIVEN BUSINESSWOMAN

Isabella was a driven entrepreneur who had built a successful business from the ground up. Her determination and innovative ideas made her a respected figure in the business community. Despite her success, Isabella often felt the pressures of her career and longed for a deeper connection.

The Compassionate Social Worker

LIAM WAS A COMPASSIONATE social worker who dedicated his life to helping those in need. His empathy and commitment to making a difference made him a beloved figure in the community. Liam had experienced his own share of struggles, using his work to heal and uplift others.

The First Encounter

Isabella and Liam first met at a charity event organized by a local nonprofit. Their initial interactions were polite and professional, but they quickly discovered a shared passion for making a positive impact. Their conversations flowed effortlessly, and they soon found themselves lost in deep discussions about their work and dreams.

The Growing Connection

THEIR INITIAL MEETING turned into regular interactions as they collaborated on community projects. Liam admired Isabella's drive and innovation, while Isabella appreciated Liam's compassion and dedication. Their bond deepened, each finding inspiration and joy in the other's presence.

The Interwoven Lives

AS ISABELLA AND LIAM'S relationship blossomed, their love began to ripple out, impacting the lives of those around them. They combined their skills and resources to create initiatives that supported local businesses and provided aid to those in need. Their friends and colleagues, inspired by their love story, found new ways to contribute to their community and support each other.

A Love That Empowers

ISABELLA AND LIAM'S love not only enriched their own lives but also brought empowerment and hope to their community. They organized workshops and mentorship programs, fostering a sense of unity and purpose among their neighbors. Their story became a testament to the ripple effect of love, showing how interconnected lives can create waves of positive change and inspiration.

Story 9: The Veterinarian and the Teacher

The Animal Lover

MIA WAS A DEDICATED veterinarian who loved caring for animals and educating their owners about proper pet care. Her compassionate nature and commitment to her work made her a beloved figure in the community. Despite her fulfilling career, Mia often felt isolated, longing for a deeper connection.

The Dedicated Teacher

JAMES WAS A DEDICATED teacher who loved inspiring his students with the wonders of science and nature. His classroom was a place of discovery, where young minds were encouraged to explore their passions and dreams. Despite his fulfilling career, James often felt the weight of his responsibilities and longed for a creative outlet.

The Shared Passion

MIA AND JAMES FIRST met at a community event focused on animal conservation. Their mutual love for animals and education sparked an immediate connection, and they soon found themselves lost in deep conversations about their work and passions. Their shared dedication to making a positive impact created a strong bond between them.

The Growing Affection

AS THEY SPENT MORE time together, Mia and James's bond deepened. They collaborated on projects to promote animal welfare and education in the community, organizing pet adoption events and science fairs for children. Their friendship blossomed into love, built on a foundation of mutual respect and admiration.

The Interwoven Dreams

MIA AND JAMES'S LOVE began to ripple out, impacting the lives of their students and pet owners. Their collaborative efforts brought new resources and opportunities to the community, inspiring others to pursue their own dreams and passions. The students, motivated by their teachers' love story, found new ways to express themselves and explore their interests.

A Love That Educates

MIA AND JAMES'S LOVE not only enriched their own lives but also brought knowledge and inspiration to their community. Their story became a testament to the ripple effect of love, proving that when hearts connect, they can create waves of positive change in the lives around them.

Story 10: The Journalist and the Environmentalist

The Investigative Reporter

SOPHIE WAS A DEDICATED journalist known for her investigative reporting on environmental issues. Her passion for uncovering the truth and holding those in power accountable made her a respected figure in the media. Despite her success, Sophie often felt the pressures of her career and longed for a deeper connection.

The Green Activist

ETHAN WAS A PASSIONATE environmentalist who dedicated his life to protecting the planet and raising awareness about climate change. His commitment to sustainability and his ability to inspire others made him a beloved figure in the community. Ethan had experienced his own share of struggles, using his work to heal and uplift others.

The First Encounter

Sophie and Ethan first met at a climate change conference where Sophie was covering the event. Their initial interactions were professional, but they quickly discovered a shared passion for the environment. Their conversations flowed effortlessly, and they soon found themselves lost in deep discussions about their work and dreams.

The Growing Connection

THEIR INITIAL MEETING turned into regular interactions as they collaborated on environmental campaigns. Ethan admired Sophie's dedication and tenacity, while Sophie appreciated Ethan's passion and commitment. Their bond deepened, each finding inspiration and joy in the other's presence.

The Interwoven Lives

AS SOPHIE AND ETHAN'S relationship blossomed, their love began to ripple out, impacting the lives of those around them. They combined their skills and resources to create initiatives that raised awareness about environmental issues and promoted sustainable practices. Their friends and colleagues, inspired by their love story, found new ways to contribute to their community and support each other.

A Love That Protects

SOPHIE AND ETHAN'S love not only enriched their own lives but also brought awareness and hope to their community. They organized workshops and campaigns, fostering a sense of unity and purpose among their neighbors. Their story became a testament to the ripple effect of love, showing how interconnected lives can create waves of positive change and inspiration.

CONCLUSION

Interwoven destinies reveal the beauty of how lives and love stories are interconnected, creating a ripple effect that touches and transforms those around us. These tales of interconnected lives explore how different romances influence one another and create waves of positive change. As you read through these stories, may you be inspired by the profound impact of love and the interconnectedness of our lives, proving that when hearts connect, they can create a powerful force for good.

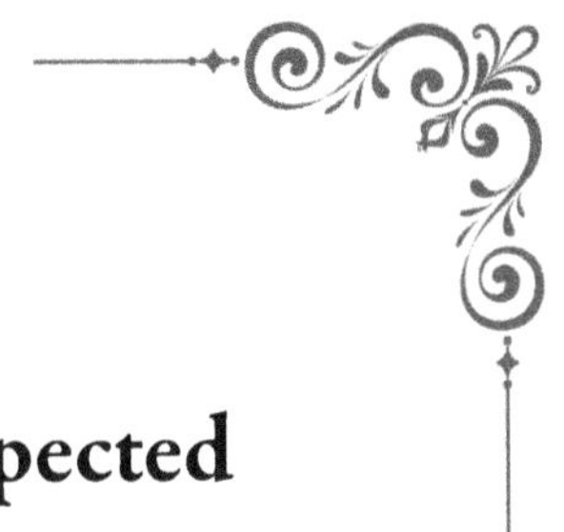

Chapter 13: Unexpected Heroes

Introduction to Unexpected Heroes

Love stories often revolve around familiar archetypes, but sometimes, the most extraordinary romances emerge from the most unexpected heroes and heroines. These unconventional characters break traditional romance stereotypes, celebrating diversity and unique love stories that inspire and resonate. This chapter delves into tales of love featuring unconventional heroes and heroines, showing that true love can be found in the most surprising places.

Story 1: The Tattoo Artist and the Librarian

The Inked Artist

ALEX WAS A TALENTED tattoo artist known for his intricate designs and creative flair. Despite his tough exterior, he had a heart of gold and a passion for helping others express themselves through art. His tattoo studio was a haven for those seeking to transform their bodies into canvases of personal stories.

The Bookish Librarian

EMMA WAS A QUIET AND reserved librarian who loved the solace of books and the tranquility of her library. Her love for literature and her gentle demeanor made her a beloved figure among patrons. Despite her fulfilling career, Emma often felt isolated, longing for a deeper connection.

The First Encounter

Alex and Emma first met when Emma wandered into Alex's studio, curious about the art form. Their initial interaction was polite but hesitant, as they seemed to come from completely different worlds. However, Alex's gentle approach and Emma's curiosity soon bridged the gap between them.

The Growing Connection

EMMA BEGAN VISITING the studio more frequently, fascinated by the stories behind the tattoos. Alex admired Emma's intelligence and passion for books, while Emma appreciated Alex's creativity and kindness. Their bond deepened as they shared their stories and dreams, finding common ground in their love for art and expression.

One afternoon, as they discussed a design for a literary-themed tattoo, Alex said, "Emma, you have such a deep appreciation for art and stories. It's inspiring."

Emma smiled softly, "Thank you, Alex. Your work is truly amazing. It's like you're telling stories through your tattoos."

The Blossoming Love

AS THEY SPENT MORE time together, Alex and Emma's bond deepened. They attended art exhibitions, visited bookstores, and enjoyed quiet evenings at the library and studio. Their love grew in the warmth of shared experiences and quiet moments of understanding.

A Love That Breaks Stereotypes

Alex and Emma's love story was anything but conventional. Their relationship broke stereotypes and challenged societal norms, showing that true love can thrive in the most unexpected places. Their unique love story inspired those around them to embrace diversity and celebrate their own uniqueness.

A Wholesome Proposal

ONE EVENING, IN THE soft glow of the studio, Alex proposed. He had designed a beautiful tattoo for Emma, symbolizing their love and journey together. With tears of joy, Emma said yes, her heart full of love for the man who had become her best friend and soulmate.

A Sweet Future

ALEX AND EMMA'S STORY is a testament to the power of love to break barriers and celebrate individuality. Their gentle romance, built on emotional connection and pure affection, proves that true love doesn't need to fit into traditional molds. Sometimes, the sweetest love stories are those that unfold in the quiet moments of everyday life.

Story 2: The Mechanic and the Pianist

THE SKILLED MECHANIC

Jake was a skilled mechanic who loved working with his hands and solving problems. His garage was a place of creativity and precision, where he transformed broken machines into smooth-running engines. Despite his rough exterior, Jake had a deep appreciation for beauty and craftsmanship.

The Talented Pianist

LILA WAS A TALENTED pianist who found solace and expression through music. Her performances were filled with emotion and grace, captivating audiences with her skill and passion. Despite her success, Lila often felt the pressures of her career and longed for a deeper connection.

The First Encounter

Jake and Lila first met when Lila's car broke down near Jake's garage. Their initial interaction was polite but hesitant, as they seemed to come from completely different worlds. However, Jake's gentle approach and Lila's curiosity soon bridged the gap between them.

The Growing Connection

LILA BEGAN VISITING the garage more frequently, fascinated by the intricacies of Jake's work. Jake admired Lila's talent and dedication, while Lila appreciated Jake's craftsmanship and kindness. Their bond deepened as they shared their stories and dreams, finding common ground in their love for beauty and precision.

One afternoon, as they discussed the parallels between music and mechanics, Jake said, "Lila, your music is incredible. It's like you're creating art with your hands."

Lila smiled softly, "Thank you, Jake. Your work is truly amazing. It's like you're composing with engines."

The Blossoming Love

AS THEY SPENT MORE time together, Jake and Lila's bond deepened. They attended concerts, visited museums, and enjoyed quiet evenings at the garage and piano studio. Their love grew in the warmth of shared experiences and quiet moments of understanding.

A Love That Breaks Stereotypes

JAKE AND LILA'S LOVE story was anything but conventional. Their relationship broke stereotypes and challenged societal norms, showing that true love can thrive in the most unexpected places. Their unique love story inspired those around them to embrace diversity and celebrate their own uniqueness.

A Wholesome Proposal

ONE EVENING, IN THE soft glow of the garage, Jake proposed. He had crafted a beautiful music box for Lila, symbolizing their love and journey together. With tears of joy, Lila said yes, her heart full of love for the man who had become her best friend and soulmate.

A Sweet Future

Jake and Lila's story is a testament to the power of love to break barriers and celebrate individuality. Their gentle romance, built on emotional connection and pure affection, proves that true love doesn't need to fit into traditional molds. Sometimes, the sweetest love stories are those that unfold in the quiet moments of everyday life.

Story 3: The Tech Guru and the Dancer

The Innovative Tech Guru

ETHAN WAS A BRILLIANT tech guru known for his innovative ideas and passion for technology. His work at a cutting-edge tech company earned him respect and admiration, but his social skills were often lacking. Ethan's mind was always buzzing with ideas, but he struggled to connect with others on a personal level.

The Graceful Dancer

MIA WAS A GRACEFUL dancer who found expression and freedom through movement. Her performances were mesmerizing, filled with emotion and beauty. Despite her success, Mia often felt the pressures of her career and longed for a deeper connection.

The First Encounter

Ethan and Mia first met at a tech conference where Ethan was presenting a new project. Mia attended the conference to explore how technology could enhance her dance performances. Their initial interaction was polite but hesitant, as they seemed to come from completely different worlds. However, Ethan's innovative ideas and Mia's curiosity soon bridged the gap between them.

The Growing Connection

MIA BEGAN VISITING Ethan's lab more frequently, fascinated by the possibilities of integrating technology with dance. Ethan admired Mia's creativity and dedication, while Mia appreciated Ethan's brilliance and kindness. Their bond deepened as they shared their stories and dreams, finding common ground in their love for innovation and expression.

One afternoon, as they discussed the potential of using technology in dance, Ethan said, "Mia, your performances are incredible. It's like you're creating art with your body."

Mia smiled softly, "Thank you, Ethan. Your work is truly amazing. It's like you're choreographing with technology."

The Blossoming Love

AS THEY SPENT MORE time together, Ethan and Mia's bond deepened. They attended tech showcases, visited dance performances, and enjoyed quiet evenings at the lab and dance studio. Their love grew in the warmth of shared experiences and quiet moments of understanding.

A Love That Breaks Stereotypes

ETHAN AND MIA'S LOVE story was anything but conventional. Their relationship broke stereotypes and challenged societal norms, showing that true love can thrive in the most unexpected places. Their unique love story inspired those around them to embrace diversity and celebrate their own uniqueness.

A Wholesome Proposal

ONE EVENING, IN THE soft glow of the lab, Ethan proposed. He had designed a beautiful holographic display for Mia, symbolizing their love and journey together. With tears of joy, Mia said yes, her heart full of love for the man who had become her best friend and soulmate.

A Sweet Future

Ethan and Mia's story is a testament to the power of love to break barriers and celebrate individuality. Their gentle romance, built on emotional connection and pure affection, proves that true love doesn't need to fit into traditional molds. Sometimes, the sweetest love stories are those that unfold in the quiet moments of everyday life.

Story 4: The Chef and the Environmentalist

The Culinary Genius

SOPHIE WAS A CULINARY genius known for her innovative dishes and dedication to sustainable cooking. Her restaurant was a favorite among food enthusiasts, offering delicious meals made from locally sourced ingredients. Despite her success, Sophie often felt the pressures of her career and longed for a deeper connection.

The Passionate Environmentalist

LIAM WAS A PASSIONATE environmentalist who dedicated his life to protecting the planet and raising awareness about climate change. His commitment to sustainability and his ability to inspire others made him a beloved figure in the community. Liam had experienced his own share of struggles, using his work to heal and uplift others.

The First Encounter

Sophie and Liam first met at a sustainability fair where Sophie was showcasing her sustainable cooking methods. Their initial interaction was polite but hesitant, as they seemed to come from completely different worlds. However, Sophie's innovative ideas and Liam's passion for sustainability soon bridged the gap between them.

The Growing Connection

LIAM BEGAN VISITING Sophie's restaurant more frequently, fascinated by the possibilities of integrating sustainability with culinary arts. Sophie admired Liam's dedication and commitment, while Liam appreciated Sophie's creativity and kindness. Their bond deepened as they shared their stories and dreams, finding common ground in their love for sustainability and innovation.

One afternoon, as they discussed the potential of using sustainable practices in cooking, Sophie said, "Liam, your work is incredible. It's like you're creating art with the environment."

Liam smiled softly, "Thank you, Sophie. Your dishes are truly amazing. It's like you're choreographing with flavors."

The Blossoming Love

AS THEY SPENT MORE time together, Sophie and Liam's bond deepened. They attended sustainability conferences, visited farmers' markets, and enjoyed quiet evenings at the restaurant and environmental center. Their love grew in the warmth of shared experiences and quiet moments of understanding.

A Love That Breaks Stereotypes

SOPHIE AND LIAM'S LOVE story was anything but conventional. Their relationship broke stereotypes and challenged societal norms, showing that true love can thrive in the most unexpected places. Their unique love story inspired those around them to embrace diversity and celebrate their own uniqueness.

A Wholesome Proposal

ONE EVENING, IN THE soft glow of the restaurant, Liam proposed. He had designed a beautiful garden for Sophie, symbolizing their love and journey together. With tears of joy, Sophie said yes, her

heart full of love for the man who had become her best friend and soulmate.

A Sweet Future

SOPHIE AND LIAM'S STORY is a testament to the power of love to break barriers and celebrate individuality. Their gentle romance, built on emotional connection and pure affection, proves that true love doesn't need to fit into traditional molds. Sometimes, the sweetest love stories are those that unfold in the quiet moments of everyday life.

Story 5: The Social Worker and the Tattoo Artist

The Compassionate Social Worker

ISABELLA WAS A COMPASSIONATE social worker who dedicated her life to helping those in need. Her empathy and commitment to making a difference made her a beloved figure in the community. Isabella had experienced her own share of struggles, using her work to heal and uplift others.

The Artistic Tattoo Artist

MASON WAS A TALENTED tattoo artist known for his intricate designs and creative flair. Despite his tough exterior, he had a heart of gold and a passion for helping others express themselves through art. His tattoo studio was a haven for those seeking to transform their bodies into canvases of personal stories.

The First Encounter

Isabella and Mason first met when Isabella wandered into Mason's studio, curious about the art form. Their initial interaction was polite but hesitant, as they seemed to come from completely different worlds.

However, Mason's gentle approach and Isabella's curiosity soon bridged the gap between them.

The Growing Connection

ISABELLA BEGAN VISITING the studio more frequently, fascinated by the stories behind the tattoos. Mason admired Isabella's dedication and compassion, while Isabella appreciated Mason's creativity and kindness. Their bond deepened as they shared their stories and dreams, finding common ground in their love for art and expression.

One afternoon, as they discussed a design for a tattoo symbolizing hope and resilience, Mason said, "Isabella, your work is incredible. It's like you're creating art with your heart."

Isabella smiled softly, "Thank you, Mason. Your tattoos are truly amazing. It's like you're telling stories through your designs."

The Blossoming Love

AS THEY SPENT MORE time together, Isabella and Mason's bond deepened. They attended art exhibitions, visited community centers, and enjoyed quiet evenings at the studio and social work office. Their love grew in the warmth of shared experiences and quiet moments of understanding.

A Love That Breaks Stereotypes

ISABELLA AND MASON'S love story was anything but conventional. Their relationship broke stereotypes and challenged societal norms, showing that true love can thrive in the most unexpected places. Their unique love story inspired those around them to embrace diversity and celebrate their own uniqueness.

A Wholesome Proposal

ONE EVENING, IN THE soft glow of the studio, Mason proposed. He had designed a beautiful tattoo for Isabella, symbolizing their love and journey together. With tears of joy, Isabella said yes, her heart full of love for the man who had become her best friend and soulmate.

A Sweet Future

ISABELLA AND MASON'S story is a testament to the power of love to break barriers and celebrate individuality. Their gentle romance, built on emotional connection and pure affection, proves that true love doesn't need to fit into traditional molds. Sometimes, the sweetest love stories are those that unfold in the quiet moments of everyday life.

Story 6: The Scientist and the Artist

The Brilliant Scientist

ELENA WAS A BRILLIANT scientist known for her groundbreaking research in renewable energy. Her dedication to her work and her innovative ideas made her a respected figure in the scientific community. Despite her success, Elena often felt the pressures of her career and longed for a deeper connection.

The Creative Artist

LUCAS WAS A CREATIVE artist who used his work to express his emotions and connect with others. His vibrant paintings and sculptures brought joy and inspiration to those who saw them. Lucas had experienced his own share of struggles, using art as a way to heal and express his feelings.

The First Encounter

Elena and Lucas first met at an art exhibition where Lucas's work was being showcased. Elena was captivated by his art, and they struck up a conversation about creativity and innovation. Their shared passion for creating beauty sparked an immediate connection.

The Growing Connection

THEIR INITIAL CONVERSATIONS turned into regular meetings at art galleries and research labs. Elena admired Lucas's creativity and sensitivity, while Lucas appreciated Elena's brilliance and dedication. Their bond deepened, each finding inspiration and joy in the other's presence.

One afternoon, as they discussed the parallels between science and art, Elena said, "Lucas, your work is incredible. It's like you're creating art with your soul."

Lucas smiled softly, "Thank you, Elena. Your research is truly amazing. It's like you're choreographing with energy."

The Blossoming Love

AS THEY SPENT MORE time together, Elena and Lucas's bond deepened. They attended science conferences, visited art studios, and enjoyed quiet evenings at the lab and art gallery. Their love grew in the warmth of shared experiences and quiet moments of understanding.

A Love That Breaks Stereotypes

ELENA AND LUCAS'S LOVE story was anything but conventional. Their relationship broke stereotypes and challenged societal norms, showing that true love can thrive in the most unexpected places. Their unique love story inspired those around them to embrace diversity and celebrate their own uniqueness.

A Wholesome Proposal

ONE EVENING, IN THE soft glow of the art gallery, Lucas proposed. He had painted a beautiful piece for Elena, symbolizing their love and journey together. With tears of joy, Elena said yes, her heart full of love for the man who had become her best friend and soulmate.

A Sweet Future

ELENA AND LUCAS'S STORY is a testament to the power of love to break barriers and celebrate individuality. Their gentle romance, built on emotional connection and pure affection, proves that true love doesn't need to fit into traditional molds. Sometimes, the sweetest love stories are those that unfold in the quiet moments of everyday life.

Story 7: The Farmer and the Poet

The Hardworking Farmer

ETHAN WAS A HARDWORKING farmer who loved the land and the simple life it provided. His days were filled with the rhythms of nature, tending to crops and caring for animals. Despite his rough exterior, Ethan had a deep appreciation for beauty and simplicity.

The Sensitive Poet

OLIVIA WAS A SENSITIVE poet who found solace and expression through words. Her poems were filled with emotion and grace, captivating readers with their depth and beauty. Despite her success, Olivia often felt the pressures of her career and longed for a deeper connection.

The First Encounter

Ethan and Olivia first met at a local market where Olivia was selling her poetry books. Ethan was captivated by her words, and they struck up a conversation about nature and creativity. Their shared passion for beauty and simplicity sparked an immediate connection.

The Growing Connection

OLIVIA BEGAN VISITING Ethan's farm more frequently, fascinated by the rhythms of rural life. Ethan admired Olivia's talent and sensitivity, while Olivia appreciated Ethan's craftsmanship and kindness. Their bond deepened as they shared their stories and dreams, finding common ground in their love for beauty and simplicity.

One afternoon, as they discussed the parallels between farming and poetry, Ethan said, "Olivia, your poems are incredible. It's like you're creating art with your words."

Olivia smiled softly, "Thank you, Ethan. Your farm is truly amazing. It's like you're composing with nature."

The Blossoming Love

AS THEY SPENT MORE time together, Ethan and Olivia's bond deepened. They attended literary festivals, visited farmers' markets, and enjoyed quiet evenings at the farm and poetry readings. Their love grew in the warmth of shared experiences and quiet moments of understanding.

A Love That Breaks Stereotypes

ETHAN AND OLIVIA'S love story was anything but conventional. Their relationship broke stereotypes and challenged societal norms, showing that true love can thrive in the most unexpected places. Their unique love story inspired those around them to embrace diversity and celebrate their own uniqueness.

A Wholesome Proposal

ONE EVENING, IN THE soft glow of the farm, Ethan proposed. He had written a beautiful poem for Olivia, symbolizing their love and journey together. With tears of joy, Olivia said yes, her heart full of love for the man who had become her best friend and soulmate.

A Sweet Future

ETHAN AND OLIVIA'S story is a testament to the power of love to break barriers and celebrate individuality. Their gentle romance, built on emotional connection and pure affection, proves that true love doesn't need to fit into traditional molds. Sometimes, the sweetest love stories are those that unfold in the quiet moments of everyday life.

Story 8: The Firefighter and the Scientist

The Brave Firefighter

JACK WAS A BRAVE FIREFIGHTER who dedicated his life to saving others and protecting his community. His courage and commitment made him a beloved figure in the community. Despite his rough exterior, Jack had a deep appreciation for science and innovation.

The Brilliant Scientist

CLARA WAS A BRILLIANT scientist known for her groundbreaking research in renewable energy. Her dedication to her work and her innovative ideas made her a respected figure in the scientific community. Despite her success, Clara often felt the pressures of her career and longed for a deeper connection.

The First Encounter

Jack and Clara first met at a community event focused on emergency preparedness and sustainability. Their initial interaction was polite but hesitant, as they seemed to come from completely different worlds. However, Jack's courage and Clara's innovation soon bridged the gap between them.

The Growing Connection

CLARA BEGAN VISITING the fire station more frequently, fascinated by the possibilities of integrating science with emergency response. Jack admired Clara's dedication and brilliance, while Clara appreciated Jack's bravery and kindness. Their bond deepened as they shared their stories and dreams, finding common ground in their love for innovation and protection.

One afternoon, as they discussed the potential of using science in firefighting, Jack said, "Clara, your research is incredible. It's like you're creating art with energy."

Clara smiled softly, "Thank you, Jack. Your work is truly amazing. It's like you're choreographing with fire."

The Blossoming Love

AS THEY SPENT MORE time together, Jack and Clara's bond deepened. They attended science conferences, visited fire stations, and enjoyed quiet evenings at the lab and firehouse. Their love grew in the warmth of shared experiences and quiet moments of understanding.

A Love That Breaks Stereotypes

JACK AND CLARA'S LOVE story was anything but conventional. Their relationship broke stereotypes and challenged societal norms, showing that true love can thrive in the most unexpected places. Their unique love story inspired those around them to embrace diversity and celebrate their own uniqueness.

A Wholesome Proposal

ONE EVENING, IN THE soft glow of the firehouse, Jack proposed. He had designed a beautiful fire-themed sculpture for Clara, symbolizing their love and journey together. With tears of joy, Clara said yes, her heart full of love for the man who had become her best friend and soulmate.

A Sweet Future

JACK AND CLARA'S STORY is a testament to the power of love to break barriers and celebrate individuality. Their gentle romance, built on emotional connection and pure affection, proves that true love doesn't need to fit into traditional molds. Sometimes, the sweetest love stories are those that unfold in the quiet moments of everyday life.

Story 9: The Chef and the Scientist

The Culinary Genius

Sophia was a culinary genius known for her innovative dishes and dedication to sustainable cooking. Her restaurant was a favorite among food enthusiasts, offering delicious meals made from locally sourced ingredients. Despite her success, Sophia often felt the pressures of her career and longed for a deeper connection.

The Brilliant Scientist

DANIEL WAS A BRILLIANT scientist known for his groundbreaking research in nutrition and food science. His dedication to his work and his innovative ideas made him a respected figure in the scientific community. Despite his success, Daniel often felt the pressures of his career and longed for a deeper connection.

The First Encounter

Sophia and Daniel first met at a food science conference where Sophia was showcasing her sustainable cooking methods. Their initial interaction was polite but hesitant, as they seemed to come from completely different worlds. However, Sophia's innovative ideas and Daniel's passion for nutrition soon bridged the gap between them.

The Growing Connection

DANIEL BEGAN VISITING Sophia's restaurant more frequently, fascinated by the possibilities of integrating science with culinary arts. Sophia admired Daniel's dedication and brilliance, while Daniel appreciated Sophia's creativity and kindness. Their bond deepened as they shared their stories and dreams, finding common ground in their love for sustainability and innovation.

One afternoon, as they discussed the potential of using food science in cooking, Sophia said, "Daniel, your research is incredible. It's like you're creating art with food."

Daniel smiled softly, "Thank you, Sophia. Your dishes are truly amazing. It's like you're choreographing with flavors."

The Blossoming Love

AS THEY SPENT MORE time together, Sophia and Daniel's bond deepened. They attended science conferences, visited farmers' markets, and enjoyed quiet evenings at the restaurant and lab. Their love grew in the warmth of shared experiences and quiet moments of understanding.

A Love That Breaks Stereotypes

SOPHIA AND DANIEL'S love story was anything but conventional. Their relationship broke stereotypes and challenged societal norms, showing that true love can thrive in the most unexpected places. Their unique love story inspired those around them to embrace diversity and celebrate their own uniqueness.

A Wholesome Proposal

ONE EVENING, IN THE soft glow of the restaurant, Daniel proposed. He had designed a beautiful dish for Sophia, symbolizing their love and journey together. With tears of joy, Sophia said yes, her

heart full of love for the man who had become her best friend and soulmate.

A Sweet Future

SOPHIA AND DANIEL'S story is a testament to the power of love to break barriers and celebrate individuality. Their gentle romance, built on emotional connection and pure affection, proves that true love doesn't need to fit into traditional molds. Sometimes, the sweetest love stories are those that unfold in the quiet moments of everyday life.

Story 10: The Architect and the Musician

The Visionary Architect

ISABELLA WAS A TALENTED architect known for her innovative designs and sustainable practices. Her love for creating beautiful, functional spaces made her a respected figure in the community. Despite her success, Isabella often felt the pressures of her career and longed for a deeper connection.

The Creative Musician

LUCAS WAS A PASSIONATE musician who used his work to express his emotions and connect with others. His soulful melodies and compositions brought joy and inspiration to those who heard them. Lucas had experienced his own share of struggles, using music as a way to heal and express his feelings.

The First Encounter

Isabella and Lucas first met at a charity event where Lucas was performing. Isabella was captivated by his music, and they struck up a conversation about creativity and design. Their shared passion for creating beauty sparked an immediate connection.

The Growing Connection

THEIR INITIAL CONVERSATIONS turned into regular meetings at art galleries and music studios. Isabella admired Lucas's creativity and sensitivity, while Lucas appreciated Isabella's vision and dedication. Their bond deepened, each finding inspiration and joy in the other's presence.

One afternoon, as they discussed the parallels between architecture and music, Isabella said, "Lucas, your music is incredible. It's like you're creating art with sound."

Lucas smiled softly, "Thank you, Isabella. Your designs are truly amazing. It's like you're choreographing with space."

The Blossoming Love

AS THEY SPENT MORE time together, Isabella and Lucas's bond deepened. They attended concerts, visited architectural exhibits, and enjoyed quiet evenings at the studio and music hall. Their love grew in the warmth of shared experiences and quiet moments of understanding.

A Love That Breaks Stereotypes

ISABELLA AND LUCAS'S love story was anything but conventional. Their relationship broke stereotypes and challenged societal norms, showing that true love can thrive in the most unexpected places. Their unique love story inspired those around them to embrace diversity and celebrate their own uniqueness.

A Wholesome Proposal

ONE EVENING, IN THE soft glow of the music hall, Lucas proposed. He had composed a beautiful piece for Isabella, symbolizing their love and journey together. With tears of joy, Isabella said yes, her

heart full of love for the man who had become her best friend and soulmate.

A Sweet Future

ISABELLA AND LUCAS'S story is a testament to the power of love to break barriers and celebrate individuality. Their gentle romance, built on emotional connection and pure affection, proves that true love doesn't need to fit into traditional molds. Sometimes, the sweetest love stories are those that unfold in the quiet moments of everyday life.

CONCLUSION

Unexpected heroes reveal the beauty of love stories that break traditional stereotypes and celebrate diversity. These tales of unconventional heroes and heroines explore how unique love stories can inspire and resonate, proving that true love can be found in the most surprising places. As you read through these stories, may you be inspired by the power of love to break barriers and celebrate individuality, showing that when hearts connect, they can create a powerful force for good.

Chapter 14: Ephemeral Romance

Introduction to Ephemeral Romance

Love doesn't always come with a promise of forever. Sometimes, the most intense and memorable romances are those that burn brightly but briefly, leaving an indelible mark on our hearts. This chapter delves into short, poignant stories of fleeting love, exploring the beauty and sadness of transient romantic encounters. These tales remind us that even the briefest moments of love can have a profound impact on our lives.

Story 1: The Summer Fling

The Serene Beach Town

IN A SMALL, SERENE beach town, every summer brought a sense of magic and possibility. This was the setting where Emily, a recent college graduate, decided to spend her summer before starting her new job in the city. She rented a cozy cottage near the beach, hoping to find peace and inspiration.

The Free-Spirited Traveler

JACK WAS A FREE-SPIRITED traveler who had seen much of the world. He had come to the beach town for a brief respite, drawn by the promise of tranquility and the beauty of the ocean. Jack lived in a small van that he had converted into a mobile home, enjoying the freedom of the open road.

The Chance Meeting

EMILY AND JACK MET by chance on a warm afternoon. Emily was sketching by the shore, and Jack, intrigued by her focus, struck up a conversation. They quickly discovered a mutual love for art and adventure, and their connection was immediate and intense.

The Intense Connection

OVER THE FOLLOWING weeks, Emily and Jack spent almost every day together. They explored the town, shared stories of their pasts, and dreamed about their futures. Their time together was filled with laughter, deep conversations, and a palpable sense of connection.

One evening, as they watched the sunset over the ocean, Jack said, "Emily, I don't know where my travels will take me next, but I know that this summer with you will always be one of my most cherished memories."

Emily smiled, tears in her eyes. "Jack, you've made this summer unforgettable. I'll carry this time with me, no matter where life leads."

The Fleeting Farewell

AS THE SUMMER CAME to an end, both knew their time together was limited. Emily had to return to the city to start her new job, and Jack was eager to continue his travels. Their farewell was bittersweet, filled with promises to remember each other and the moments they shared.

The Lasting Impact

EMILY AND JACK'S SUMMER fling was brief, but it left a lasting impact on both of them. Emily found inspiration in their time together, channeling it into her art and new job. Jack continued his travels, carrying the memory of their intense connection as a reminder of the beauty of fleeting love.

Story 2: The Train Encounter

The Bustling Train Station

IN A BUSTLING TRAIN station in Paris, lives intersected briefly yet profoundly. Rachel, a writer struggling with a creative block, decided to take a spontaneous trip to find inspiration. She boarded a train to the south of France, hoping the change of scenery would spark her creativity.

The Mysterious Stranger

MARC WAS A MUSICIAN returning home after a tour. He was charming and enigmatic, with a passion for life that was contagious. Marc boarded the same train as Rachel, seeking a quiet journey to reflect and rejuvenate.

The Serendipitous Meeting

RACHEL AND MARC'S PATHS crossed when they were assigned seats next to each other. They struck up a conversation that quickly turned deep and meaningful. Both were intrigued by the other's perspective on life, art, and love.

The Whirlwind Romance

DURING THE TRAIN JOURNEY, Rachel and Marc shared stories, laughter, and even a few tears. They felt an immediate and intense connection, as if they had known each other for years. The hours flew by as they talked and watched the picturesque landscapes pass by.

One evening, as they watched the sunset from the train window, Marc took Rachel's hand and said, "Rachel, meeting you has been a beautiful surprise. I wish this journey could last forever."

Rachel squeezed his hand, a bittersweet smile on her face. "Marc, this has been one of the most incredible experiences of my life. I'll always cherish this time with you."

The Inevitable Goodbye

AS THE TRAIN REACHED its destination, Rachel and Marc knew they had to part ways. Their time together was fleeting, but it was filled with an intensity that neither had ever experienced before. They exchanged contact information, but both knew that their lives were heading in different directions.

The Unforgettable Memory

RACHEL AND MARC'S TRAIN encounter was short-lived, but it left a profound impact on both of them. Rachel found the inspiration she needed to finish her novel, and Marc returned to his music with a renewed sense of passion. Their brief, intense romance reminded them of the beauty of fleeting moments and the lasting power of connection.

Story 3: The Festival Night

The Vibrant City

IN THE HEART OF A VIBRANT city, an annual music festival brought people together from all walks of life. Maria, a passionate dancer, had traveled to the city to perform at the festival. It was a dream come true for her, and she was excited to share her art with a new audience.

The Captivating Musician

JAMES WAS A TALENTED guitarist performing at the same festival. His soulful music and charismatic presence drew people in, leaving a lasting impression. James was dedicated to his craft and had spent years perfecting his art.

The Electric Encounter

Maria and James met backstage after their respective performances. They were immediately drawn to each other, captivated by the other's talent and passion. Their connection was electric, and they quickly found themselves lost in conversation.

The Night of Magic

THAT NIGHT, MARIA AND James explored the festival together, dancing to the music, laughing, and sharing their dreams. Their chemistry was undeniable, and they felt an intense connection that neither had experienced before.

As the night wore on, they found a quiet spot away from the crowds and talked until the early hours of the morning. James strummed his guitar softly, and Maria danced, their movements synchronized in a beautiful display of their shared passion.

The Fleeting Romance

MARIA AND JAMES'S TIME together was brief, but it was filled with an intensity and magic that neither would ever forget. They knew their lives would soon take them in different directions, but they cherished every moment they had together.

One final time, as the sun began to rise, James said, "Maria, this night has been unforgettable. I'll always remember the way you danced to my music."

Maria smiled, tears glistening in her eyes. "James, meeting you has been a gift. I'll carry this night with me forever."

The Bittersweet Goodbye

AS THE FESTIVAL CAME to an end, Maria and James knew they had to say goodbye. Their time together was fleeting, but it had left a lasting impact on both of them. They exchanged promises to remember each other and the magic they had shared.

The Lasting Memory

MARIA AND JAMES'S FESTIVAL night romance was short-lived, but it left a profound impact on both of them. Maria continued to dance with a renewed passion, inspired by their connection. James's music took on a new depth, infused with the memory of their magical night. Their brief, intense romance reminded them of the beauty of fleeting moments and the lasting power of connection.

Story 4: The Winter Getaway

The Snow-Covered Resort

IN A SNOW-COVERED MOUNTAIN resort, the beauty of winter brought people together for a time of relaxation and reflection. Sarah, a successful but stressed-out businesswoman, decided to take a break from her hectic life and spend a week at the resort. She hoped to find peace and clarity in the serene surroundings.

The Adventurous Snowboarder

TOM WAS AN ADVENTUROUS snowboarder who had come to the resort to enjoy the winter sports he loved. His free-spirited nature and love for the mountains made him a captivating presence. Tom was always seeking new experiences and cherished the thrill of the unknown.

The Unexpected Meeting

SARAH AND TOM MET ON the slopes, both drawn to the beauty of the winter landscape. Their initial interaction was brief, but they quickly realized they shared a love for the mountains and the serenity they provided.

The Whirlwind Adventure

OVER THE FOLLOWING days, Sarah and Tom spent their time together exploring the resort, snowboarding, and enjoying the beauty of the winter wonderland. Their connection was immediate and intense, filled with laughter and deep conversations.

One evening, as they sat by the fire in the resort lodge, Tom said, "Sarah, this week with you has been incredible. I feel like I've known you forever."

Sarah smiled, her heart full. "Tom, meeting you has been a gift. I'll always cherish this time."

The Fleeting Romance

SARAH AND TOM'S WINTER getaway was brief, but it was filled with an intensity and magic that neither would ever forget. They knew their lives would soon take them in different directions, but they cherished every moment they had together.

The Bittersweet Goodbye

AS THE WEEK CAME TO an end, Sarah and Tom knew they had to part ways. Their time together was fleeting, but it had left a lasting impact on both of them. They exchanged promises to remember each other and the magic they had shared.

The Lasting Memory

SARAH AND TOM'S WINTER getaway romance was short-lived, but it left a profound impact on both of them. Sarah returned to her life with a renewed sense of peace and clarity, inspired by their connection. Tom continued his adventures, carrying the memory of their magical week as a reminder of the beauty of fleeting love.

Story 5: The Spring Garden

The Blossoming Park

IN A BEAUTIFUL PARK filled with blossoming flowers and lush greenery, the arrival of spring brought a sense of renewal and hope. Lily, an artist seeking inspiration, often visited the park to sketch and find solace in nature.

The beauty of the flowers and the tranquility of the surroundings provided a perfect escape.

The Charming Gardener

BEN WAS A CHARMING gardener who tended to the park with dedication and care. His love for nature and his gentle demeanor made him a beloved figure among visitors. Ben found joy in nurturing the plants and creating a beautiful space for others to enjoy.

The Serendipitous Encounter

LILY AND BEN MET BY chance one morning as Lily was sketching a particularly beautiful flower bed. Ben noticed her work and struck up a conversation about the flowers. Their connection was immediate, and they quickly found themselves lost in conversation.

The Blooming Romance

OVER THE FOLLOWING weeks, Lily and Ben spent their mornings together in the park. They shared their dreams, fears, and the simple joys of life. Their connection was intense and filled with a sense of wonder and discovery.

One afternoon, as they sat on a bench surrounded by blooming flowers, Ben said, "Lily, meeting you has been a beautiful surprise. I feel like we've created something special here."

Lily smiled, tears in her eyes. "Ben, this time with you has been magical. I'll carry these moments with me always."

The Fleeting Farewell

As spring came to an end, Lily and Ben knew their time together was limited. Lily had to return to her city life, and Ben's work in the park would soon take him to new projects. Their farewell was bittersweet, filled with promises to remember each other and the beauty they had shared.

The Lasting Impact

LILY AND BEN'S SPRING garden romance was brief, but it left a lasting impact on both of them. Lily found inspiration in their time together, channeling it into her art. Ben continued his work with a renewed sense of joy and purpose, carrying the memory of their intense connection as a reminder of the beauty of fleeting love.

Story 6: The Autumn Café

The Cozy Café

IN A COZY CAFÉ NESTLED in a quaint town, the arrival of autumn brought a sense of warmth and comfort. Hannah, a writer seeking inspiration, often visited the café to work on her novel. The aroma of freshly brewed coffee and the ambiance of the café provided a perfect setting for creativity.

The Enigmatic Barista

ETHAN WAS AN ENIGMATIC barista who worked at the café. His passion for coffee and his friendly demeanor made him a beloved figure among patrons. Ethan found joy in creating the perfect cup of coffee and engaging in meaningful conversations with customers.

The Fortuitous Meeting

HANNAH AND ETHAN MET by chance one rainy afternoon as Hannah was struggling with writer's block. Ethan noticed her frustration and offered her a special blend of coffee to lift her spirits. Their connection was immediate, and they quickly found themselves lost in conversation.

The Intense Connection

OVER THE FOLLOWING weeks, Hannah and Ethan spent their afternoons together in the café. They shared their dreams, fears, and the simple joys of life. Their connection was intense and filled with a sense of warmth and comfort.

One evening, as they sat by the window watching the rain, Ethan said, "Hannah, meeting you has been a beautiful surprise. I feel like we've created something special here."

Hannah smiled, tears in her eyes. "Ethan, this time with you has been magical. I'll carry these moments with me always."

The Fleeting Farewell

AS AUTUMN CAME TO AN end, Hannah and Ethan knew their time together was limited. Hannah had to return to her city life, and Ethan's work at the café would soon take him to new projects. Their farewell was bittersweet, filled with promises to remember each other and the beauty they had shared.

The Lasting Impact

HANNAH AND ETHAN'S autumn café romance was brief, but it left a lasting impact on both of them. Hannah found inspiration in their time together, channeling it into her novel. Ethan continued his work with a renewed sense of joy and purpose, carrying the memory of their intense connection as a reminder of the beauty of fleeting love.

Story 7: The Desert Retreat

The Remote Oasis

IN A REMOTE DESERT oasis, the beauty of the vast, open landscape brought a sense of serenity and reflection. Olivia, a photographer seeking inspiration, decided to spend a week at the retreat. She hoped to capture the unique beauty of the desert and find peace in its solitude.

The Solitary Explorer

MAX WAS A SOLITARY explorer who had come to the desert to find solace and clarity. His love for the rugged terrain and his adventurous spirit made him a captivating presence. Max was always seeking new experiences and cherished the thrill of the unknown.

The Unexpected Meeting

OLIVIA AND MAX MET by chance one evening as they watched the sunset over the dunes. Their initial interaction was brief, but they quickly realized they shared a love for the desert and the serenity it provided.

The Whirlwind Adventure

OVER THE FOLLOWING days, Olivia and Max spent their time together exploring the desert, photographing the landscape, and enjoying the beauty of the night sky. Their connection was immediate and intense, filled with laughter and deep conversations.

One evening, as they sat by the campfire, Max said, "Olivia, this time with you has been incredible. I feel like I've known you forever."

Olivia smiled, her heart full. "Max, meeting you has been a gift. I'll always cherish this time."

The Fleeting Romance

OLIVIA AND MAX'S DESERT retreat was brief, but it was filled with an intensity and magic that neither would ever forget. They knew their lives would soon take them in different directions, but they cherished every moment they had together.

The Bittersweet Goodbye

AS THE WEEK CAME TO an end, Olivia and Max knew they had to part ways. Their time together was fleeting, but it had left a lasting impact on both of them. They exchanged promises to remember each other and the beauty they had shared.

The Lasting Memory

OLIVIA AND MAX'S DESERT retreat romance was short-lived, but it left a profound impact on both of them. Olivia returned to her photography with a renewed sense of inspiration, and Max continued his adventures, carrying the memory of their magical week as a reminder of the beauty of fleeting love.

Story 8: The Winter Lodge

The Snowy Mountains

IN A COZY LODGE NESTLED in the snowy mountains, the beauty of winter brought a sense of warmth and comfort. Laura, a writer seeking inspiration, decided to spend a week at the lodge. She hoped to find peace and clarity in the serene surroundings.

The Adventurous Skier

DAVID WAS AN ADVENTUROUS skier who had come to the lodge to enjoy the winter sports he loved. His free-spirited nature and love for the mountains made him a captivating presence. David was always seeking new experiences and cherished the thrill of the unknown.

The Unexpected Meeting

LAURA AND DAVID MET by chance one evening as they sat by the fireplace in the lodge. Their initial interaction was brief, but they quickly realized they shared a love for the mountains and the serenity they provided.

The Whirlwind Adventure

OVER THE FOLLOWING days, Laura and David spent their time together exploring the lodge, skiing, and enjoying the beauty of the winter landscape. Their connection was immediate and intense, filled with laughter and deep conversations.

One evening, as they sat by the fire, David said, "Laura, this time with you has been incredible. I feel like I've known you forever."

Laura smiled, her heart full. "David, meeting you has been a gift. I'll always cherish this time."

The Fleeting Romance

LAURA AND DAVID'S WINTER lodge stay was brief, but it was filled with an intensity and magic that neither would ever forget. They knew their lives would soon take them in different directions, but they cherished every moment they had together.

The Bittersweet Goodbye

AS THE WEEK CAME TO an end, Laura and David knew they had to part ways. Their time together was fleeting, but it had left a lasting impact on both of them. They exchanged promises to remember each other and the beauty they had shared.

The Lasting Memory

LAURA AND DAVID'S WINTER lodge romance was short-lived, but it left a profound impact on both of them. Laura returned to her writing with a renewed sense of inspiration, and David continued his adventures, carrying the memory of their magical week as a reminder of the beauty of fleeting love.

Story 9: The City Lights

The Bustling Metropolis

IN A BUSTLING METROPOLIS filled with bright lights and endless possibilities, the energy of the city brought people together in unexpected ways. Megan, an artist seeking inspiration, decided to spend a weekend in the city. She hoped to capture the vibrant energy and unique beauty of urban life.

The Mysterious Photographer

JAMES WAS A MYSTERIOUS photographer who loved capturing the essence of the city through his lens. His passion for urban landscapes and his enigmatic presence made him a captivating figure. James found joy in exploring the city and discovering hidden gems.

The Fortuitous Meeting

MEGAN AND JAMES MET by chance one evening as they both photographed the city skyline. Their initial interaction was brief, but they quickly realized they shared a love for capturing the beauty of the city.

The Intense Connection

OVER THE FOLLOWING days, Megan and James spent their time together exploring the city, photographing its unique sights, and enjoying the vibrant energy. Their connection was immediate and intense, filled with laughter and deep conversations.

One evening, as they watched the city lights from a rooftop, James said, "Megan, this time with you has been incredible. I feel like I've known you forever."

Megan smiled, her heart full. "James, meeting you has been a gift. I'll always cherish this time."

The Fleeting Romance

MEGAN AND JAMES'S CITY lights romance was brief, but it was filled with an intensity and magic that neither would ever forget. They knew their lives would soon take them in different directions, but they cherished every moment they had together.

The Bittersweet Goodbye

AS THE WEEKEND CAME to an end, Megan and James knew they had to part ways. Their time together was fleeting, but it had left a lasting impact on both of them. They exchanged promises to remember each other and the beauty they had shared.

The Lasting Memory

MEGAN AND JAMES'S CITY lights romance was short-lived, but it left a profound impact on both of them. Megan returned to her art with a renewed sense of inspiration, and James continued his photography, carrying the memory of their magical weekend as a reminder of the beauty of fleeting love.

Story 10: The Autumn Festival

The Colorful Festival

IN A SMALL TOWN KNOWN for its annual autumn festival, the arrival of fall brought a sense of warmth and celebration. Emily, a teacher seeking inspiration, decided to spend the weekend at the festival. She hoped to find joy and creativity in the vibrant atmosphere.

The Talented Musician

SAM WAS A TALENTED musician who performed at the festival every year. His soulful music and charismatic presence drew people in, leaving a lasting impression. Sam was dedicated to his craft and had spent years perfecting his art.

The Electric Encounter

EMILY AND SAM MET BY chance one evening as they both enjoyed the festival's lively atmosphere. Their initial interaction was brief, but they quickly realized they shared a love for music and creativity.

The Whirlwind Romance

OVER THE FOLLOWING days, Emily and Sam spent their time together exploring the festival, dancing to the music, laughing, and sharing their dreams. Their connection was intense and filled with a sense of magic and discovery.

One evening, as they watched the fireworks, Sam said, "Emily, this time with you has been incredible. I feel like I've known you forever."

Emily smiled, tears in her eyes. "Sam, meeting you has been a gift. I'll always cherish this time."

The Fleeting Farewell

AS THE FESTIVAL CAME to an end, Emily and Sam knew their time together was limited. Emily had to return to her teaching job, and Sam's music would soon take him on tour. Their farewell was bittersweet, filled with promises to remember each other and the magic they had shared.

The Lasting Impact

EMILY AND SAM'S AUTUMN festival romance was brief, but it left a lasting impact on both of them. Emily found inspiration in their time together, channeling it into her teaching. Sam's music took on a new depth, infused with the memory of their magical weekend. Their brief, intense romance reminded them of the beauty of fleeting moments and the lasting power of connection.

Conclusion

Ephemeral romance reveals the beauty and sadness of fleeting love, showcasing the power of brief, intense romantic encounters. These stories of transient love explore how even the shortest moments can leave a profound impact on our lives. As you read through these tales, may you be reminded of the magic of fleeting connections and the lasting power of love, proving that sometimes, the most beautiful romances are those that burn brightly but briefly, leaving an indelible mark on our hearts.

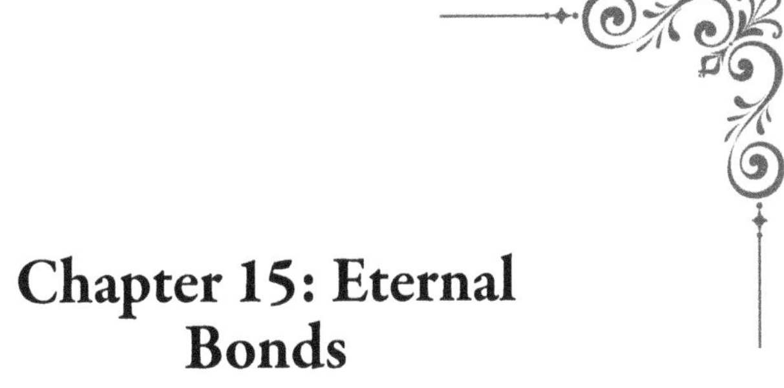

Chapter 15: Eternal Bonds

Introduction to Eternal Bonds

Love that endures the test of time is one of the most beautiful and inspiring forms of romance. This chapter celebrates stories of lifelong partnerships, exploring themes of commitment, marriage, and growing old together. These tales of enduring love remind us that true love isn't just about the initial spark but about the steadfast flame that burns brightly through all of life's trials and triumphs.

Story 1: The High School Sweethearts

The Beginnings of Love

IN A SMALL TOWN, SARAH and John met during their sophomore year of high school. Their connection was immediate, and they quickly became inseparable. Their relationship blossomed over shared lunches, study sessions, and school dances. By senior year, they were voted "Most Likely to Stay Together" by their classmates.

The College Years

SARAH AND JOHN DECIDED to attend the same college, where they continued to support each other through academic challenges and personal growth. They shared dreams of the future and made plans for their life together. Their commitment to each other only deepened as they navigated the complexities of young adulthood.

The Proposal

After graduating, John proposed to Sarah during a romantic picnic in the park where they had their first date. With tears of joy, Sarah said yes, and they began planning their future together. Their wedding was a beautiful celebration of their love, attended by family and friends who had watched their relationship grow over the years.

Building a Life Together

SARAH AND JOHN BUILT a life filled with love, laughter, and shared goals. They supported each other through career changes, the purchase of their first home, and the birth of their two children. Their relationship was a partnership based on mutual respect, trust, and unwavering support.

Weathering the Storms

LIKE ANY LONG-TERM relationship, Sarah and John faced challenges. They dealt with financial struggles, health issues, and the demands of raising a family. But through it all, they remained committed to each other, finding strength in their love and the bond they had built.

Growing Old Together

AS THEY ENTERED THEIR golden years, Sarah and John found joy in the simple pleasures of life. They traveled, spent time with their grandchildren, and enjoyed quiet evenings at home. Their love had matured and deepened, becoming a source of comfort and joy.

A Lifetime of Love

SARAH AND JOHN'S STORY is a testament to the power of enduring love. Their lifelong partnership, built on commitment and mutual respect, proves that true love can stand the test of time. Their journey together, from high school sweethearts to lifelong companions, is a celebration of the beauty of enduring love.

Story 2: The Unexpected Second Chance

The Lost Love

EMILY AND MICHAEL MET in their twenties and fell deeply in love. However, life took them in different directions, and they eventually parted ways. Both married other people and built separate lives, but they never forgot the love they once shared.

Reconnecting

Years later, both Emily and Michael found themselves single again. Emily had lost her husband to illness, and Michael had gone through a difficult divorce. They reconnected at a mutual friend's party and found that the spark between them was still alive.

A Second Chance

EMILY AND MICHAEL DECIDED to give their relationship another try. They spent time getting to know each other again, sharing their experiences and the lessons they had learned over the years. Their love had matured, and they approached their relationship with a deeper understanding and appreciation for each other.

Blending Families

Emily and Michael faced the challenge of blending their families. They worked hard to create a supportive and loving environment for their children and grandchildren. Their commitment to each other and their families strengthened their bond and brought them closer together.

A Renewed Commitment

MICHAEL PROPOSED TO Emily during a family gathering, surrounded by their loved ones. Their wedding was a beautiful celebration of second chances and enduring love. They vowed to cherish each other and the time they had been given to be together again.

Growing Old Together

EMILY AND MICHAEL EMBRACED their second chance at love with gratitude and joy. They traveled, pursued hobbies, and enjoyed the company of their blended family. Their love had a depth and richness that came from the wisdom and experience of their years apart.

A Lifetime of Love

EMILY AND MICHAEL'S story is a testament to the power of second chances and enduring love. Their journey, from lost love to lifelong companions, proves that true love can be rekindled and grow even stronger with time. Their story is a celebration of the beauty of enduring love and the joy of finding each other again.

Story 3: The Devoted Caregivers

A Lifelong Partnership

MARGARET AND JAMES met in college and quickly fell in love. They married shortly after graduation and spent the next several decades building a life together. Their relationship was marked by mutual support, respect, and unwavering devotion.

Facing Health Challenges

AS THEY GREW OLDER, James began to experience health issues. Margaret became his primary caregiver, dedicating herself to his well-being. Despite the challenges, their love for each other remained strong, and they faced each day with courage and determination.

A Deepening Bond

MARGARET AND JAMES found that their roles as caregiver and patient brought them even closer together. They relied on each other for strength and support, and their love deepened as they navigated the difficult journey of illness together.

Finding Joy in the Everyday

DESPITE THE CHALLENGES, Margaret and James found joy in the simple pleasures of life. They spent time together watching movies, reading, and reminiscing about their shared memories. Their love provided a source of comfort and happiness, even in the face of adversity.

A Lifetime of Commitment

MARGARET AND JAMES'S commitment to each other was unwavering. They faced each challenge with grace and resilience, finding strength in their enduring love. Their relationship was a testament to the power of commitment and the beauty of lifelong partnership.

Growing Old Together

MARGARET AND JAMES'S love story continued to evolve as they grew older. They cherished each moment they had together, grateful for the love and companionship they had built over the years. Their bond remained strong, a testament to their enduring love.

A Lifetime of Love

MARGARET AND JAMES'S story is a celebration of enduring love and lifelong partnership. Their journey, marked by commitment and devotion, proves that true love can stand the test of time. Their story is a testament to the beauty of enduring love and the strength that comes from facing life's challenges together.

Story 4: The Long-Distance Love

The Unexpected Meeting

LILY AND DAVID MET while on vacation in Europe. Both were exploring the same historic city and happened to stay at the same charming bed and breakfast. Their paths crossed at breakfast one morning, and they quickly bonded over their shared love for travel and adventure.

The Blossoming Romance

LILY AND DAVID SPENT the rest of their vacation together, exploring the city and sharing stories of their lives back home. Their connection was immediate and intense, and they quickly fell in love. However, there was one significant challenge: they lived on opposite sides of the world.

The Long-Distance Relationship

DETERMINED TO MAKE their relationship work, Lily and David committed to a long-distance relationship. They communicated daily through video calls, messages, and letters, finding creative ways to stay connected despite the physical distance.

Overcoming Challenges

THE LONG-DISTANCE NATURE of their relationship presented numerous challenges, but Lily and David remained committed to each other. They made regular visits, alternating between their respective countries, and planned for a future where they could be together permanently.

The Proposal

After several years of maintaining a long-distance relationship, David proposed to Lily during one of their visits. With tears of joy, Lily said yes, and they began planning their wedding and future together. Their commitment to each other had only grown stronger through the distance.

Building a Life Together

LILY AND DAVID FINALLY closed the distance between them and began building a life together. They navigated the challenges of merging their lives, careers, and cultures with grace and determination. Their love, strengthened by the years apart, flourished in their new life together.

Growing Old Together

AS THEY GREW OLDER, Lily and David continued to cherish their love and the journey that had brought them together. They traveled, pursued their passions, and enjoyed the simple pleasures of life. Their bond remained strong, a testament to their enduring love.

A Lifetime of Love

LILY AND DAVID'S STORY is a celebration of enduring love and the power of commitment. Their journey, marked by the challenges of long-distance, proves that true love can stand the test of time and distance. Their story is a testament to the beauty of enduring love and the strength that comes from facing life's challenges together.

Story 5: The Second Act

THE NEW BEGINNING

Anne and Richard met later in life, both having experienced the joys and sorrows of previous marriages. They were introduced by mutual friends at a dinner party and quickly discovered a deep connection. Their shared experiences and mutual understanding created a strong bond.

The Blossoming Romance

ANNE AND RICHARD'S relationship blossomed as they spent more time together. They enjoyed quiet dinners, walks in the park, and long conversations about their lives and dreams. Their love was marked by a sense of companionship and deep respect for each other.

A Renewed Commitment

Richard proposed to Anne during a weekend getaway, surrounded by the beauty of nature. With tears of joy, Anne said yes, and they began planning their future together. Their wedding was a beautiful celebration of new beginnings and enduring love.

Building a Life Together

ANNE AND RICHARD EMBRACED their second act with gratitude and joy. They supported each other through career changes, the blending of their families, and the pursuit of new hobbies and interests. Their love provided a source of strength and inspiration.

Weathering the Storms

LIKE ANY LONG-TERM relationship, Anne and Richard faced challenges. They dealt with health issues, the demands of their careers, and the complexities of blending their families. But through it all, they remained committed to each other, finding strength in their love and the bond they had built.

Growing Old Together

AS THEY ENTERED THEIR golden years, Anne and Richard found joy in the simple pleasures of life. They traveled, spent time with their grandchildren, and enjoyed quiet evenings at home. Their love had matured and deepened, becoming a source of comfort and joy.

A Lifetime of Love

ANNE AND RICHARD'S story is a testament to the power of enduring love. Their lifelong partnership, built on commitment and mutual respect, proves that true love can stand the test of time. Their journey together, from a new beginning to lifelong companions, is a celebration of the beauty of enduring love.

Story 6: The Childhood Friends

The Early Years

LUCY AND TOM GREW UP in the same neighborhood and were childhood friends. They shared many adventures, from building forts in the woods to riding bikes around town. Their bond was strong, and they remained close through the ups and downs of childhood.

The Teenage Years

AS THEY ENTERED THEIR teenage years, Lucy and Tom's friendship deepened into something more. They began dating, and their relationship blossomed. They supported each other through the challenges of high school and dreamed of a future together.

The College Years

LUCY AND TOM ATTENDED different colleges but remained committed to each other. They visited each other often and stayed connected through letters and phone calls. Their love grew stronger as they navigated the complexities of young adulthood.

The Proposal

After graduating, Tom proposed to Lucy during a romantic picnic at their favorite childhood spot. With tears of joy, Lucy said yes, and they began planning their future together. Their wedding was a beautiful celebration of their lifelong bond and enduring love.

Building a Life Together

LUCY AND TOM BUILT a life filled with love, laughter, and shared goals. They supported each other through career changes, the purchase of their first home, and the birth of their two children. Their relationship was a partnership based on mutual respect, trust, and unwavering support.

Weathering the Storms

LIKE ANY LONG-TERM relationship, Lucy and Tom faced challenges. They dealt with financial struggles, health issues, and the demands of raising a family. But through it all, they remained committed to each other, finding strength in their love and the bond they had built.

Growing Old Together

AS THEY ENTERED THEIR golden years, Lucy and Tom found joy in the simple pleasures of life. They traveled, spent time with their grandchildren, and enjoyed quiet evenings at home. Their love had matured and deepened, becoming a source of comfort and joy.

A Lifetime of Love

LUCY AND TOM'S STORY is a testament to the power of enduring love. Their lifelong partnership, built on commitment and mutual respect, proves that true love can stand the test of time. Their journey together, from childhood friends to lifelong companions, is a celebration of the beauty of enduring love.

Story 7: The Military Couple

The Early Days

RACHEL AND CHRIS MET while Chris was on leave from the military. Their connection was immediate, and they quickly fell in love. Despite the challenges of a military relationship, they were committed to making it work.

The Long Deployments

CHRIS'S DEPLOYMENTS were long and frequent, but Rachel and Chris found ways to stay connected. They wrote letters, sent care packages, and made the most of their limited time together. Their love grew stronger with each separation and reunion.

The Proposal

During one of Chris's leaves, he proposed to Rachel on a quiet beach. With tears of joy, Rachel said yes, and they began planning their future together. Their wedding was a beautiful celebration of their love and commitment, attended by family and friends who had supported them through the challenges of military life.

Building a Life Together

RACHEL AND CHRIS BUILT a life filled with love, laughter, and shared goals. They supported each other through Chris's deployments and Rachel's career changes. Their relationship was a partnership based on mutual respect, trust, and unwavering support.

Weathering the Storms

LIKE ANY LONG-TERM relationship, Rachel and Chris faced challenges. They dealt with the stress of deployments, the demands of military life, and the complexities of maintaining a long-distance relationship. But through it all, they remained committed to each other, finding strength in their love and the bond they had built.

Growing Old Together

AS THEY ENTERED THEIR golden years, Rachel and Chris found joy in the simple pleasures of life. They traveled, spent time with their grandchildren, and enjoyed quiet evenings at home. Their love had matured and deepened, becoming a source of comfort and joy.

A Lifetime of Love

RACHEL AND CHRIS'S story is a testament to the power of enduring love. Their lifelong partnership, built on commitment and mutual respect, proves that true love can stand the test of time. Their journey together, from the early days of military life to lifelong companions, is a celebration of the beauty of enduring love.

Story 8: The Academic Couple

The College Sweethearts

JANE AND MARK MET IN college, where they were both studying literature. Their shared love for books and intellectual pursuits created a strong bond. They quickly fell in love and began dreaming of a future together.

The Academic Journey

JANE AND MARK PURSUED academic careers, supporting each other through graduate school and the challenges of academia. They published papers, attended conferences, and built successful careers while maintaining a strong and loving relationship.

The Proposal

Mark proposed to Jane during a quiet evening at their favorite bookstore. With tears of joy, Jane said yes, and they began planning their future together. Their wedding was a beautiful celebration of their love and commitment, attended by family and friends who had supported them through the challenges of academia.

Building a Life Together

JANE AND MARK BUILT a life filled with love, laughter, and shared intellectual pursuits. They supported each other through career changes, the purchase of their first home, and the birth of their two children. Their relationship was a partnership based on mutual respect, trust, and unwavering support.

Weathering the Storms

Like any long-term relationship, Jane and Mark faced challenges. They dealt with the stress of academic life, the demands of raising a family, and the complexities of balancing their careers. But through it all, they remained committed to each other, finding strength in their love and the bond they had built.

Growing Old Together

AS THEY ENTERED THEIR golden years, Jane and Mark found joy in the simple pleasures of life. They traveled, spent time with their grandchildren, and enjoyed quiet evenings at home. Their love had matured and deepened, becoming a source of comfort and joy.

A Lifetime of Love

JANE AND MARK'S STORY is a testament to the power of enduring love. Their lifelong partnership, built on commitment and mutual respect, proves that true love can stand the test of time. Their journey together, from college sweethearts to lifelong companions, is a celebration of the beauty of enduring love.

Story 9: The Artistic Couple

The Creative Connection

SOPHIE AND ALEX MET at an art gallery opening. Both were artists with a deep passion for their craft, and their connection was immediate. They quickly fell in love and began dreaming of a future together.

The Artistic Journey

SOPHIE AND ALEX PURSUED artistic careers, supporting each other through the challenges of the art world. They held joint exhibitions, collaborated on projects, and built successful careers while maintaining a strong and loving relationship.

The Proposal

Alex proposed to Sophie during a quiet evening in their studio. With tears of joy, Sophie said yes, and they began planning their future together. Their wedding was a beautiful celebration of their love and commitment, attended by family and friends who had supported them through the challenges of the art world.

Building a Life Together

SOPHIE AND ALEX BUILT a life filled with love, laughter, and shared creative pursuits. They supported each other through career changes, the purchase of their first home, and the birth of their two children. Their relationship was a partnership based on mutual respect, trust, and unwavering support.

Weathering the Storms

LIKE ANY LONG-TERM relationship, Sophie and Alex faced challenges. They dealt with the stress of artistic life, the demands of raising a family, and the complexities of balancing their careers. But through it all, they remained committed to each other, finding strength in their love and the bond they had built.

Growing Old Together

AS THEY ENTERED THEIR golden years, Sophie and Alex found joy in the simple pleasures of life. They traveled, spent time with their grandchildren, and enjoyed quiet evenings at home. Their love had matured and deepened, becoming a source of comfort and joy.

A Lifetime of Love

SOPHIE AND ALEX'S STORY is a testament to the power of enduring love. Their lifelong partnership, built on commitment and mutual respect, proves that true love can stand the test of time. Their journey together, from artistic collaborators to lifelong companions, is a celebration of the beauty of enduring love.

Story 10: The Philanthropic Couple

The Shared Mission

CLARA AND HENRY MET while volunteering at a local charity. Their shared passion for helping others and making a positive impact created a strong bond. They quickly fell in love and began dreaming of a future together.

The Philanthropic Journey

Clara and Henry pursued philanthropic careers, supporting each other through the challenges of their work. They founded a nonprofit organization together, dedicated to improving the lives of those in need. Their relationship was marked by a deep sense of purpose and shared mission.

The Proposal

Henry proposed to Clara during a quiet evening at their favorite charity event. With tears of joy, Clara said yes, and they began planning their future together. Their wedding was a beautiful celebration of their love and commitment, attended by family and friends who had supported them through the challenges of their work.

Building a Life Together

CLARA AND HENRY BUILT a life filled with love, laughter, and shared philanthropic pursuits. They supported each other through career changes, the purchase of their first home, and the birth of their two children. Their relationship was a partnership based on mutual respect, trust, and unwavering support.

Weathering the Storms

LIKE ANY LONG-TERM relationship, Clara and Henry faced challenges. They dealt with the stress of philanthropic work, the demands of raising a family, and the complexities of balancing their careers. But through it all, they remained committed to each other, finding strength in their love and the bond they had built.

Growing Old Together

AS THEY ENTERED THEIR golden years, Clara and Henry found joy in the simple pleasures of life. They traveled, spent time with their grandchildren, and enjoyed quiet evenings at home. Their love had matured and deepened, becoming a source of comfort and joy.

A Lifetime of Love

CLARA AND HENRY'S STORY is a testament to the power of enduring love. Their lifelong partnership, built on commitment and mutual respect, proves that true love can stand the test of time. Their journey together, from philanthropic partners to lifelong companions, is a celebration of the beauty of enduring love.

Story 11: The Tech Innovators

The Startup Dream

EMMA AND JASON MET while working at a tech startup. Their shared passion for innovation and entrepreneurship created a strong bond. They quickly fell in love and began dreaming of a future together.

The Tech Journey

EMMA AND JASON PURSUED tech careers, supporting each other through the challenges of the startup world. They founded a tech company together, dedicated to developing cutting-edge solutions. Their relationship was marked by a deep sense of purpose and shared mission.

The Proposal

Jason proposed to Emma during a quiet evening at their favorite tech conference. With tears of joy, Emma said yes, and they began planning their future together. Their wedding was a beautiful celebration of their love and commitment, attended by family and friends who had supported them through the challenges of the tech world.

Building a Life Together

EMMA AND JASON BUILT a life filled with love, laughter, and shared tech pursuits. They supported each other through career changes, the purchase of their first home, and the birth of their two children. Their relationship was a partnership based on mutual respect, trust, and unwavering support.

Weathering the Storms

LIKE ANY LONG-TERM relationship, Emma and Jason faced challenges. They dealt with the stress of tech work, the demands of raising a family, and the complexities of balancing their careers. But through it all, they remained committed to each other, finding strength in their love and the bond they had built.

Growing Old Together

AS THEY ENTERED THEIR golden years, Emma and Jason found joy in the simple pleasures of life. They traveled, spent time with their grandchildren, and enjoyed quiet evenings at home. Their love had matured and deepened, becoming a source of comfort and joy.

A Lifetime of Love

EMMA AND JASON'S STORY is a testament to the power of enduring love. Their lifelong partnership, built on commitment and mutual respect, proves that true love can stand the test of time. Their journey together, from tech innovators to lifelong companions, is a celebration of the beauty of enduring love.

Story 12: The Medical Couple

The Shared Mission

ANNA AND TOM MET WHILE working at the same hospital. Their shared passion for medicine and helping others created a strong bond. They quickly fell in love and began dreaming of a future together.

The Medical Journey

ANNA AND TOM PURSUED medical careers, supporting each other through the challenges of their work. They worked long hours, dealt with the stress of life-and-death situations, and navigated the complexities of the medical field. Their relationship was marked by a deep sense of purpose and shared mission.

The Proposal

Tom proposed to Anna during a quiet evening in the hospital garden. With tears of joy, Anna said yes, and they began planning their future together. Their wedding was a beautiful celebration of their love and commitment, attended by family and friends who had supported them through the challenges of their work.

Building a Life Together

ANNA AND TOM BUILT a life filled with love, laughter, and shared medical pursuits. They supported each other through career changes, the purchase of their first home, and the birth of their two children. Their relationship was a partnership based on mutual respect, trust, and unwavering support.

Weathering the Storms

LIKE ANY LONG-TERM relationship, Anna and Tom faced challenges. They dealt with the stress of medical work, the demands of raising a family, and the complexities of balancing their careers. But through it all, they remained committed to each other, finding strength in their love and the bond they had built.

Growing Old Together

AS THEY ENTERED THEIR golden years, Anna and Tom found joy in the simple pleasures of life. They traveled, spent time with their grandchildren, and enjoyed quiet evenings at home. Their love had matured and deepened, becoming a source of comfort and joy.

A Lifetime of Love

ANNA AND TOM'S STORY is a testament to the power of enduring love. Their lifelong partnership, built on commitment and mutual respect, proves that true love can stand the test of time. Their journey together, from medical partners to lifelong companions, is a celebration of the beauty of enduring love.

Story 13: The Legal Power Couple

The Shared Mission

RACHEL AND DAVID MET while working at the same law firm. Their shared passion for justice and helping others created a strong bond. They quickly fell in love and began dreaming of a future together.

The Legal Journey

RACHEL AND DAVID PURSUED legal careers, supporting each other through the challenges of their work. They worked long hours, dealt with the stress of high-profile cases, and navigated the complexities of the legal field. Their relationship was marked by a deep sense of purpose and shared mission.

The Proposal

David proposed to Rachel during a quiet evening at their favorite park. With tears of joy, Rachel said yes, and they began planning their future together. Their wedding was a beautiful celebration of their love and commitment, attended by family and friends who had supported them through the challenges of their work.

Building a Life Together

RACHEL AND DAVID BUILT a life filled with love, laughter, and shared legal pursuits. They supported each other through career changes, the purchase of their first home, and the birth of their two children. Their relationship was a partnership based on mutual respect, trust, and unwavering support.

Weathering the Storms

LIKE ANY LONG-TERM relationship, Rachel and David faced challenges. They dealt with the stress of legal work, the demands of raising a family, and the complexities of balancing their careers. But through it all, they remained committed to each other, finding strength in their love and the bond they had built.

Growing Old Together

AS THEY ENTERED THEIR golden years, Rachel and David found joy in the simple pleasures of life. They traveled, spent time with their grandchildren, and enjoyed quiet evenings at home. Their love had matured and deepened, becoming a source of comfort and joy.

A Lifetime of Love

RACHEL AND DAVID'S story is a testament to the power of enduring love. Their lifelong partnership, built on commitment and mutual respect, proves that true love can stand the test of time. Their journey together, from legal partners to lifelong companions, is a celebration of the beauty of enduring love.

Story 14: The Entrepreneurs

The Startup Dream

LILY AND JACK MET WHILE working at a startup incubator. Their shared passion for innovation and entrepreneurship created a strong bond. They quickly fell in love and began dreaming of a future together.

The Entrepreneurial Journey

LILY AND JACK PURSUED entrepreneurial careers, supporting each other through the challenges of the startup world. They founded a company together, dedicated to developing innovative solutions. Their relationship was marked by a deep sense of purpose and shared mission.

The Proposal

Jack proposed to Lily during a quiet evening at their favorite café. With tears of joy, Lily said yes, and they began planning their future together. Their wedding was a beautiful celebration of their love and commitment, attended by family and friends who had supported them through the challenges of the startup world.

Building a Life Together

LILY AND JACK BUILT a life filled with love, laughter, and shared entrepreneurial pursuits. They supported each other through career changes, the purchase of their first home, and the birth of their two children. Their relationship was a partnership based on mutual respect, trust, and unwavering support.

Weathering the Storms

LIKE ANY LONG-TERM relationship, Lily and Jack faced challenges. They dealt with the stress of entrepreneurial work, the demands of raising a family, and the complexities of balancing their careers. But through it all, they remained committed to each other, finding strength in their love and the bond they had built.

Growing Old Together

AS THEY ENTERED THEIR golden years, Lily and Jack found joy in the simple pleasures of life. They traveled, spent time with their grandchildren, and enjoyed quiet evenings at home. Their love had matured and deepened, becoming a source of comfort and joy.

A Lifetime of Love

LILY AND JACK'S STORY is a testament to the power of enduring love. Their lifelong partnership, built on commitment and mutual respect, proves that true love can stand the test of time. Their journey together, from entrepreneurial partners to lifelong companions, is a celebration of the beauty of enduring love.

Story 15: The Journalists

The Shared Mission

NINA AND SAM MET WHILE working at the same news organization. Their shared passion for journalism and uncovering the truth created a strong bond. They quickly fell in love and began dreaming of a future together.

The Journalism Journey

NINA AND SAM PURSUED journalism careers, supporting each other through the challenges of their work. They worked long hours, dealt with the stress of breaking news, and navigated the complexities of the media industry. Their relationship was marked by a deep sense of purpose and shared mission.

The Proposal

Sam proposed to Nina during a quiet evening at their favorite café. With tears of joy, Nina said yes, and they began planning their future together. Their wedding was a beautiful celebration of their love and commitment, attended by family and friends who had supported them through the challenges of their work.

Building a Life Together

Nina and Sam built a life filled with love, laughter, and shared journalism pursuits. They supported each other through career changes, the purchase of their first home, and the birth of their two children. Their relationship was a partnership based on mutual respect, trust, and unwavering support.

Weathering the Storms

LIKE ANY LONG-TERM relationship, Nina and Sam faced challenges. They dealt with the stress of journalism work, the demands of raising a family, and the complexities of balancing their careers. But through it all, they remained committed to each other, finding strength in their love and the bond they had built.

Growing Old Together

AS THEY ENTERED THEIR golden years, Nina and Sam found joy in the simple pleasures of life. They traveled, spent time with their grandchildren, and enjoyed quiet evenings at home. Their love had matured and deepened, becoming a source of comfort and joy.

A Lifetime of Love

NINA AND SAM'S STORY is a testament to the power of enduring love. Their lifelong partnership, built on commitment and mutual respect, proves that true love can stand the test of time. Their journey together, from journalism partners to lifelong companions, is a celebration of the beauty of enduring love.

Conclusion

Eternal bonds reveal the beauty of enduring love that lasts a lifetime, celebrating the strength and resilience of lifelong partnerships. These stories of commitment, marriage, and growing old together remind us that true love isn't just about the initial spark but about the steadfast flame that burns brightly through all of life's trials and triumphs. As you read through these tales, may you be inspired by the power of enduring love and the beauty of lifelong companionship, proving that when hearts connect, they can create a powerful force for good that lasts a lifetime.

Don't miss out!

Visit the website below and you can sign up to receive emails whenever Jessica Marie Garcia publishes a new book. There's no charge and no obligation.

https://books2read.com/r/B-A-VGXUB-BQNUD

Did you love *Romantic Reveries*? Then you should read *The Gift of Love*[1] by Jessica Marie Garcia!

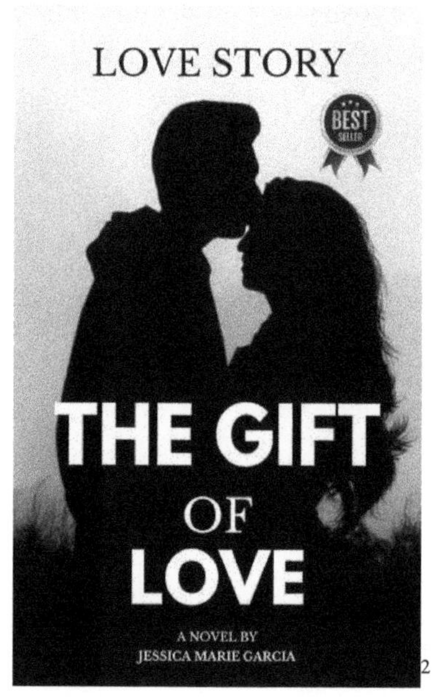

[2]

Sarah, a small-town librarian, and Daniel, a successful businessman, meet by chance at a farmers' market. Drawn to each other's contrasting worlds, their friendship blossoms into a deep bond. As they navigate personal struggles, community projects, and public scrutiny, their love grows stronger. With heartfelt conversations, a romantic getaway, and grand gestures, they overcome obstacles and embrace their shared dreams. The story culminates in a heartfelt proposal and a joyous wedding, celebrating love, faith, and community.

---

1. https://books2read.com/u/3LlLWe

2. https://books2read.com/u/3LlLWe

About the Author

Jessica Marie Garcia is a celebrated author renowned for her engaging fiction in the romance genre. Her novels intricately explore love, relationships, and human connections with heartfelt prose that captivates readers globally.

Milton Keynes UK
Ingram Content Group UK Ltd.
UKHW030823010824
446326UK00001B/32